# Isaac Asimov

Isaac Asimov, world maestro of science fiction, was born in Russia near Smolensk in 1920 and brought to the United States by his parents three years later. He grew up in Brooklyn where he went to grammar school and at the age of eight he gained his citizen papers. A remarkable memory helped him finish high school before he was sixteen. He then went on to Columbia University and resolved to become a chemist rather than follow the medical career his father had in mind for him. He graduated in chemistry and after a short spell in the Army he gained his doctorate in 1949 and qual-ified as an instructor in biochemistry at Boston University School of Medicine where he became Associate Professor in 1955, doing research in nucleic acid. Increasingly, however, the pressures of chemical research conflicted with his aspira-tions in the literary field, and in 1958 he retired to full-time authorship while retaining his connection with the University.

Asimov's fantastic career as a science fiction writer began in 1939 with the appearance of a short story, *Marooned Off Vesta*, in *Amazing Stories*. Thereafter he became a regular contributor to the leading SF magazines of the day including *Astounding*, *Astonishing Stories*, *Super Science Stories* and *Galaxy*. He won the Hugo Award four times and the Nebula Award once. With nearly five hundred books to his credit and several hundred articles, Asimov's output was prolific by any standards. Apart from his many world-famous science fiction works, Asimov also wrote highly suc-cessful detective mystery stories, a four-volume *History of North America*, a two-volume *Guide to the Bible*, a biographi-cal dictionary, encyclopaedias, textbooks and an impressive list of books on many aspects of science, as well as two vol-umes of autobiography.

Isaac Asimov died in 1992 at the age of 72.

BY THE SAME AUTHOR

The Foundation Saga

Prelude to Foundation
Foundation
Foundation and Empire
Second Foundation
Foundation's Edge
Foundation and Earth

Galactic Empire Novels

The Currents of Space
Pebble in the Sky

Earth is Room Enough
The Martian Way
The End of Eternity
The Winds of Change

Asimov's Mysteries
The Gods Themselves
Nightfall One
Nightfall Two
Buy Jupiter
The Bicentennial Man
Nine Tomorrows

Robot Stories and Novels

I, Robot
The Rest of the Robots
The Complete Robot
The Caves of Steel

The Naked Sun
The Robots of Dawn
Robots and Empire

The Early Asimov: Volume 1
The Early Asimov: Volume 2
The Early Asimov: Volume 3

Nebula Award Stories 8
  (editor)
The Science Fictional Solar
  System (editor, with
  Martin Harry Greenberg
  and Charles G. Waugh)

Non-fiction

The Stars in their Courses
The Left Hand of the Electron
Asimov on Science Fiction
The Sun Shines Bright
Counting the Eons
Far As Human Eye Could See

Detection

Tales of the Black Widowers
More Tales of the Black
  Widowers
Casebook of the Black
  Widowers
Authorised Murder
The Union Club Mysteries

$\boxed{Voyager}$

ISAAC ASIMOV

---

# Second Foundation

HarperCollins*Publishers*

www.voyager-books.com

This paperback edition 1995
7  9  8

Previously published in paperback by
HarperCollinsScience Fiction and Fantasy 1994 (Reprinted once)
and by Grafton 1964 (Reprinted thirty-five times)

*Second Foundation* is based upon published material originally
copyrighted by Street & Smith Publications Inc. 1948, 1949

ISBN 0 586 01713 5

Set in Plantin

Printed in Great Britain by
Caledonian International Book Manufacturing Ltd, Glasgow

to Marcia, John, and Stan

# SECOND FOUNDATION

# PROLOGUE

The First Galactic Empire had endured for tens of thousands of years. It had included all the planets of the Galaxy in a centralized rule, sometimes tyrannical, sometimes benevolent, always orderly. Human beings had forgotten that any other form of existence could be.

All except Hari Seldon.

Hari Seldon was the last great scientist of the First Empire. It was he who brought the science of psycho-history to its full development. Psycho-history was the quintessence of sociology; it was the science of human behaviour reduced to mathematical equations.

The individual human being is unpredictable, but the reactions of human mobs, Seldon found, could be treated statistically. The larger the mob, the greater the accuracy that could be achieved. And the size of the human masses that Seldon worked with was no less than the population of the Galaxy which in his time was numbered in the quintillions.

It was Seldon, then, who foresaw, against all common sense and popular belief, that the brilliant Empire which seemed so strong was in a state of irremediable decay and decline. He foresaw (or he solved his equations and interpreted its symbols, which amounts to the same thing) that left to itself, the Galaxy would pass through a thirty thousand year period of misery and anarchy before a unified government would rise once more.

He set about to remedy the situation, to bring about a state of affairs that would restore peace and civilization in a single thousand of years. Carefully, he set up two colonies of scientists that he called 'Foundations.' With deliberate intention, he set them up 'at opposite ends of the Galaxy.' One

Foundation was set up in the full daylight of publicity. The existence of the other, the Second Foundation, was drowned in silence.

In *Foundation* (Gnome, 1951) and *Foundation and Empire* (Gnome, 1952) are told the first three centuries of the history of the First Foundation. It began as a small community of Encyclopedists lost in the emptiness of the outer periphery of the Galaxy. Periodically, it faced a crisis in which the variables of human intercourse, of the social and economic currents of the time constricted about it. Its freedom to move lay along only one certain line and when it moved in that direction, a new horizon of development opened before it. All had been planned by Hari Seldon, long dead now.

The First Foundation, with its superior science, took over the barbarized planets that surrounded it. It faced the anarchic Warlords that broke away from the dying Empire and beat them. It faced the remnant of the Empire itself under its last strong Emperor and its last strong General and beat it.

Then it faced something which Hari Seldon could not foresee, the overwhelming power of a single human being, a Mutant. The creature known as the Mule was born with the ability to mould men's emotions and to shape their minds. His bitterest opponents were made into his devoted servants. Armies could not, *would* not fight him. Before him, the First Foundation fell and Seldon's schemes lay partly in ruins.

There was left the mysterious Second Foundation, the goal of all searches. The Mule must find it to make his conquest of the Galaxy complete. The faithful of what was left of the First Foundation must find it for quite another reason. But where was it? That no one knew.

This, then, is the story of the search for the Second Foundation!

# Part I

# SEARCH BY THE MULE

# 1

# TWO MEN AND THE MULE

THE MULE *It was after the fall of the First Foundation that the constructive aspects of the Mule's regime took shape. After the definite break-up of the first Galactic Empire, it was he who first presented history with a unified volume of space truly imperial in scope. The earlier commercial empire of the fallen Foundation had been diverse and loosely knit, despite the impalpable backing of the predictions of psycho-history. It was not to be compared with the tightly controlled 'Union of Worlds' under the Mule, comprising as it did, one-tenth the volume of the Galaxy and one-fifteenth of its population. Particularly during the era of the so called Search...*

ENCYCLOPEDIA GALACTICA*

There is much more that the Encyclopedia has to say on the subject of the Mule and his Empire but almost all of it is not germane to the issue at immediate hand, and most of it is considerably too dry for our purposes in any case. Mainly, the article concerns itself at this point with the economic conditions that led to the rise of the 'First Citizen of the Union' – the Mule's official title – and with the economic consequences thereof.

If, at any time, the writer of the article is mildly astonished at the colossal haste with which the Mule rose from nothing to vast dominion in five years, he conceals it. If he is further surprised at the sudden cessation of expansion in favour of a five-year consolidation of territory, he hides the fact.

*All quotations from the Encyclopedia Galactica here reproduced are taken from the 116th Edition published in 1020 F.E. by the Encyclopedia Galactica Publishing Co., Terminus, with permission of the publishers.

We therefore abandon the Encyclopedia and continue on our own path for our own purposes and take up the history of the Great Interregnum – between the first and Second Galactic Empires – at the end of that five years of consolidation.

Politically, the Union is quiet. Economically, it is prosperous. Few would care to exchange the peace of the Mule's steady grip for the chaos that had preceded. On the worlds that five years previously had known the Foundation, there might be a nostalgic regret, but no more. The Foundation's leaders were dead, where useless; and Converted, where useful.

And of the Converted, the most useful was Han Pritcher, now lieutenant general.

In the days of the Foundation, Han Pritcher had been a captain and a member of the underground Democratic Opposition. When the Foundation fell to the Mule without a fight, Pritcher fought the Mule. Until, that is, he was Converted.

The Conversion was not the ordinary one brought on by the power of superior reason. Han Pritcher knew that well enough. He had been changed because the Mule was a mutant with mental powers quite capable of adjusting the conditions of ordinary humans to suit himself. But that satisfied him completely. That was as it should be. The very contentment with the Conversion was a prime symptom of it, but Han Pritcher was no longer even curious about the matter.

And now that he was returning from his fifth major expedition into the boundlessness of the Galaxy outside the Union, it was with something approaching artless joy that the veteran spaceman and Intelligence agent considered his approaching audience with the 'First Citizen.' His hard face, gouged out of a dark, grainless wood that did not seem to be capable of smiling without cracking, didn't show it – but the outward indications were unnecessary. The Mule could see the emotions within, down to the smallest, much as an ordinary man could see the twitch of an eyebrow.

14

Pritcher left his air car at the old vice-regal hangars and entered the palace grounds on foot as was required. He walked one mile along the arrowed highway – which was empty and silent. Pritcher knew that over the square miles of palace grounds, there was not one guard, not one soldier, not one armed man.

The Mule had need of no protection.

The Mule was his own best, all-powerful protector.

Pritcher's footsteps beat softly in his own ears, as the palace reared its gleaming, incredibly light and incredibly strong metallic walls before him in the daring, overblown, near-hectic arches that characterized the architecture of the Late Empire. It brooded strongly over the empty grounds, over the crowded city on the horizon.

Within the palace was that one man – by himself – on whose inhuman mental attributes depended the new aristocracy, and the whole structure of the Union.

The huge, smooth door swung massively open at the general's approach, and he entered. He stepped on to the wide, sweeping ramp that moved upward under him. He rose swiftly in the noiseless elevator. He stood before the small plain door of the Mule's own room in the highest glitter of the palace spires.

It opened—

Bail Channis was young, and Bail Channis was Unconverted. That is, in plainer language, his emotional make-up had been unadjusted by the Mule. It remained exactly as it had been formed by the original shape of its heredity and the subsequent modifications of his environment. And that satisfied him, too.

At not quite thirty, he was in marvellously good odour in the capital. He was handsome and quick-witted – therefore successful in society. He was intelligent and self-possessed – therefore successful with the Mule. And he was thoroughly pleased at both successes.

And now, for the first time, the Mule had summoned him to personal audience.

His legs carried him down the long, glittering highway that led tautly to the sponge-aluminium spires that had been once the residence of the viceroy of Kalgan, who ruled under the old emperors; and that had been later the residence of the independent princes of Kalgan, who ruled in their own name, and that was now the residence of the First Citizen of the Union, who ruled over an empire of his own.

Channis hummed softly to himself. He did not doubt what this was all about. The Second Foundation, naturally! That all-embracing bogey, the mere consideration of which had thrown the Mule back from his policy of limitless expansion into static caution. The official term was 'consolidation.'

Now there were rumours – you couldn't stop rumours. The Mule was to begin the offensive once more. The Mule had discovered the whereabouts of the Second Foundation, and would attack. The Mule had come to an agreement with the Second Foundation and divided the Galaxy. The Mule had decided the Second Foundation did not exist and would take over all the Galaxy.

No use listing all the varieties one heard in the anterooms. It was not even the first time such rumours had circulated. But now they seemed to have more body in them, and all the free, expansive souls who thrived on war, military adventure, and political chaos and withered in times of stability and stagnant peace were joyful.

Bail Channis was one of these. He did not fear the mysterious Second Foundation. For that matter, he did not fear the Mule, and boasted of it. Some, perhaps, who disapproved of one at once so young and so well-off, waited darkly for the reckoning with the gay ladies' man who employed his wit openly at the expense of the Mule's physical appearance and sequestered life. None dared join him and few dared laugh, but when nothing happened to him, his reputation rose accordingly.

Channis was improvising words to the tune he was humming. Nonsense words with the recurrent refrain: 'Second Foundation threatens the Nation and all of Creation.'

16

He was at the palace.

The huge, smooth door swung massively open at his approach and he entered. He stepped on to the wide, sweeping ramp that moved upward under him. He rose swiftly in the noiseless elevator. He stood before the small plain door of the Mule's own room in the highest glitter of the palace spires.

It opened—

The man who had no name other than the Mule, and no title other than First Citizen looked out through the one-way transparency of the wall to the light and lofty city on the horizon.

In the darkening twilight, the stars were emerging, and not one but owed allegiance to him.

He smiled with fleeting bitterness at the thought. The allegiance they owed was to a personality few had ever seen.

He was not a man to look at, the Mule – not a man to look at without derision. Not more than one hundred and twenty pounds was stretched out into his five-foot-eight length. His limbs were bony stalks that jutted out of his scrawniness in graceless angularity. And his thin face was nearly drowned out in the prominence of a fleshy beak that thrust three inches outward.

Only his eyes played false with the general farce that was the Mule. In their softness – a strange softness for the Galaxy's greatest conqueror – sadness was never entirely subdued.

In the city was to be found all the gaiety of a luxurious capital on a luxurious world. He might have established his capital on the Foundation, the strongest of his now-conquered enemies, but it was far out on the very rim of the Galaxy. Kalgan, more centrally located, with a long tradition as aristocracy's playground, suited him better – strategically.

But in its traditional gaiety, enhanced by unheard-of prosperity, he found no peace.

They feared him and obeyed him and, perhaps, even respected him – from a goodly distance. But who could look at

17

him without contempt? Only those he had Converted. And of what value was their artificial loyalty? It lacked flavour. He might have adopted titles, and enforced ritual and invented elaborations, but even that would have changed nothing. Better – or at least, no worse – to be simply the First Citizen – and to hide himself.

There was a sudden surge of rebellion within him – strong and brutal. Not a portion of the Galaxy must be denied him. For five years he had remained silent and buried here on Kalgan because of the eternal, misty, space-ridden menace of the unseen, unheard, unknown Second Foundation. He was thirty-two. Not old – but he felt old. His body, whatever its mutant mental powers, was physically weak.

Every star! Every star he could see – and every star he couldn't see. It must all be his!

Revenge on all. On a humanity of which he wasn't a part. On a Galaxy in which he didn't fit.

The cool, overhead warning light flickered. He could follow the progress of the man who had entered the palace, and simultaneously, as though his mutant sense had been enhanced and sensitized in the lonely twilight, he felt the wash of emotional content touch the fibres of his brain.

He recognized the identity without an effort. It was Pritcher.

Captain Pritcher of the one-time Foundation. The Captain Pritcher who had been ignored and passed over by the bureaucrats of that decaying government. The Captain Pritcher whose job as petty spy he had wiped out and whom he had lifted from its slime. The Captain Pritcher whom he had made first colonel and then general; whose scope of activity he had made Galaxy-wide.

The now-General Pritcher who was, iron rebel though he began, completely loyal. And yet with all that, not loyal because of benefits gained, not loyal out of gratitude, not loyal as a fair return – but loyal only through the artifice of Conversion.

18

The Mule was conscious of that strong unalterable surface layer of loyalty and love that coloured every swirl and eddy of the emotionality of Han Pritcher – the layer he had himself implanted five years before. Far underneath there were the original traces of stubborn individuality, impatience of rule, idealism – but even he, himself, could scarcely detect them any longer.

The door behind him opened, and he turned. The transparency of the wall faded to opacity, and the purple evening light gave way to the whitely blazing glow of atomic power.

Han Pritcher took the seat indicated. There was neither bowing, nor kneeling nor the use of honorifics in private audiences with the Mule. The Mule was merely 'First Citizen.' He was addressed as 'sir.' You sat in his presence, and you could turn your back on him if it so happened that you did.

To Han Pritcher this was all evidence of the sure and confident power of the man. He was warmly satisfied with it.

The Mule said: 'Your final report reached me yesterday. I can't deny that I find it somewhat depressing, Pritcher.'

The general's eyebrows closed upon each other: 'Yes, I imagine so – but I don't see to what other conclusions I could have come. There just isn't any Second Foundation, sir.'

And the Mule considered and then slowly shook his head, as he had done many a time before: 'There's the evidence of Ebling Mis. There is always the evidence of Ebling Mis.'

It was not a new story. Pritcher said without qualification: 'Mis may have been the greatest psychologist of the Foundation, but he was a baby compared to Hari Seldon. At the time he was investigating Seldon's works, he was under the artificial stimulation of your own brain control. You may have pushed him too far. He might have been wrong. Sir, he *must* have been wrong.'

The Mule sighed, his lugubrious face thrust forward on its thin stalk of a neck. 'If only he had lived another minute. He was on the point of telling me where the Second Foundation was. He *knew*, I'm telling you. I need not have retreated. I need not have waited and waited. So much time lost. Five years gone for nothing.'

Pritcher could not have been censorious over the weak longing of his ruler; his controlled mental make-up forbade that. He was disturbed instead; vaguely uneasy. He said: 'But what alternative explanation can there possibly be, sir? Five times I've gone out. You yourself have plotted the routes. And I've left no asteroid unturned. It was three hundred years ago – that Hari Seldon of the old Empire supposedly established two Foundations to act as nuclei of a new Empire to replace the dying old one. One hundred years after Seldon, the First Foundation – the one we know so well – was known through all the Periphery. One hundred fifty years after Seldon – at the time of the last battle with the old Empire – it was known throughout the Galaxy. And now it's three hundred years – and where should this mysterious Second be? In no eddy of the Galactic stream has it been heard of.'

'Ebling Mis said it kept itself secret. Only secrecy can turn its weakness to strength.'

'Secrecy as deep as this is past possibility without nonexistence as well.'

The Mule looked up, large eyes sharp and wary. 'No. It *does* exist.' A bony finger pointed sharply. 'There is going to be a slight change in tactics.'

Pritcher frowned. 'You plan to leave yourself? I would scarcely advise it.'

'No, of course not. You will have to go out once again – one last time. But with another in joint command.'

There was a silence, and Pritcher's voice was hard, 'Who, sir?'

'There's a young man here in Kalgan. Bail Channis.'

'I've never heard of him, sir.'

'No, I imagine not. But he's got an agile mind, he's ambitious – and he's *not* Converted.'

Pritcher's long jaw trembled for a bare instant, 'I fail to see the advantage in that.'

'There is one, Pritcher. You're a resourceful and experienced man. You have given me good service. But you are Converted. Your motivation is simply an enforced and helpless loyalty to myself. When you lost your native motivations, you lost something, some subtle drive, that I cannot possibly replace.'

'I don't feel that, sir,' said Pritcher, grimly. 'I recall myself quite well as I was in the days when I was an enemy of yours. I feel none the inferior.'

'Naturally not,' and the Mule's mouth twitched into a smile. 'Your judgement in this matter is scarcely objective. This Channis, now, is ambitious – for himself. He is completely trustworthy – out of no loyalty but to himself. He knows that it is on my coat-tails that he rides and he would do anything to increase my power that the ride might be long and far and that the destination might be glorious. If he goes with you, there is just that added push behind *his* seeking – that push for himself.'

'Then,' said Pritcher, still insistent, 'why not remove my own Conversion, if you think that will improve me. I can scarcely be mistrusted, now.'

'That never, Pritcher. While you are within arm's reach, or blaster reach, of myself, you will remain firmly held in Conversion. If I were to release you this minute, I would be dead the next.'

The general's nostrils flared. 'I am hurt that you should think so.'

'I don't mean to hurt you, but it is impossible for you to realize what your feelings would be if free to form themselves along the lines of your natural motivation. The human mind resents control. The ordinary human hypnotist cannot hypnotize a person against his will for that reason. I can, because I'm not a hypnotist, and, believe me, Pritcher, the resentment that you cannot show and do not even know you possess is something I wouldn't want to face.'

Pritcher's head bowed. Futility wrenched him and left him

21

grey and haggard inside. He said with an effort: 'But how can you trust this man. I mean, completely – as you can trust me in my Conversion.'

'Well, I suppose I can't entirely. That is why you must go with him. You see, Pritcher,' and the Mule buried himself in the large armchair against the soft back of which he looked like an angularly animated toothpick, 'if he *should* stumble on the Second Foundation – if it *should* occur to him that an arrangement with them might be more profitable than with me – You understand?'

A profoundly satisfied light blazed in Pritcher's eyes. 'That is better, sir.'

'Exactly. But remember, he must have a free rein as far as possible.'

'Certainly.'

'And ... uh ... Pritcher. The young man is handsome, pleasant, and extremely charming. Don't let him fool you. He's a dangerous and unscrupulous character. Don't get in his way unless you're prepared to meet him properly. That's all.'

The Mule was alone again. He let the lights die and the wall before him kicked to transparency again. The sky was purple now, and the city was a smudge of light on the horizon.

What was it all for? And if he *were* the master of all there was what then? Would it really stop men like Pritcher from being straight and tall, self-confident, strong? Would Bail Channis lose his looks? Would he himself be other than he was?

He cursed his doubts. What was he really after?

The cool, overhead warning light flickered. He could follow the progress of the man who had entered the palace and, almost against his will, he felt the soft wash of emotional content touch the fibres of his brain.

He recognized the identity without an effort. It was Channis. Here the Mule saw no uniformity, but the primitive diversity of a strong mind, untouched and unmoulded except by the manifold disorganizations of the Universe. It writhed in

22

floods and waves. There was caution on the surface, a thin, smoothing effect, but with touches of cynical ribaldry in the hidden eddies of it. And underneath there was the strong flow of self-interest and self-love, with a gush of cruel humour here and there, and a deep, still pool of ambition underlying all.

The Mule felt that he could reach out and dam the current, wrench the pool from its basin and turn it in another course, dry up one flow and begin another. But what of it? If he could bend Channis' curly head in the profoundest adoration, would that change his own grotesquerie that made him shun the day and love the night, that made him a recluse inside an empire that was unconditionally his?

The door behind him opened, and he turned. The transparency of the wall faded to opacity, and the darkness gave way to the whitely blazing artifice of atomic power.

Bail Channis sat down lightly and said: 'This is a not-quite-unexpected honour, sir.'

The Mule rubbed his proboscis with all four fingers at once and sounded a bit irritable in his response. 'Why so, young man?'

'A hunch, I suppose. Unless I want to admit that I've been listening to rumours.'

'Rumours? Which one of the several dozen varieties are you referring to?'

'Those that say a renewal of the Galactic Offensive is being planned. It is a hope with me that such is true and that I might play an appropriate part.'

'Then you think there *is* a Second Foundation?'

'Why not? It could make things so much more interesting.'

'And you find interest in it as well?'

'Certainly. In the very mystery of it! What better subject could you find for conjecture? The newspaper supplements are full of nothing else lately – which is probably significant. The *Cosmos* had one of its feature writers compose a weirdie about a world consisting of beings of pure mind – the Second

23

Foundation, you see – who had developed mental force to energies large enough to compete with any known to physical science. Spaceships could be blasted light-years away, planets could be turned out of their orbits—'

'Interesting. Yes. But do *you* have any notions on the subject? Do you subscribe to this mind-power notion?'

'Galaxy, no! Do you think creatures like that would stay on their own planet? No, sir. I think the Second Foundation remains hidden because it is weaker than we think.'

'In that case, I can explain myself very easily. How would you like to head an expedition to locate the Second Foundation?'

For a moment Channis seemed caught up by the sudden rush of events at just a little greater speed than he was prepared for. His tongue had apparently skidded to a halt in a lengthening silence.

The Mule said dryly: 'Well?'

Channis corrugated his forehead. 'Certainly. But where am I to go? Have you any information available?'

'General Pritcher will be with you—'

'Then I'm *not* to head it?'

'Judge for yourself when I'm done. Listen, you're not of the Foundation. You're a native of Kalgan, aren't you? Yes. Well, then, your knowledge of the Seldon plan may be vague. When the first Galactic Empire was falling, Hari Seldon and a group of psychohistorians, analyzing the future course of history by mathematical tools no longer available in these degenerate times, set up two Foundations, one at each end of the Galaxy, in such a way that the economic and sociological forces that were slowly evolving, would make them serve as foci for the Second Empire. Hari Seldon planned on a thousand years to accomplish that – and it would have taken thirty thousand without the Foundations. But he couldn't count on *me*. I am a mutant and I am unpredictable by psychohistory which can only deal with the average reactions of numbers. Do you understand?'

24

'Perfectly, sir. But how does that involve me?'

'You'll understand shortly. I intend to unite the Galaxy now – and reach Seldon's thousand-year goal in three hundred. One Foundation – the world of physical scientists – is still flourishing under *me*. Under the prosperity and order of the Union, the atomic weapons they have developed are capable of dealing with anything in the Galaxy – except perhaps the Second Foundation. So I must know more about it. General Pritcher is of the definite opinion that it does not exist at all. I know otherwise.'

Channis said delicately: 'How do you know, sir?'

And the Mule's words were suddenly liquid indignation: 'Because minds under my control have been interfered with. Delicately! Subtly! But not so subtly that I couldn't notice. And these interferences are increasing, and hitting valuable men at important times. Do you wonder now that a certain discretion has kept me motionless these years?

'That is your importance. General Pritcher is the best man left me, so he is no longer safe. Of course, he does not know that. But *you* are Unconverted and therefore not instantly detectable as a Mule's man. You may fool the Second Foundation longer than one of my own men would – perhaps just sufficiently longer. Do you understand?'

'Um-m-m. Yes. But pardon me, sir, if I question you. How are these men of yours disturbed, so that I might detect change in General Pritcher, in case any occurs. Are they Unconverted again? Do they become disloyal?'

'No. I told you it was subtle. It's more disturbing than that, because it's harder to detect and sometimes I have to wait before acting, uncertain whether a key man is being normally erratic or has been tampered with. Their loyalty is left intact, but initiative and ingenuity are rubbed out. I'm left with a perfectly normal person, apparently, but one completely useless. In the last year, six have been so treated. Six of my best.' A corner of his mouth lifted. 'They're in charge of training bases now – and my most earnest wishes go with them

25

that no emergencies come up for them to decide upon.'

'Suppose, sir . . . suppose it were not the Second Foundation. What if it were another, such as yourself – another mutant?'

'The planning is too careful, too long range. A single man would be in a greater hurry. No, it is a world, and you are to be my weapon against it.'

Channis' eyes shone as he said: I'm delighted at the chance.'

But the Mule caught the sudden emotional upwelling. He said: 'Yes, apparently it occurs to you, that you will perform a unique service, worthy of a unique reward – perhaps even that of being my successor. Quite so. But there are unique punishments, too, you know. My emotional gymnastics are not confined to the creation of loyalty alone.'

And the little smile on his thin lips was grim, as Channis leaped out of his seat in horror.

For just an instant, just one, flashing instant, Channis had felt the pang of an overwhelming grief close over him. It had slammed down with a physical pain that had blackened his mind unbearably, and then lifted. Now nothing was left but the strong wash of anger.

The Mule said: 'Anger won't help . . . yes, you're covering it up now, aren't you? But I can see it. So just remember – *that* sort of business can be made more intense and kept up. I've killed men by emotional control, and there's no death crueler.'

He paused: 'That's all!'

The Mule was alone again. He let the lights die and the wall before him kicked to transparency again. The sky was black, and the rising body of the Galactic lens was spreading its bespanglement across the velvet depths of space.

All that haze of nebula was a mass of stars so numerous that they melted one into the other and left nothing but a cloud of light.

And all to be his—

And now but one last arrangement to make, and he could sleep.

The Executive Council of the Second Foundation was in session. To us they are merely voices. Neither the exact scene of the meeting nor the identity of those present are essential at the point.

Nor, strictly speaking, can we even consider an exact reproduction of any part of the session – unless we wish to sacrifice completely even the minimum comprehensibility we have a right to expect.

We deal here with psychologists – and not merely psychologists. Let us say, rather, scientists with a psychological orientation. That is, men whose fundamental conception of scientific philosophy is pointed in an entirely different direction from all of the orientations we know. The 'psychology' of scientists brought up among the axioms deduced from the observational habits of physical science has only the vaguest relationship to PSYCHOLOGY.

Which is about as far as I can go in explaining colour to a blind man – with myself as blind as the audience.

The point being made is that the minds assembled understood thoroughly the workings of each other, not only by general theory but by the specific application over a long period of these theories to particular individuals. Speech as known to us was unnecessary. A fragment of a sentence amounted almost to long winded redundancy. A gesture, a grunt, the curve of a facial line – even a significantly timed pause yielded informational juice.

The liberty is taken, therefore, of freely translating a small portion of the conference into the extremely specific word-combinations necessary to minds oriented from childhood to a physical science philosophy, even at the risk of losing the more delicate nuances.

There was one 'voice' predominant, and that belonged to the individual known simply as the First Speaker.

He said: 'It is apparently quite definite now as to what

27

stopped the Mule in his first mad rush. I can't say that the matter reflects credit upon ... well, upon the organization of the situation. Apparently, he almost located us, by means of the artificially heightened brain-energy of what they call a "psychologist" on the First Foundation. This psychologist was killed just before he could communicate his discovery to the Mule. The events leading to that killing were completely fortuitous for all calculations below Phase Three. Suppose you take over.'

It was the Fifth Speaker who was indicated by an inflection of the voice. He said, in grim nuances: 'It is certain that the situation was mishandled. We are, of course, highly vulnerable under mass attack, particularly an attack led by such a mental phenomenon as the Mule. Shortly after he first achieved Galactic eminence with the conquest of the First Foundation, half a year after to be exact, he was on Trantor. Within another half year he would have been here and the odds would have been stupendously against us – 96.3 plus or minus 0.05% to be exact. We have spent considerable time analyzing the forces that stopped him. We know, of course, what was driving him on so in the first place. The internal ramifications of his physical deformity and mental uniqueness are obvious to all of us. However, it was only through penetration to Phase Three that we could determine – *after the fact* – the possibility of his anomalous action in the presence of another human being who had an honest affection for him.

'And since such an anomalous action would depend upon the presence of such another human being at the appropriate time, to that extent the whole affair was fortuitous. Our agents are certain that it was a girl that killed the Mule's psychologist – a girl for whom the Mule felt trust out of sentiment, and whom he, therefore, did not control mentally – simply because she liked him.

'Since that event – and for those who want the details, a mathematical treatment of the subject has been drawn up for the Central Library – which warned us, we have held the Mule

28

off by unorthodox methods with which we daily risk Seldon's entire scheme of history. That is all.'

The First Speaker paused an instant to allow the individuals assembled to absorb the full implications. He said: 'The situation is then highly unstable. With Seldon's original scheme bent to the fracture point – and I must emphasize that we have blundered badly in this whole matter, in our horrible lack of foresight – we are faced with an irreversible breakdown of the Plan. Time is passing us by. I think there is only one solution left us – and even that is risky.

'We must allow the Mule to find us – in a sense.'

Another pause, in which he gathered the reactions, then: 'I repeat – in a sense!'

# TWO MEN WITHOUT THE MULE

The ship was in near-readiness. Nothing lacked, but the destination. The Mule had suggested a return to Trantor – the world that was the hulk of an incomparable Galactic metropolis of the hugest Empire mankind had ever known – the dead world that had been capital of all the stars.

Pritcher disapproved. It was an old path – sucked dry.

He found Bail Channis in the ship's navigation room. The young man's curly hair was just sufficiently dishevelled to allow a single curl to droop over the forehead – as if it had been carefully placed there – and even teeth showed in a smile that matched it. Vaguely, the stiff officer felt himself harden against the other.

Channis' excitement was evident, 'Pritcher, it's too far a coincidence.'

The general said coldly: 'I'm not aware of the subject of conversation.'

'Oh— Well, then drag up a chair, old man, and let's get into it. I've been going over your notes. I find them excellent.'

'How ... pleasant that you do.'

'But I'm wondering if you've come to the conclusions I have. Have you ever tried analyzing the problem deductively? I mean, it's all very well to comb the stars at random, and to have done all you did in five expeditions is quite a bit of star-hopping. That's obvious. But have you calculated how long it would take to go through every known world at this rate?'

'Yes. Several times.' Pritcher felt no urge to meet the young man halfway, but there was the importance of filching the other's mind – the other's uncontrolled, and hence, unpredictable, mind.

'Well, then, suppose we're analytical about it and try to

30

decide just what we're looking for?'

'The Second Foundation,' said Pritcher, grimly.

'A Foundation of psychologists,' corrected Channis, 'who are as weak in physical science as the First Foundation was weak in psychology. Well, you're from the First Foundation, which I'm not. The implications are probably obvious to you. We must find a world which rules by virtue of mental skills, and yet which is very backwards scientifically.'

'Is that necessarily so?' questioned Pritcher, quietly. 'Our own "Union of Worlds" isn't backwards scientifically, even though our ruler owes his strength to his mental powers.'

'Because he has the skills of the First Foundation to draw upon,' came the slightly impatient answer, 'and that is the only such reservoir of knowledge in the Galaxy. The Second Foundation must live among the dry crumbs of the broken Galactic Empire. There are no pickings there.'

'So then you postulate mental power sufficient to establish their rule over a group of worlds and physical helplessness as well?'

'*Comparative* physical helplessness. Against the decadent neighbouring areas, they are competent to defend themselves. Against the resurgent forces of the Mule, with his background of a mature atomic economy, they cannot stand. Else, why is their location so well-hidden, both at the start by the founder, Hari Seldon, and now by themselves. Your own First Foundation made no secret of its existence and did not have it made for them, when they were an undefended single city on a lonely planet three hundred years ago.'

The smooth lines of Pritcher's dark face twitched sardonically. 'And now that you've finished your deep analysis, would you like a list of all the kingdoms, republics, planet states and dictatorships of one sort or another in that political wilderness out there that correspond to your description and to several factors besides?'

'All this has been considered then?' Channis lost none of his brashness.

31

'You won't find it here, naturally, but we have a completely worked out guide to the political units of the Opposing Periphery. Really, did you suppose the Mule would work entirely hit-and-miss?'

'Well, then,' and the young man's voice rose in a burst of energy, 'what of the Oligarchy of Tazenda?'

Pritcher touched his ear thoughtfully, 'Tazenda? Oh, I think I know it. They are not in the Periphery, are they? It seems to me they're fully a third of the way towards the centre of the Galaxy.'

'Yes. What of that?'

'The records we have place the Second Foundation at the other end of the Galaxy. Space knows it's the only thing we have to go on. Why talk of Tazenda anyway? Its angular deviation from the First Foundation radian is only about one hundred ten to one hundred twenty degrees anyway. Nowhere near one hundred eighty.'

'There's another point in the records. The Second Foundation was established at "Star's End."'

'No such region in the Galaxy has ever been located.'

'Because it was a local name, suppressed later for greater secrecy. Or maybe one invented for the purpose by Seldon and his group. Yet there's some relationship between "Star's End" and "Tazenda," don't you think?'

'A vague similarity in sound? Insufficient.'

'Have you ever been there?'

'No.'

'Yet it is mentioned in your records.'

'Where? Oh, yes, but that was merely to take on food and water. There was certainly nothing remarkable about the world.'

'Did you land at the ruling planet? The centre of government?'

'I couldn't possibly say.'

Channis brooded about it under the other's cold gaze. Then, 'Would you look at the Lens with me for a moment?'

'Certainly.'

\*    \*    \*

The Lens was perhaps the newest feature of the interstellar cruisers of the day. Actually, it was a complicated calculating machine which could throw on a screen a reproduction of the night sky as seen from any given point of the Galaxy.

Channis adjusted the co-ordinate points and the wall lights of the pilot room were extinguished. In the dim red light at the control board of the Lens, Channis' face glowed ruddily. Pritcher sat in the pilot seat, long legs crossed, face lost in the gloom.

Slowly, as the induction period passed, the points of light brightened on the screen. And then they were thick and bright with the generously populated star-groupings of the Galaxy's centre.

'This,' explained Channis, 'is the winter night-sky as seen from Trantor. That is the important point that, as far as I know, has been neglected so far in your search. All intelligent orientation must start from Trantor as zero point. Trantor was the capital of the Galactic Empire. Even more so scientifically and culturally, than politically. And therefore, the significance of any descriptive name should stem, nine times out of ten, from a Trantorian orientation. You'll remember in this connection that, although Seldon was from Helicon, towards the Periphery, his group worked on Trantor itself.'

'What is it you're trying to show me?' Pritcher's level voice plunged icily into the gathering enthusiasm of the other.

'The map will explain it. Do you see the dark nebula?' The shadow of his arm fell upon the screen, which took on the be-spanglement of the Galaxy. The pointing finger ended on a tiny patch of black that seemed a hole in the speckled fabric of light. 'The stellagraphical records call it Pellot's Nebula. Watch it. I'm going to expand the image.'

Pritcher had watched the phenomenon of Lens Image expansion before but he still caught his breath. It was like being at the visiplate of a spaceship storming through a horribly crowded Galaxy without entering hyperspace. The stars diverged towards them from a common centre, flared outwards and tumbled off the edge of the screen. Single points

33

became double, then globular. Hazy patches dissolved into myriad points. And always that illusion of motion.

Channis spoke through it all, 'You'll notice that we are moving along the direct line from Trantor to Pellot's Nebula, so that in effect we are still looking at a stellar orientation equivalent to that of Trantor. There is probably a slight error because of the gravitic deviation of light that I haven't the math to calculate for, but I'm sure it can't be significant.'

The darkness was spreading over the screen. As the rate of magnification slowed, the stars slipped off the four ends of the screen in a regretful leave-taking. At the rims of the growing nebula, the brilliant universe of stars shone abruptly in token for that light which was merely hidden behind the swirling unradiating atom fragments of sodium and calcium that filled cubic parsecs of space.

And Channis pointed again, 'This has been called "The Mouth" by the inhabitants of that region of space. And that is significant because it is only from the Trantorian orientation that it looks like a mouth.' What he indicated was a rift in the body of the Nebula, shaped like a ragged, grinning mouth in profile, outlined by the blazing glory of the starlight with which it was filled.

'Follow "The Mouth,"' said Channis, 'Follow "The Mouth" towards the gullet as it narrows down to a thin, splintering line of light.'

Again the screen expanded a trifle, until the Nebula stretched away from 'The Mouth' to block off all the screen but that narrow trickle and Channis' finger silently followed it down, to where it straggled to a halt, and then, as his finger continued moving onward, to a spot where one single star sparked lonesomely, and there his finger halted, for beyond that was blackness, unrelieved.

'"Star's End,"' said the young man, simply. 'The fabric of the Nebula is thin there and the light of that one star finds its way through in just that one direction – to shine on Trantor.'

'You're trying to tell me that—' the voice of the Mule's

34

general died in suspicion.

'I'm not trying. That *is* Tazenda – Star's End.'

The lights went on. The Lens flicked off. Pritcher reached Channis in three long strides, 'What made you think of this?'

And Channis leaned back in his chair with a queerly puzzled expression on his face. 'It was accidental. I'd like to take intellectual credit for this, but it was only accidental. In any case, however it happens, it fits. According to our references, Tazenda is an oligarchy. It rules twenty-seven inhabited planets. It is not advanced scientifically. And most of all, it is an obscure world that has adhered to a strict neutrality in the local politics of that stellar region, and is not expansionist. I think we ought to see it.'

'Have you informed the Mule of this?'

'No. Nor shall we. We're in space now, about to make the first hop.'

Pritcher, in sudden horror, sprang to the visiplate. Cold space met his eyes when he adjusted it. He gazed fixedly at the view, then turned. Automatically, his hand reached for the hard, comfortable curve of the butt of his blaster.

'By whose order?'

'By my order, general' – it was the first time Channis had ever used the other's title – 'while I was engaging you here. You probably felt no acceleration, because it came at the moment I was expanding the field of the Lens and you undoubtedly imagined it to be an illusion of the apparent star motion.'

'Why — Just what are you doing? What was the point of your nonsense about Tazenda, then?'

'That was no nonsense. I was completely serious. We're going there. We left today because we were scheduled to leave three days from now. General, you don't believe there is a Second Foundation, and I do. *You* are merely following the Mule's orders without faith; *I* recognize a serious danger. The Second Foundation has now had five years to prepare. How

35

they've prepared, I don't know, but what if they have agents on Kalgan. If I carry about in my mind the knowledge of the whereabouts of the Second Foundation, they may discover that. My life might be no longer safe, and I have a great affection for my life. Even on a thin and remote possibility such as that, I would rather play safe. So no one knows of Tazenda but you, and you found out only after we were out in space. And even so, there is the question of the crew.' Channis was smiling again, ironically, in obviously complete control of the situation.

Pritcher's hand fell away from his blaster, and for a moment a vague discomfort pierced him. What kept *him* from action? What deadened *him*? There was a time when he was a rebellious and unpromoted captain of the First Foundation's commercial empire, when it would have been *himself* rather than Channis who would have taken prompt and daring action such as that. Was the Mule right? Was his controlled mind so concerned with obedience as to lose initiative? He felt a thickening despondency drive him down into a strange lassitude.

He said, 'Well done! However, you will consult me in the future before making decisions of this nature.'

The flickering signal caught his attention.

'That's the engine room,' said Channis, casually. 'They warmed up on five minutes' notice and I asked them to let me know if there was any trouble. Want to hold the fort?'

Pritcher nodded mutely, and cogitated in the sudden loneliness on the evils of approaching fifty. The visiplate was sparsely starred. The main body of the Galaxy misted one end. What if he were free of the Mule's influence—

But he recoiled in horror at the thought.

Chief Engineer Huxlani looked sharply at the young, ununiformed man who carried himself with the assurance of a Fleet officer and seemed to be in a position of authority. Huxlani, as a regular Fleet man from the days his chin had dripped milk, generally confused authority with specific insignia.

But the Mule had appointed this man, and the Mule was, of course, the last word. The only word for that matter. Not even subconsciously did he question that. Emotional control went deep.

He handed Channis the little oval object without a word.

Channis lifted it, and smiled engagingly.

'You're a Foundation man, aren't you, chief?'

'Yes, sir. I served in the Foundation Fleet eighteen years before the First Citizen took over.'

'Foundation training in engineering?'

'Qualified Technician, First Class – Central School on Anacreon.'

'Good enough. And you found this on the communication circuit, where I asked you to look?'

'Yes, sir.'

'Does it belong there?'

'No, sir.'

'Then what is it?'

'A hypertracer, sir.'

'That's not enough. I'm not a Foundation man. What is it?'

'It's a device to allow the ship to be traced through hyperspace.'

'In other words we can be followed anywhere.'

'Yes, sir.'

'All right. It's a recent invention, isn't it? It was developed by one of the Research Institutes set up by the First Citizen, wasn't it?'

'I believe so, sir.'

'And its workings are a government secret. Right?'

'I believe so, sir.'

'Yet here it is. Intriguing.'

Channis tossed the hypertracer methodically from hand to hand for a few seconds. Then, sharply, he held it out, 'Take it, then, and put it back exactly where you found it and exactly how you found it. Understand? And then forget this incident. Entirely!'

The chief choked down his near-automatic salute, turned sharply and left.

\*　　\*　　\*

The ship bounded through the Galaxy, its path a wide-spaced dotted line through the stars. The dots, referred to, were the scant stretches of ten to sixty light-seconds spent in normal space and between them stretched the hundred-and-up light-year gaps that represented the 'hops' through hyperspace.

Bail Channis sat at the control panel of the Lens and felt again the involuntary surge of near-worship at the contemplation of it. He was not a Foundation man and the interplay of forces at the twist of a knob or the breaking of a contact was not second nature to him.

Not that the Lens ought quite to bore even a Foundation man. Within its unbelievably compact body were enough electronic circuits to pin point accurately a hundred million separate stars in exact relationship to each other. And as if that were not a feat in itself, it was further capable of translating any given portion of the Galactic Field along any of the three spatial axes or to rotate any portion of the Field about a centre.

It was because of that, that the Lens had performed a near-revolution in interstellar travel. In the younger days of interstellar travel, the calculation of each 'hop' through hyperspace meant any amount of work from a day to a week – and the larger portion of such work was the more or less precise calculation of 'Ship's Position' on the Galactic scale of reference. Essentially that meant the accurate observation of at least three widely-spaced stars, the position of which, with reference to the arbitrary Galactic triple-zero, were known.

And it is the word 'known,' that is the catch. To any who know the star field well from one certain reference point, stars are as individual as people. Jump ten parsecs, however, and not even your own sun is recognizable. It may not even be visible.

The answer was, of course, spectroscopic analysis. For centuries, the main object of interstellar engineering was the analysis of the 'light signature' of more and more stars in greater and greater detail. With this, and the growing precision of the 'hop,' itself, standard routes of travel through the Galaxy were adopted and interstellar travel became less of an art and more of a science.

And yet, even under the Foundation with improved calculating machines and a new method of mechanically scanning the star field for a known 'light signature,' it sometimes took days to locate three stars and then calculate positions in regions not previously familiar to the pilot.

It was the Lens that changed all that. For one thing it required only a single known star. For another, even a space tyro such as Channis could operate it.

The nearest sizeable star at the moment was Vincetori, according to 'hop' calculations, and on the visiplate now, a bright star was centred. Channis hoped that it was Vincetori.

The field screen of the Lens was thrown directly next that of the visiplate and with careful fingers, Channis punched out the co-ordinates of Vincetori. He closed a relay, and the star field sprang to bright view. In it, too, a bright star was centred, but otherwise there seemed no relationship. He adjusted the Lens along the Z-axis and expanded the Field to where the photometer showed both centred stars to be of equal brightness.

Channis looked for a second star, sizeably bright, on the visiplate and found one on the field screen to correspond. Slowly, he rotated the screen to similar angular deflection. He twisted his mouth and rejected the result with a grimace. Again he rotated and another bright star was brought into position, and a third. And then he grinned. That did it. Perhaps a specialist with trained relationship perception might have clicked first try, but he'd settle for three.

That was the adjustment. In the final step, the two fields overlapped and merged into a sea of not-quite-rightness. Most of the stars were close doubles. But the fine adjustment did not take long. The double stars melted together, one field remained, and the 'Ship's Position' could now be read directly off the dials. The entire procedure had taken less than half an hour.

Channis found Han Pritcher in his private quarters. The general was quite apparently preparing for bed. He looked up.

'News?'

'Not particularly. We'll be at Tazenda in another hop.'

'I know.'

'I don't want to bother you if you're turning in, but have you looked through the film we picked up in Cil?'

Han Pritcher cast a disparaging look at the article in question, where it lay in its black case upon his low bookshelf, 'Yes.'

'And what do you think?'

'I think that if there was ever any science to History, it has been quite lost in this region of the Galaxy.'

Channis grinned broadly, 'I know what you mean. Rather barren, isn't it?'

'Not if you enjoy personal chronicles of rulers. Probably unreliable, I should say, in both directions. Where history concerns mainly personalities, the drawings become either black or white according to the interests of the writer. I find it all remarkably useless.'

'But there is talk about Tazenda. That's the point I tried to make when I gave you the film. It's the only one I could find that even mentioned them.'

'All right. They have good rulers and bad. They've conquered a few planets, won some battles, lost a few. There is nothing distinctive about them. I don't think much of your theory, Channis.'

'But you've missed a few points. Didn't you notice that they never formed coalitions? They always remained completely outside the politics of this corner of the star swarm. As you say, they conquered a few planets, but then they stopped – and that without any startling defeat of consequence. It's just as if they spread out enough to protect themselves, but not enough to attract attention.'

'Very well,' came the unemotional response. 'I have no objection to landing. At the worst – a little lost time.'

'Oh, no. At the worst – complete defeat. If it *is* the Second Foundation. Remember it would be a world of space-knows-how-many Mules.'

'What do you plan to do?'

'Land on some minor subject planet. Find out as much as we can about Tazenda first, then improvise from that.'

'All right. No objection. If you don't mind now, I *would* like the light out.'

Channis left with a wave of his hand.

And in the darkness of a tiny room in an island of driving metal lost in the vastness of space, General Han Pritcher remained awake, following the thoughts that led him through such fantastic reaches.

If everything he had so painfully decided were true – and how all the facts were beginning to fit – then Tazenda *was* the Second Foundation. There was no way out. But how? How?

*Could* it be Tazenda? An ordinary world? One without distinction? A slum lost amid the wreckage of an Empire? A splinter among the fragments? He remembered, as from a distance, the Mule's shrivelled face and his thin voice as he used to speak of the old Foundation psychologist, Ebling Mis, the one man who had – maybe – learned the secret of the Second Foundation.

Pritcher recalled the tension of the Mule's words: 'It was as if astonishment had overwhelmed Mis. It was as though something about the Second Foundation had surpassed all his expectations, had driven in a direction completely different from what he might have assumed. If I could only have read his thoughts rather than his emotions. Yet the emotions were plain – and above everything else was this vast surprise.'

Surprise was the keynote. Something supremely astonishing! And now came this boy, this grinning youngster, glibly joyful about Tazenda and its undistinguished subnormality. And he had to be right. He *had* to. Otherwise, nothing made sense.

Pritcher's last conscious thought had a touch of grimness. That hypertracer along the Etheric tube was still there. He had checked it one hour back, with Channis well out of the way.

It was a casual meeting in the anteroom of the Council Chamber – just a few moments before passing into the Chamber to take up the business of the day – and the few thoughts flashed back and forth quickly.

'So the Mule is on his way.'

'That's what I hear, too. Risky! Mighty risky!'

'Not if affairs adhere to the functions set up.'

'The Mule is not an ordinary man – and it is difficult to manipulate his chosen instruments without detection by him. The controlled minds are difficult to touch. They say he's caught on to a few cases.'

'Yes, I don't see how that can be avoided.'

'Uncontrolled minds are easier. But so few are in positions of authority under him—'

They entered the Chamber. Others of the Second Foundation followed them.

# 3

# TWO MEN AND A PEASANT

Rossem is one of those marginal worlds usually neglected in Galactic history and scarcely ever obtruding itself upon the notice of men of the myriad happier planets.

In the latter days of the Galactic Empire, a few political prisoners had inhabited its wastes, while an observatory and a small Naval garrison served to keep it from complete desertion. Later, in the evil days of strife, even before the time of Hari Seldon, the weaker sort of men, tired of the periodic decades of insecurity and danger; weary of sacked planets and a ghostly succession of ephemeral emperors making their way to the Purple for a few wicked, fruitless years – these men fled the populated centres and sought shelter in the barren nooks of the Galaxy.

Along the chilly wastes of Rossem, villages huddled. Its sun was a small ruddy niggard that clutched its dribble of heat to itself, while snow beat thinly down for nine months of the year. The tough native grain lay dormant in the soil those snow filled months, then grew and ripened in almost panic speed, when the sun's reluctant radiation brought the temperature to nearly fifty.

Small, goatlike animals cropped the grasslands, kicking the thin snow aside with tiny, tri-hooved feet.

The men of Rossem had, thus, their bread and their milk – and when they could spare an animal – even their meat. The darkly ominous forests that gnarled their way over half of the equatorial region of the planet supplied a tough, fine-grained wood for housing. This wood, together with certain furs and minerals, was even worth exporting, and the ships of the Empire came at times and brought in exchange farm machinery, atomic heaters, even televisor sets. The last was not really incongruous, for the long winter imposed a lonely hibernation upon the peasant.

Imperial history flowed past the peasants of Rossem. The trading ships might bring news in impatient spurts; occasionally new fugitives would arrive – at one time, a relatively large group arrived in a body and remained – and these usually had news of the Galaxy.

It was then that the Rossemites learned of sweeping battles and decimated populations or of tyrannical emperors and rebellious viceroys. And they would sigh and shake their heads, and draw their fur collars closer about their bearded faces as they sat about the village square in the weak sun and philosophized on the evil of men.

Then after a while, no trading ships arrived at all, and life grew harder. Supplies of foreign, soft food, of tobacco, of machinery stopped. Vague word from scraps gathered on the televisor brought increasingly disturbing news. And finally it spread that Trantor had been sacked. The great capital world of all the Galaxy, the splendid, storied, unapproachable and incomparable home of the emperors had been despoiled and ruined and brought to utter destruction.

It was something inconceivable, and to many of the peasants of Rossem, scratching away at their fields, it might well seem that the end of the Galaxy was at hand.

And then one day not unlike other days a ship arrived again. The old men of each village nodded wisely and lifted their old eyelids to whisper that thus it had been in their father's time – but it wasn't, quite.

This ship was not an Imperial ship. The glowing Spaceship-and-Sun of the Empire was missing from its prow. It was a stubby affair made of scraps of older ships – and the men within called themselves soldiers of Tazenda.

The peasants were confused. They had not heard of Tazenda, but they greeted the soldiers nevertheless in the traditional fashion of hospitality. The newcomers inquired closely as to the nature of the planet, the number of its inhabitants, the number of its cities – a word mistaken by the peasants to mean 'villages' to the confusion of all concerned – its type of economy and so on.

Other ships came and proclamations were issued all over the world that Tazenda was now the ruling world, that tax-collecting stations would be established girdling the equator – the inhabited region – that percentages of grain and furs according to certain numerical formulae would be collected annually.

The Rossemites had blinked solemnly, uncertain of the word 'taxes.' When collection time came, many had paid, or had stood by in confusion while the uniformed, other wordlings loaded the harvested corn and the pelts on to the broad ground-cars.

Here and there indignant peasants banded together and brought out ancient hunting weapons – but of this nothing ever came. Grumblingly they had disbanded when the men of Tazenda came and with dismay watched their hard struggle for existence become harder.

But a new equilibrium was reached. The Tazendian governor lived dourly in the village of Gentri, from which all Rossemites were barred. He and the officials under him were dim otherworld beings that rarely impinged on the Rossemite ken. The tax farmers, Rossemites in the employ of Tazenda, came periodically, but they were creatures of custom now – and the peasant had learned how to hide his grain and drive his cattle into the forest, and refrain from having his hut appear too ostentatiously prosperous. Then with a dull, uncomprehending expression he would greet all sharp questioning as to his assets by merely pointing at what they could see.

Even that grew less, and taxes decreased, almost as if Tazenda wearied of extorting pennies from such a world.

Trading sprang up and perhaps Tazenda found that more profitable. The men of Rossem no longer received in exchange the polished creations of the Empire, but even Tazendian

45

machines and Tazendian food was better than the native stuff. And there were clothes for the women of other than grey homespun, which was a very important thing.

So once again, Galactic history glided past peacefully enough, and the peasants scrabbled life out of the hard soil.

Narovi blew into his beard as he stepped out of his cottage. The first snows were sifting across the hard ground and the sky was a dull, overcast pink. He squinted carefully upward and decided that no real storm was in sight. He could travel to Gentri without much trouble and get rid of his surplus grain in return for enough canned food to last the winter.

He roared back through the door, which he opened a crack for the purpose: 'Has the car been fed its fuel, yunker?'

A voice shouted from within, and then Narovi's oldest son, his short, red beard not yet completely outgrown its boyish sparseness, joined him.

'The car,' he said, sullenly, 'is fuelled and rides well, but for the bad condition of the axles. For that I am of no blame. I have told you it needs expert repairs.'

The old man stepped back and surveyed his son through lowering eyebrows, then thrust his hairy chin outward: 'And is the fault mine? Where and in what manner may I achieve expert repairs? Has the harvest then been anything but scanty for five years? Have my herds escaped the pest? Have the pelts climbed of themselves—'

'Narovi!' The well-known voice from within stopped him in mid-word. He grumbled, 'Well, well – and now your mother must insert herself into the affairs of a father and his son. Bring out the car, and see to it that the storage trailers are securely attached.'

He pounded his gloved hands together, and looked upward again. The dimly-ruddy clouds were gathering and the grey sky that showed in the rifts bore no warmth. The sun was hidden.

He was at the point of looking away, when his dropping eyes

caught and his finger almost automatically rose on high while his mouth fell open in a shout, in complete disregard of the cold air.

'Wife,' he called vigorously, 'Old woman – come here.'

An indignant head appeared at a window. The woman's eyes followed his finger, gaped. With a cry, she dashed down the wooden stairs, snatching up an old wrap and a square of linen as she went. She emerged with the linen wrapped insecurely over her head and ears, and the wrap dangling from her shoulders.

She snuffled: 'It is a ship from outer space.'

And Narovi remarked impatiently: 'And what else could it be? We have visitors, old woman, visitors!'

The ship was sinking slowly to a landing on the bare frozen field in the northern portions of Narovi's farm.

'But what shall we do?' gasped the woman. 'Can we offer these people hospitality? Is the dirt floor of our hovel to be theirs and the pickings of last week's hoecake?'

'Shall they then go to our neighbours?' Narovi purpled past the crimson induced by the cold and his arms in their sleek fur covering lunged out and seized the woman's brawny shoulders.

'Wife of my soul,' he purred, 'you will take the two chairs from our room downstairs; you will see that a fat youngling is slaughtered and roasted with tubers; you will bake a fresh hoecake. I go now to greet these men of power from outer space ... and ... and—' He paused, placed his great cap awry, and scratched hesitantly. 'Yes, I shall bring my jug of brewed grain as well. Hearty drink is pleasant.'

The woman's mouth had flapped idly during this speech. Nothing came out. And when that stage passed, it was only a discordant screech that issued.

Narovi lifted a finger, 'Old woman, what was it the village Elders said a sc'nnight since? Eh? Stir your memory. The Elders went from farm to farm – themselves! Imagine the importance of it! – to ask us that should any ships from outer space land, they were to be informed immediately *on the orders of the governor.*

47

'And now shall I not seize the opportunity to win into the good graces of those in power? Regard that ship. Have you ever seen its like? These men from the outer world are rich, great. The governor himself sends such urgent messages concerning them that the Elders walk from farm to farm in the cooling weather. Perhaps the message is sent throughout all Rossem that these men are greatly desired by the Lords of Tazenda – and it is on my farm that they are landing.'

He fairly hopped for anxiety, 'The proper hospitality now – the mention of my name to the governor – and what may not be ours?'

His wife was suddenly aware of the cold biting through her thin house-clothing. She leaped towards the door, shouting over her shoulders, 'Leave then quickly.'

But she was speaking to a man who was even then racing towards the segment of the horizon against which the ship sank.

Neither the cold of the world, nor its bleak, empty spaces worried General Han Pritcher. Nor the poverty of their surroundings, nor the perspiring peasant himself.

What did bother him was the question of the wisdom of their tactics? He and Channis were alone here.

The ship, left in space, could take care of itself in ordinary circumstances, but still, he felt unsafe. It was Channis, of course, who was responsible for this move. He looked across at the young man and caught him winking cheerfully at the gap in the furred partition, in which a woman's peeping eyes and gaping mouth momentarily appeared.

Channis, at least, seemed completely at ease. That fact Pritcher savoured with a vinegary satisfaction. His game had not much longer to proceed exactly as he wished it. Yet, meanwhile their wrist ultrawave sender-receivers were their only connection with the ship.

And then the peasant host smiled enormously and bobbed his head several times and said in a voice oily with respect,

'Noble Lords, I crave leave to tell you that my eldest son – a good, worthy lad whom my poverty prevents from educating as his wisdom deserves – has informed me that the Elders will arrive soon. I trust your stay here has been as pleasant as my humble means – for I am poverty-stricken, though a hard-working, honest, and humble farmer, as anyone here will tell you – could afford.'

'Elders?' said Channis, lightly. 'The chief men of the region here?'

'So they are, Noble Lords, and honest, worthy men all of them, for our entire village is known throughout Rossem as a just and righteous spot – though living is hard and the returns of the fields and forests meagre. Perhaps you will mention to the Elders, Noble Lords, of my respect and honour for travellers and it may happen that they will request a new motor wagon for our household as the old one can scarcely creep and upon the remnant of it depends our livelihood.'

He looked humbly eager and Han Pritcher nodded with the properly aloof condescension required of the role of 'Noble Lords' bestowed upon them.

'A report of your hospitality shall reach the ears of your Elders.'

Pritcher seized the next moments of isolation to speak to the apparently half-sleeping Channis.

'I am not particularly fond of this meeting of the Elders,' he said. 'Have you any thoughts on the subject?'

Channis seemed surprised. 'No. What worries you?'

'It seems we have better things to do than to become conspicuous here.'

Channis spoke hastily, in a low monotoned voice: 'It may be necessary to risk becoming conspicuous in our next moves. We won't find the type of men we want, Pritcher, by simply reaching out a hand into a dark bag and groping. Men who rule by tricks of the mind need not necessarily be men in obvious power. In the first place, the psychologists of the Second Foundation are probably a very small minority of the total population, just as on your own First Foundation, the technicians and scientists formed a minority. The ordinary inhabitants are probably just that – very ordinary. The psychologists may even be well hidden, and the men in the apparently ruling position may honestly think they are the true masters. Our solution to that problem may be found here on this frozen lump of a planet.'

'I don't follow that at all.'

'Why, see here, it's obvious enough. Tazenda is probably a huge world of millions or hundreds of millions. How could we identify the psychologists among them and be able to report truly to the Mule that we have located the Second Foundation? But here, on this tiny peasant world and subject planet, all the Tazendian rulers, our host informs us, are concentrated in their chief village of Gentri. There may be only a few hundred of them there, Pritcher, and among them *must* be one or more of the men of the Second Foundation. We will go there eventually, but let us see the Elders first – it's a logical step on the way.'

They drew apart easily, as their black-bearded host tumbled into the room again, obviously agitated.

'Noble Lords, the Elders are arriving. I crave leave to beg you once more to mention a word, perhaps, on my behalf—' He almost bent double in a paroxysm of fawning.

'We shall certainly remember you,' said Channis. 'Are these your Elders?'

They apparently were. There were three.

One approached. He bowed with a dignified respect and said: 'We are honoured. Transportation has been provided. Respected sirs, and we hope for the pleasure of your company at our Meeting Hall.'


THIRD INTERLUDE

The First Speaker gazed wistfully at the night sky. Wispy clouds scudded across the faint stargleams. Space looked actively hostile. It was cold and awful at best but now it contained that strange creature, the Mule, and the very content seemed to darken and thicken it into ominous threat.

The meeting was over. It had not been long. There had been the doubts and questionings inspired by the difficult mathematical problem of dealing with a mental mutant of uncertain makeup. All the extreme permutations had had to be considered.

Were they even yet certain? Somewhere in this region of space – within reaching distance as Galactic spaces go – was the Mule. What would he do?

It was easy enough to handle his men. They reacted – and were reacting – according to plan.

But what of the Mule himself?

# 4

# TWO MEN AND THE ELDERS

The Elders of this particular region of Rossem were not exactly what one might have expected. They were not a mere extrapolation of the peasantry; older, more authoritative, less friendly.

Not at all.

The dignity that had marked them at first meeting had grown in impression till it had reached the mark of being their predominant characteristic.

They sat about their oval table like so many grave and slow-moving thinkers. Most were a trifle past their physical prime, though the few who possessed beards wore them short and neatly arranged. Still, enough appeared younger than forty to make it quite obvious that 'Elders' was a term of respect rather than entirely a literal description of age.

The two from outer space were at the head of the table and in the solemn silence that accompanied a rather frugal meal that seemed ceremonious rather than nourishing, absorbed the new, contrasting atmosphere.

After the meal and after one or two respectful remarks – too short and simple to be called speeches – had been made by those of the Elders apparently held most in esteem, an informality forced itself upon the assembly.

It was as if the dignity of greeting foreign personages had finally given way to the amiable rustic qualities of curiosity and friendliness.

They crowded around the two strangers and the flood of questions came.

They asked if it were difficult to handle a spaceship, how many men were required for the job, if better motors could be made for their ground-cars, if it was true that it rarely snowed on other worlds as was said to be the case with Tazenda, how many people lived on their world, if it was as large as Tazenda, if it was far away, how their clothes were woven and what gave them the metallic shimmer, why they did not wear furs, if they shaved every day, what sort of stone was that in Pritcher's ring— The list stretched out.

And almost always the questions were addressed to Pritcher as though, as the elder, they automatically invested him with the greater authority. Pritcher found himself forced to answer at greater and greater length. It was like an immersion in a crowd of children. Their questions were those of utter and disarming wonder. Their eagerness to know was completely irresistible and would not be denied.

Pritcher explained that spaceships were not difficult to handle and that crews varied with the size, from one to many, that the motors of their ground cars were unknown in detail to him but could doubtless be improved, that the climates of worlds varied almost infinitely, that many hundreds of millions lived on his world but that it was far smaller and more insignificant than the great empire of Tazenda, that their clothes were woven of silicone plastics in which metallic luster was artificially produced by proper orientation of the surface molecules, and that they could be artificially heated so that furs were unnecessary, that they shaved every day, that the stone in his ring was an amethyst. The list stretched out. He found himself thawing to these naïve provincials against his will.

And always as he answered there was a rapid chatter among the Elders, as though they debated the information gained. It was difficult to follow these inner discussions of theirs for they lapsed into their own accented version of the universal Galactic language that, through long separation from the currents of living speech, had become archaic.

Almost, one might say, their curt comments among themselves hovered on the edge of understanding, but just managed to elude the clutching tendrils of comprehension.

Until finally Channis interrupted to say, 'Good sirs, you

must answer us for a while, for we are strangers and would be very much interested to know all we can of Tazenda.'

And what happened then was that a great silence fell and each of the hitherto voluble Elders grew silent. Their hands, which had been moving in such rapid and delicate accompaniment to their words as though to give them greater scope and varied shades of meaning, fell suddenly limp. They stared furtively at one another, apparently quite willing to let the other have all the floor.

Pritcher interposed quickly, 'My companion asks this in friendliness, for the fame of Tazenda fills the Galaxy and we, of course, shall inform the governor of the loyalty and love of the Elders of Rossem.'

No sigh of relief was heard but faces brightened. An Elder stroked his beard with thumb and forefinger, straightening its slight curl with a gentle pressure, and said: 'We are faithful servants of the Lords of Tazenda.'

Pritcher's annoyance at Channis' bald question subsided. It was apparent, at least, that the age that he had felt creeping over him of late had not yet deprived him of his own capacity for making smooth the blunders of others.

He continued: 'We do not know, in our far part of the universe, much of the past history of the Lords of Tazenda. We presume they have ruled benevolently here for a long time.'

The same Elder who spoke before, answered. In a soft, automatic way he had become spokesman. He said: 'Not the grandfather of the oldest can recall a time in which the Lords were absent.'

'It has been a time of peace?'

'It has been a time of peace!' He hesitated. 'The governor is a strong and powerful Lord who would not hesitate to punish traitors. None of us are traitors, of course.'

'He has punished some in the past, I imagine, as they deserve.'

Again hesitation, 'None here have ever been traitors, or our fathers or our fathers' fathers. But on other worlds, there have been such, and death followed for them quickly. It is not good to think of for we are humble men who are poor farmers and not concerned with matters of politics.'

The anxiety of his voice, the universal concern in the eyes of all of them was obvious.

Pritcher said smoothly: 'Could you inform us as to how we can arrange an audience with your governor.'

And instantly an element of sudden bewilderment entered the situation.

For after a long moment, the elder said: 'Why, did you not know? The governor will be here tomorrow. He has expected you. It has been a great honour for us. We ... we hope earnestly that you will report to him satisfactorily as to our loyalty to him.'

Pritcher's smile scarcely twitched. 'Expected us?'

The Elder looked wonderingly from one to the other. 'Why ... it is now a week since we have been waiting for you.'

Their quarters were undoubtedly luxurious for the world. Pritcher had lived in worse. Channis showed nothing but indifference to externals.

But there was an element of tension between them of a different nature than hitherto. Pritcher felt the time approaching for a definite decision and yet there was still the desirability of additional waiting. To see the governor first would be to increase the gamble to dangerous dimensions and yet to win that gamble might multi-double the winnings. He felt a surge of anger at the slight crease between Channis' eyebrows, the delicate uncertainty with which the young man's lower lip presented itself to an upper tooth. He detested the useless play-acting and yearned for an end to it.

He said: 'We seem to be anticipated.'

'Yes,' said Channis, simply.

'Just that? You have no contribution of greater pith to make. We come here and find that the governor expects us. Presumably we shall find from the governor that Tazenda itself

55

expects us. Of what value then is our entire mission?'

Channis looked up, without endeavouring to conceal the weary note in his voice: 'To expect us is one thing; to know who we are and what we came for, is another.'

'Do you expect to conceal these things from men of the Second Foundation?'

'Perhaps. Why not? Are you ready to throw your hand in? Suppose our ship was detected in space. Is it unusual for a realm to maintain frontier observation posts? Even if we were ordinary strangers, we would be of interest.'

'Sufficient interest for a governor to come to us rather than the reverse?'

Channis shrugged: 'We'll have to meet that problem later. Let us see what this governor is like.'

Pritcher bared his teeth in a bloodless kind of scowl. The situation was becoming ridiculous.

Channis proceeded with an artificial animation: 'At least we know one thing. Tazenda is the Second Foundation or a million shreds of evidence are unanimously pointing the wrong way. How do you interpret the obvious terror in which these natives hold Tazenda? I see no signs of political domination. Their groups of Elders apparently meet freely and without interference of any sort. The taxation they speak of doesn't seem at all extensive to me or efficiently carried through. The natives speak much of poverty but seem sturdy and well-fed. The houses are uncouth and their villages rude, but are obviously adequate for the purpose.

'In fact, the world fascinates me. I have never seen a more forbidding one, yet I am convinced there is no suffering among the population and that their uncomplicated lives manage to contain a well-balanced happiness lacking in the sophisticated populations of the advanced centres.'

'Are you an admirer of peasant virtues, then?'

'The stars forbid.' Channis seemed amused at the idea. 'I merely point out the significance of all this. Apparently, Tazenda is an efficient administrator – efficient in a sense far different from the efficiency of the Old Empire or of the First Foundation, or even of our own Union. All these have brought mechanical efficiency to their subjects at the cost of more intangible values. Tazenda brings happiness and sufficiency. Don't you see that the whole orientation of their domination is different? It is not physical, but psychological.'

'Really?' Pritcher allowed himself irony. 'And the terror with which the Elders spoke of the punishment of treason by these kind hearted psychologist administrators? How does that suit your thesis?'

'Were they the objects of the punishment? They speak of punishment only of others. It is as if knowledge of punishment has been so well implanted in them that punishment itself need never be used. The proper mental attitudes are so inserted into their minds that I am certain that not a Tazendian soldier exists on the planet. Don't you *see* all this?'

'I'll see perhaps,' said Pritcher, coldly, 'when I see the governor. And what, by the way, if *our* mentalities are handled?'

Channis replied with brutal contempt: '*You* should be accustomed to *that*.'

Pritcher whitened perceptibly, and, with an effort, turned away. They spoke to one another no more that day.

It was in the silent windlessness of the frigid night, as he listened to the soft, sleeping motions of the other, that Pritcher silently adjusted his wrist-transmitter to the ultrawave region for which Channis' was unadjustable and, with noiseless touches of his fingernail, contacted the ship.

The answer came in little periods of noiseless vibration that barely lifted themselves above the sensory threshold.

Twice Pritcher asked: 'Any communications at all yet?'

Twice the answer came: 'None. We wait always.'

He got out of bed. It was cold in the room and he pulled the furry blanket around him as he sat in the chair and stared out at the crowding stars so different in the brightness and complexity of their arrangement from the even fog of the Galactic Lens that dominated the night sky of his native Periphery.

Somewhere there between the stars was the answer to the complications that overwhelmed him, and he felt the yearning for that solution to arrive and end things.

For a moment he wondered again if the Mule were right – if Conversion had robbed him of the firm sharp edge of self-reliance. Or was it simply age and the fluctuations of these last years?

He didn't really care.

He was tired.

The governor of Rossem arrived with minor ostentation. His only companion was the uniformed man at the controls of the ground-car.

The ground-car itself was of lush design but to Pritcher it appeared inefficient. It turned clumsily; more than once it apparently balked at what might have been a too-rapid change of gears. It was obvious at once from its design that it ran on chemical, and not on atomic, fuel.

The Tazendian governor stepped softly on to the thin layer of snow and advanced between two lines of respectful Elders. He did not look on them but entered quickly. They followed after him.

From the quarters assigned to them, the two men of the Mule's Union watched. He – the governor – was thickset, rather stocky, short, unimpressive.

But what of that?

Pritcher cursed himself for a failure of nerve. His face, to be sure, remained icily calm. There was no humiliation before Channis – but he knew very well that his blood pressure had heightened and his throat had become dry.

It was not a case of physical fear. He was not one of those dull-witted, unimaginative men of nerveless meat who were too stupid ever to be afraid – but physical fear he could account for and discount.

58

But this was different. It was the other fear.

He glanced quickly at Channis. The young man glanced idly at the nails of one hand and poked leisurely at some trifling unevenness.

Something inside Pritcher became vastly indignant. What had Channis to fear of mental handling?

Pritcher caught a mental breath and tried to think back. How had he been before the Mule had Converted him from the diehard Democrat that he was. It was hard to remember. He could not place himself mentally. He could not break the clinging wires that bound him emotionally to the Mule. Intellectually, he could remember that he had once tried to assassinate the Mule but not for all the straining he could endure, could he remember his emotions at the time. That might be the self-defence of his own mind, however, for at the intuitive thought of what those emotions might have been – not realizing the details, but merely comprehending the drift of it – his stomach grew queasy.

What if the governor tampered with his mind?

What if the insubstantial mental tendrils of a Second Foundationer insinuated itself down the emotional crevices of his makeup and pulled them apart and rejoined them—

There had been no sensation the first time. There had been no pain, no mental jar – not even a feeling of discontinuity. He had always loved the Mule. If there had ever been a time long before – as long before as five short years – when he had thought he hadn't loved him, that he had hated him – that was just a horrid illusion. The thought of that illusion embarrassed him.

But there had been no pain.

Would meeting the governor duplicate that? Would all that had gone before – all his service for the Mule – all his life's orientation – join the hazy, other-life dream that held the word, Democracy. The Mule also a dream, and only to Tazenda, his loyalty—

Sharply, he turned away.

There was that strong desire to retch.

And then Channis' voice clashed on his ear, 'I think this is it, general.'

Pritcher turned again. An Elder had opened the door silently and stood with a dignified and calm respect upon the threshold.

He said, 'His Excellency, Governor of Rossem, in the name of the Lords of Tazenda, is pleased to present his permission for an audience and request your appearance before him.'

'Sure thing,' and Channis tightened his belt with a jerk and adjusted a Rossemian hood over his head.

Pritcher's jaw set. *This* was the beginning of the real gamble.

The governor of Rossem was not of formidable appearance. For one thing, he was bareheaded, and his thinning hair, light brown, tending to grey, lent him mildness. His bony eye-ridges lowered at them, and his eyes, set in a fine network of surrounding wrinkles, seemed calculating, but his fresh-cropped chin was soft and small and, by the universal convention of followers of the pseudoscience of reading character by facial bony structure, seemed 'weak.'

Pritcher avoided the eyes and watched the chin. He didn't know whether that would be effective – if anything would be.

The governor's voice was high-pitched, indifferent: 'Welcome to Tazenda. We greet you in peace. You have eaten?'

His hand – long fingers, gnarled veins – waved almost regally at the U-shaped table.

They bowed and sat down. The governor sat at the outer side of the base of the U, they on the inner; along both arms sat the double row of silent Elders.

The governor spoke in short, abrupt sentences – praising the food as Tazendian importations – and it had indeed a quality different if, somehow, not so much better, than the rougher food of the Elders – disparaging Rossemian weather, referring with an attempt at casualness to the intricacies of space travel.

Channis talked little, Pritcher not at all.

Then it was over. The small, stewed fruits were finished; the napkins used and discarded, and the governor leaned back.

His small eyes sparkled.

'I have inquired as to your ship. Naturally, I would like to see that it receives due care and overhaul. I am told its whereabouts are unknown.'

'True,' Channis replied lightly. 'We have left it in space. It is a large ship, suitable for long journeys in sometimes hostile regions, and we felt that landing it here might give rise to doubts as to our peaceful intentions. We preferred to land alone, unarmed.'

'A friendly act,' commented the governor, without conviction. 'A large ship, you say?'

'Not a vessel of war, excellency.'

'Ha, hum. Where is it you come from?'

'A small world of the Santanni sector, your excellency. It may be you are not aware of its existence for it lacks importance. We are interested in establishing trade relationships.'

'Trade, eh? And what have you to sell?'

'Machines of all sorts, excellency. In return, food, wood, ores—'

'Ha, hum.' The governor seemed doubtful. 'I know little of these matters. Perhaps mutual profit may be arranged. Perhaps, after I have examined your credentials at length – for much information will be required by my government before matters may proceed, you understand – and after I have looked over your ship, it would be advisable for you to proceed to Tazenda.'

There was no answer to that, and the governor's attitude iced perceptibly.

'It is necessary that I see your ship, however.'

Channis said distantly: 'The ship, unfortunately, is undergoing repairs at the moment. If your excellency would not object to giving us forty-eight hours, it will be at your service.'

'I am not accustomed to waiting.'

For the first time, Pritcher met the glare of the other, eye to

61

eye, and his breath exploded softly inside him. For a moment, he had the sensation of drowning, but then his eyes tore away.

Channis did not waver. He said: 'The ship cannot be landed for forty-eight hours, excellency. We are here and unarmed. Can you doubt our honest intentions?'

There was a long silence, and then the governor said gruffly: 'Tell me of the world from which you come.'

That was all. It passed with that. There was no more unpleasantness. The governor, having fulfilled his official duty, apparently lost interest and the audience died a full death.

And when it was *all* over, Pritcher found himself back in their quarters and took stock of himself.

Carefully – holding his breath – he 'felt' his emotions. Certainly he seemed no different to himself, but *would* he feel any difference? Had he felt different after the Mule's conversion? Had not everything seemed natural? As it should have been.

He experimented.

With cold purpose, he shouted inside the silent caverns of his mind, and the shout was, 'The Second Foundation must be discovered and destroyed.'

And the emotion that accompanied it was honest hate. There was not as much as a hesitation involved in it.

And then it was in his mind to substitute the word 'Mule' for the phrase 'Second Foundation' and his breath caught at the mere emotion and his tongue clogged.

So far, good.

But had he been handled otherwise – more subtly? Had tiny changes been made? Changes that he couldn't detect because their very existence warped his judgement.

There was no way to tell.

But he still felt absolute loyalty to the Mule! If that were unchanged, nothing else really mattered.

He turned his mind to action again. Channis was busy at his

end of the room. Pritcher's thumbnail idled at his wrist communicator.

And then at the response that came he felt a wave of relief surge over him and leave him weak.

The quiet muscles of his face did not betray him, but inside he was shouting with joy – and when Channis turned to face him, he knew that the farce was about over.


## FOURTH INTERLUDE

The two Speakers passed each other on the road and one stopped the other.

'I have word from the First Speaker.'

There was a half-apprehensive flicker in the other's eyes. 'Intersection point?'

'Yes! May we live to see the dawn!'

# 5

# ONE MAN AND THE MULE

There was no sign in any of Channis' actions that he was aware of any subtle change in the attitude of Pritcher and in their relations to each other. He leaned back on the hard wooden bench and spread-eagled his feet out in front of him.

'What did you make of the governor?'

Pritcher shrugged: 'Nothing at all. He certainly seemed no mental genius to me. A very poor specimen of the Second Foundation, if that's what he was supposed to be.'

'I don't think he was, you know. I'm not sure what to make of it. Suppose you were a Second Foundationer,' Channis grew thoughtful, 'what would *you* do? Suppose you had an idea of our purpose here. How would you handle us?'

'Conversion, of course.'

'Like the Mule?' Channis looked up, sharply. 'Would we know if they *had* converted us? I wonder— And what if they were simply psychologists, but very clever ones.'

'In that case, I'd have us killed rather quickly.'

'And our ship? No.' Channis wagged a forefinger. 'We're playing a bluff, Pritcher, old man. It can only be a bluff. Even if they have emotional control down pat, we – you and I – are only fronts. It's the Mule they must fight, and they're being just as careful of us as we are of them. I'm assuming that they know who we are.'

Pritcher stared coldly: 'What do you intend doing?'

'Wait.' The word was bitten off. 'Let them come to us. They're worried, maybe about the ship, but probably about the Mule. They bluffed with the governor. It didn't work. We stayed pat. The next person they'll send *will* be a Second Foundationer, and he'll propose a deal of some sort.'

'And then?'

'And then we make the deal.'

'I don't think so.'

'Because you think it will double-cross the Mule? It won't.'

'No, the Mule could handle your double-crosses, any you could invent. But I still don't think so.'

'Because you think then we couldn't double-cross the Foundationers?'

'Perhaps not. But that's not the reason.'

Channis let his glance drop to what the other held in his fist, and said grimly: 'You mean *that's* the reason.'

Pritcher cradled his blaster, 'That's right. You are under arrest.'

'Why?'

'For treason to the First Citizen of the Union.'

Channis' lips hardened upon one another: 'What's going on?'

'Treason! As I said. And correction of the matter, on my part.'

'Your proof? Or evidence, assumptions, daydreams? Are you mad?'

'No. Are you? Do you think the Mule sends out unweaned youngsters on ridiculous swashbuckling missions for nothing? It was queer to me at the time. But I wasted time in doubting myself. Why should he send *you*? Because you smile and dress well? Because you're twenty eight.'

'Perhaps because I can be trusted. Or aren't you in the market for logical reasons?'

'Or perhaps because you can't be trusted. Which is logical enough, as it turns out.'

'Are we matching paradoxes, or is this all a word game to see who can say the least in the most words?'

And the blaster advanced, with Pritcher after it. He stood erect before the younger man: 'Stand up!'

Channis did so, in no particular hurry, and felt the muzzle of the blaster touch his belt with no shrinking of the stomach muscles.

Pritcher said: 'What the Mule wanted was to find the Second Foundation. He had failed and I had failed, and the secret that neither of us can find is a well-hidden one. So there was one outstanding possibility left – and that was to find a seeker who already knew the hiding-place.'

'Is that I?'

'Apparently it was. I didn't know then, of course, but though my mind must be slowing, it still points in the right direction. How easily we found Star's End! How miraculously you examined the correct Field Region of the Lens from among an infinite number of possibilities! And having done so, how nicely we observe just the correct point for observation! You clumsy fool! Did you so underestimate me that no combination of impossible fortuities struck you as being too much for me to swallow?'

'You mean I've been too successful?'

'Too successful by half for any loyal man.'

'Because the standards of success you set me were so low?'

And the blaster prodded, though in the face that confronted Channis only the cold glitter of the eyes betrayed the growing anger: 'Because you are in the pay of the Second Foundation.'

'Pay?' – infinite contempt. 'Prove that.'

'Or under the mental influence.'

'Without the Mule's knowledge? Ridiculous.'

'*With* the Mule's knowledge. Exactly my point, my young dullard. *With* the Mule's knowledge. Do you suppose else that you would be given a ship to play with? You led us to the Second Foundation as you were supposed to do.'

'I thresh a kernel of something or other out of this immensity of chaff. May I ask why I'm supposed to be doing all this? If I were a traitor, why should I lead you to the Second Foundation? Why not hither and yon through the Galaxy, skipping gaily, finding no more than you ever did?'

'For the sake of the ship. And because the men of the Second Foundation quite obviously need atomic warfare for self-defence.'

'You'll have to do better than that. One ship won't mean anything to them, and if they think they'll learn science from it and build atomic power plants next year, they are very, very simple Second Foundationers, indeed. On the same order of simplicity as yourself, I should say.'

'You will have the opportunity to explain that to the Mule.'

'We're going back to Kalgan?'

'On the contrary. We're staying here. And the Mule will join us in fifteen minutes – more or less. Do you think he hasn't followed us, my sharp-witted, nimble-minded lump of self-admiration? You have played the decoy well in reverse. You may not have led our victims to us, but you have certainly led us to our victims.'

'May I sit down,' said Channis, 'and explain something to you in picture drawings? Please?'

'You will remain standing.'

'At that, I can say it as well standing. You think the Mule followed us because of the hypertracer on the communication circuit?'

The blaster might have wavered. Channis wouldn't have sworn to it. He said: 'You don't look surprised. But I don't waste time doubting that you feel surprised Yes, I knew about it. And now, having shown you that I knew of something you didn't think I did, I'll tell you something you don't know, that I know you don't.'

'You allow yourself too many preliminaries, Channis. I should think your sense of invention was more smoothly greased.'

'There's no invention to this. There have been traitors, of course, or enemy agents, if you prefer that term. But the Mule knew of that in a rather curious way. It seems, you see, that some of his Converted men had been tampered with.'

The blaster did waver that time. Unmistakably.

'I emphasize that, Pritcher. It was why he needed me. I was an Unconverted man. Didn't he emphasize to you that he

67

needed an Unconverted? Whether he gave you the real reason or not?'

'Try something else, Channis. If I were against the Mule, I'd know it.' Quietly, rapidly, Pritcher was feeling his mind. It felt the same. It felt the same. Obviously the man was lying.

'You mean you feel loyal to the Mule. Perhaps. Loyalty wasn't tampered with. Too easily detectable, the Mule said. But how do you feel mentally? Sluggish? Since you started this trip, have you always felt normal? Or have you felt strange sometimes, as though you weren't quite yourself? What are you trying to do, bore a hole through me without touching the trigger?'

Pritcher withdrew his blaster half an inch, 'What are you trying to say?'

'I say that you've been tampered with. You've been handled. You didn't see the Mule install that hypertracer. You didn't see anyone do it. You just found it there, and assumed it was the Mule, and ever since you've been assuming he was following us. Sure, the wrist receiver you're wearing contacts the ship on a wave length mine isn't good for. Do you think I didn't know that?' He was speaking quickly now, angrily. His cloak of indifference had dissolved into savagery. 'But it's not the Mule that's coming towards us from out there. It's not the Mule.'

'Who, if not?'

'Well, who do you suppose? I found that hypertracer, the day we left. But I didn't think it was the Mule. *He* had no reason for indirection at that point. Don't you see the nonsense of it? If I were a traitor and he knew that, I could be Converted as easily as you were, and he would have the secret of the location of the Second Foundation out of my mind without sending me half across the Galaxy. Can *you* keep a secret from the Mule? And if I *didn't* know, then I couldn't lead him to it. So why send me in either case?

'Obviously, that hypertracer must have been put there by an agent of the Second Foundation. *That's* who's coming towards us now. And would you have been fooled if your precious mind hadn't been tampered with? What kind of normality have you that you imagine immense folly to be wisdom? *Me* bring a ship to the Second Foundation? What would they do with a ship?

'It's *you* they want, Pritcher. You know more about the Union than anyone but the Mule, and you're not dangerous to them while he is. That's why they put the direction of search into my mind. Of course, it was completely impossible for me to find Tazenda by random searchings of the Lens. I knew that. But I knew there was the Second Foundation after us, and I knew they engineered it. Why not play their game? It was a battle of bluffs. They wanted us and I wanted their location – and space take the one that couldn't outbluff the other.

'But it's we that will lose as long as you hold that blaster on me. And it obviously isn't your idea. It's theirs. Give me the blaster, Pritcher. I know it seems wrong to you, but it isn't your mind speaking, it's the Second Foundation within you. Give me the blaster, Pritcher, and we'll face what's coming now, together.'

Pritcher faced a growing confusion in horror. Plausibility! Could he be so wrong? Why this eternal doubt of himself? Why wasn't he sure? What made Channis sound so plausible?

Plausibility!

Or was it his own tortured mind fighting the invasion of the alien.

Was he split in two?

Hazily, he saw Channis standing before him, hand outstretched – and suddenly, he knew he was going to give him the blaster.

And as the muscles of his arm were on the point of contracting in the proper manner to do so, the door opened, not hastily, behind him – and he turned.

There are perhaps men in the Galaxy who can be confused for one another even by men at their peaceful leisure. Correspondingly, there may be conditions of mind when even unlikely pairs may be mis-recognized. But the Mule rises above any combination of the two factors.

Not all Pritcher's agony of mind prevented the instantaneous mental flood of cool vigour that engulfed him.

Physically, the Mule could not dominate any situation. Nor did he dominate this one.

He was rather a ridiculous figure in his layers of clothing that thickened him past his normality without allowing him to reach normal dimensions even so. His face was muffled and the usually dominant beak covered what was left in a cold-red prominence.

Probably as a vision of rescue, no greater incongruity could exist.

He said: 'Keep your blaster, Pritcher.'

Then he turned to Channis, who had shrugged and seated himself: 'The emotional context here seems rather confusing and considerably in conflict. What's this about someone other than myself following you?'

Pritcher intervened sharply: 'Was a hypertracer placed upon our ship by your orders, sir?'

The Mule turned cool eyes upon him, 'Certainly. Is it very likely that any organization in the Galaxy other than the Union of Worlds would have access to it?'

'He said—'

'Well, he's here, general. Indirect quotation is not necessary. Have you been saying anything, Channis?'

'Yes. But mistakes apparently, sir. It has been my opinion that the tracer was put there by someone in the pay of the Second Foundation and that we had been led here for some purpose of theirs, which I was prepared to counter. I was under the further impression that the general was more or less in their hands.'

'You sound as if you think so no longer.'

'I'm afraid not. Or it would not have been you at the door.'

'Well, then, let us thresh this out.' The Mule peeled off the outer layers of padded, and electrically heated clothing. 'Do you mind if I sit down as well? Now – we are safe here and perfectly free of any danger of intrusion. No native of this lump of ice will have any desire to approach this place. I assure you of that,' and there was a grim earnestness about his insistence upon his powers.

Channis showed his disgust. 'Why privacy? Is someone going to serve tea and bring out the dancing girls?'

'Scarcely. What was this theory of yours, young man? A Second Foundationer was tracing you with a device which no one but I have and – how did you say you found this place?'

'Apparently, sir, it seems obvious, in order to account for known facts, that certain notions have been put into my head—'

'By these same Second Foundationers?'

'No one else, I imagine.'

'Then it did not occur to you that if a Second Foundationer could force, or entice, or inveigle you into going to the Second Foundation for purposes of his own – and I assume you imagined he used methods similar to mine, though, mind you, I can implant only emotions, not ideas – it did not occur to you that if he could do that there was little necessity to put a hyper-tracer on you.'

And Channis looked up sharply and met his sovereign's large eyes with sudden startle. Pritcher grunted and a visible relaxation showed itself in his shoulders.

'No,' said Channis, 'that hadn't occurred to me.'

'Or that if they were obliged to trace you, they couldn't feel capable of directing you, and that, undirected, you could have precious little chance of finding your way here as you did. Did *that* occur to you?'

'That, neither.'

'Why not? Has your intellectual level receded to a so-much-greater-than-probable degree?'

'The only answer is a question, sir. Are you joining General Pritcher in accusing me of being a traitor?'

'You have a defence in case I am?'

'Only the one I presented to the general. If I were a traitor

71

and knew the whereabouts of the Second Foundation, you could Convert me and learn the knowledge directly. If you felt it necessary to trace me, then I hadn't the knowledge beforehand and wasn't a traitor. So I answer your paradox with another.'

'Then your conclusion?'

'That I am not a traitor.'

'To which I must agree, since your argument is irrefutable.'

'Then may I ask why you had us secretly followed?'

'Because to all the facts there is a third explanation. Both you and Pritcher explained some facts in your own individual ways, but not all. I – if you can spare me the time – will explain all. And in a rather short time, so there is little danger of boredom. Sit down, Pritcher, and give me your blaster. There is no danger of attack on us any longer. None from in here and none from out there. None in fact even from the Second Foundation. Thanks to you, Channis.'

The room was lit in the usual Rossemian fashion of electrically heated wire. A single bulb was suspended from the ceiling and in its dim yellow glow, the three cast their individual shadows.

The Mule said: 'Since I felt it necessary to trace Channis, it was obvious I expect to gain something thereby. Since he went to the Second Foundation with a startling speed and directness, we can reasonably assume that that was what I was expecting to happen. Since I did not gain the knowledge from him directly, something must have been preventing me. Those are the facts. Channis, of course, knows the answer. So do I. Do you see it, Pritcher?'

And Pritcher said doggedly: 'No, sir.'

'Then I'll explain. Only one kind of man can both know the location of the Second Foundation and prevent me from learning it. Channis, I'm afraid you're a Second Foundationer yourself.'

And Channis' elbows rested on his knees as he leaned forward, and through stiff and angry lips said: 'What is your

72

direct evidence? Deduction has proven wrong twice today.'

'There is direct evidence, too, Channis. It was easy enough. I told you that my men had been tampered with. The tamperer must have been, obviously, someone who was a) Unconverted, and b) fairly close to the centre of things. The field was large but not entirely unlimited. You were too successful, Channis. People liked you too much. You got along too well. I wondered—

'And then I summoned you to take over this expedition and it didn't set you back. I watched your emotions. It didn't bother you. You overplayed the confidence there, Channis. No man of real competence could have avoided a dash of uncertainty at a job like that. Since your mind did avoid it, it was either a foolish job or a controlled one.

'It was easy to test the alternatives. I seized your mind at a moment of relaxation and filled it with grief for an instant and then removed it. You were angry afterwards with such accomplished art that I could have sworn it was a natural reaction, but for that which went first. For when I wrenched at your emotions, for just one instant, for one tiny instant before you could catch yourself, your mind resisted. It was all I needed to know.

'No one could have resisted me, even for that tiny instant, without control similar to mine.'

Channis' voice was low and bitter: 'Well, then? Now what?'

'And now you die – as a Second Foundationer. Quite necessary, as I believe you realize.'

And once again Channis stared into the muzzle of a blaster. A muzzle guided this time by a mind, not like Pritcher's capable of offhand twisting to suit himself, but by one as mature as his own and as resistant to force as his own.

And the period of time allotted him for a correction of events was small.


What followed thereafter is difficult to describe by one with the normal complement of senses and the normal incapacity for emotional control.

Essentially, this is what Channis realized in the tiny space of time involved in the pushing of the Mule's thumb upon the trigger contact.

The Mule's current emotional makeup was one of a hard and polished determination, unmisted by hesitation in the least. Had Channis been sufficiently interested afterwards to calculate the time involved from the determination to shoot to the arrival of the disintegrating energies, he might have realized that his leeway was about one-fifth of a second.

That was barely time.

What the Mule realized in that same tiny space of time was that the emotional potential of Channis' brain had surged suddenly upwards without his own mind feeling any impact and that, simultaneously, a flood of pure, thrilling hatred cascaded upon him from an unexpected direction.

It was that new emotional element that jerked his thumb off the contact. Nothing else could have done it, and almost together with his change of action, came complete realization of the new situation.

It was a tableau that endured far less than the significance adhering to it should require from a dramatic standpoint. There was the Mule, thumb off the blaster, staring intently upon Channis. There was Channis, taut, not quite daring to breathe yet. And there was Pritcher, convulsed in his chair; every muscle at a spasmodic breaking point; every tendon writhing in an effort to hurl forward; his face twisted at last out of schooled woodenness into an unrecognizable death mask of horrid hate; and his eyes only and entirely and supremely upon the Mule.

Only a word or two passed between Channis and the Mule – only a word or two and that utterly revealing stream of emotional consciousness that remains forever the true interplay of understanding between such as they. For the sake of our own limits, it is necessary to translate into words what went on, then, and thenceforward.

Channis said, tensely: 'You're between two fires, First

Citizen. You can't control two minds simultaneously, not when one of them is mine – so you have your choice. Pritcher is free of your Conversion now. I've snapped the bonds. He's the old Pritcher; the one who tried to kill you once; the one who thinks you're the enemy of all that is free and right and holy; and he's the one besides who knows that you've debased him to helpless adulation for five years. I'm holding him back now by suppressing his will, but if you kill me, that ends, and in considerably less time than you could shift your blaster or even your will – he will kill you.'

The Mule quite plainly realized that. He did not move.

Channis continued: 'If you turn to place him under control, to kill him, to do anything, you won't ever be quick enough to turn again to stop me.'

The Mule still did not move. Only a soft sigh of realization.

'So,' said Channis, 'throw down your blaster, and let us be on even terms again, and you can have Pritcher back.'

'I made a mistake,' said the Mule, finally. 'It was wrong to have a third party present when I confronted you. It introduced one variable too many. It is a mistake that must be paid for, I suppose.'

He dropped the blaster carelessly, and kicked it to the other end of the room. Simultaneously, Pritcher crumbled into profound sleep.

'He'll be normal when he awakes,' said the Mule, indifferently.

The entire exchange from the time the Mule's thumb had begun pressing the trigger-contact to the time he dropped the blaster had occupied just under a second and a half of time.

But just beneath the borders of consciousness, for a time just above the borders of detection, Channis caught a fugitive emotional gleam in the Mule's mind. And it was still one of sure and confident triumph.

# 6

# ONE MAN, THE MULE – AND ANOTHER

Two men, apparently relaxed and entirely at ease, poles apart physically – with every nerve that served as emotional detector quivering tensely.

The Mule, for the first time in long years, had insufficient surety of his own way. Channis knew that, though he could protect himself for the moment, it was an effort – and that the attack upon him was none such for his opponent. In a test of endurance, Channis knew he would lose.

But it was deadly to think of that. To give away to the Mule an emotional weakness would be to hand him a weapon. There was already that glimpse of something – a winner's something – in the Mule's mind.

To gain time—

Why did the others delay? Was that the source of the Mule's confidence? What did his opponent know that he didn't? The mind he watched told nothing. If only he could read ideas. And yet—

Channis braked his own mental whirling roughly. There was only that; to gain time—

Channis said: 'Since it is decided, and not denied by myself after our little duel over Pritcher, that I am a Second Foundationer, suppose you tell me why I came to Tazenda.'

'Oh, no,' and the Mule laughed, with high-pitched confidence, 'I am not Pritcher. I need make no explanations to you. You had what you thought were reasons. Whatever they were, your actions suited me, and so I inquire no further.'

'Yet there must be such gaps in your conception of the story. Is Tazenda the Second Foundation you expected to find? Pritcher spoke much of your other attempt at finding it, and of your psychologist tool, Ebling Mis. He babbled a bit sometimes under my ... uh ... slight encouragement. Think back on Ebling Mis, First Citizen.'

'Why should I?' Confidence!

Channis felt that confidence edge out into the open, as if with the passage of time, any anxiety the Mule might be having was increasingly vanishing.

He said, firmly restraining the rush of desperation: 'You lack curiosity, then? Pritcher told me of Mis' vast surprise at *something*. There was his terribly drastic urging for speed, for a rapid warning of the Second Foundation? Why? Why? Ebling Mis died. The Second Foundation was not warned. And yet the Second Foundation exists.'

The Mule smiled in real pleasure, and with a sudden and surprising dash of cruelty that Channis felt advance and suddenly withdraw: 'But apparently the Second Foundation *was* warned. Else how and why did one Bail Channis arrive on Kalgan to handle my men and to assume the rather thankless task of outwitting me. The warning came too late, that is all.'

'Then,' and Channis allowed pity to drench outward from him, 'you don't even know what the Second Foundation is, or anything of the deeper meaning of all that has been going on.'

To gain time!

The Mule felt the other's pity, and his eyes narrowed with instant hostility. He rubbed his nose in his familiar four-fingered gesture, and snapped: 'Amuse yourself, then. What *of* the Second Foundation?'

Channis spoke deliberately, in words rather than in emotional symbology. He said: 'From what I have heard, it was the mystery that surrounded the Second Foundation that most puzzled Mis. Hari Seldon founded his two units so differently. The First Foundation was a splurge that in two centuries dazzled half the Galaxy. And the Second was an abyss that was dark.

'You won't understand why that was, unless you can once again feel the intellectual atmosphere of the days of the dying Empire. It was a time of absolutes, of the great final generalities, at least in thought. It was a sign of decaying culture, of course, that dams had been built against the further development of ideas. It was his revolt against these dams that made Seldon famous. It was that one last spark of youthful creation in him that lit the Empire in a sunset glow and dimly foreshadowed the rising sun of the Second Empire.'

'Very dramatic. So what?'

'So he created his Foundations according to the laws of psychohistory, but who knew better than he that even those laws were relative. *He* never created a finish product. Finished products are for decadent minds. His was an evolving mechanism and the Second Foundation was the instrument of that evolution. *We*, First Citizen of your Temporary Union of Worlds, *we* are of the guardians of Seldon's Plan. Only we!'

'Are you trying to talk yourself into courage,' inquired the Mule, contemptuously, 'or are you trying to impress me? For the Second Foundation, Seldon's Plan, the Second Empire all impresses me not the least, nor touches any spring of compassion, sympathy, responsibility, nor any other source of emotional aid you may be trying to tap in me. And in any case, poor fool, speak of the Second Foundation in the past tense, for it is destroyed.'

Channis felt the emotional potential that pressed upon his mind rise in intensity as the Mule rose from his chair and approached. He fought back furiously, but something crept relentlessly on within him, battering and bending his mind back – and back.

He felt the wall behind him, and the Mule faced him, skinny arms akimbo, lips smiling terribly beneath that mountain of nose.

The Mule said: 'Your game is through, Channis. The game of all of you – of all the men of what used to be the Second Foundation. Used to be! *Used to be*!

'What were you sitting here waiting for all this time, with your babble to Pritcher, when you might have struck him down and taken the blaster from him without the least effort of

78

physical force? You were waiting for me, weren't you, waiting to greet me in a situation that would not too arouse my suspicions.

'Too bad for you that I needed no arousal. I knew you. I knew you well, Channis of the Second Foundation.

'But what are you waiting for now? You still throw words at me desperately, as though the mere sound of your voice would freeze me to my seat. And all the while you speak, something in your mind is waiting and waiting and is still waiting. But no one is coming. None of those you expect – none of your allies. You are alone here, Channis, and you will remain alone. Do you know why?

'It is because your Second Foundation miscalculated me to the very dregs of the end. I knew their plan early. They thought I would follow you here and be proper meat for their cooking. You were to be a decoy indeed – a decoy for a poor, foolish weakling mutant, so hot on the trail of Empire that he would fall blindly into an obvious pit. But am I their prisoner?

'I wonder if it occurred to them that I'd scarcely be here without my fleet – against the artillery of any unit of which they are entirely and pitifully helpless? Did it occur to them that I would not pause for discussion or wait for events?

'My ships were launched against Tazenda twelve hours ago and they are quite, quite through with their mission. Tazenda is laid in ruins; its centres of population are wiped out. There was no resistance. The Second Foundation no longer exists, Channis – and I, the queer, ugly weakling, am the ruler of the Galaxy.'

Channis could do nothing but shake his head feebly. 'No – No—'

'Yes – Yes—' mimicked the Mule. 'And if you are the last one alive, and you may be, that will not be for long either.'

And then there followed a short, pregnant pause, and Channis almost howled with the sudden pain of that tearing penetration of the innermost tissues of his mind.

The Mule drew back and muttered: 'Not enough. You do

not pass the test after all. Your despair is pretence. Your fear is not the broad overwhelming that adheres to the destruction of an ideal, but the puny seeping fear of personal destruction.'

And the Mule's weak hand seized Channis by the throat in a puny grip that Channis was somehow unable to break.

'You are my insurance, Channis. You are my director and safeguard against any underestimation I may make.' The Mule's eyes bore down upon him. Insistent— Demanding—

'Have I calculated rightly, Channis? Have I outwitted your men of the Second Foundation? Tazenda *is* destroyed, Channis, tremendously destroyed; so why is your despair pretence? Where is the reality? I must have reality and truth! Talk, Channis, talk. Have I penetrated then, not deeply enough? Does the danger still esist? *Talk, Channis.* Where have I done wrong?'

Channis felt the words drag out of his mouth. They did not come willingly. He clenched his teeth against them. He bit his tongue. He tensed every muscle of his throat.

And they came out – gasping – pulled out by force and tearing his throat and tongue and teeth on the way.

'Truth,' he squeaked, 'truth—'

'Yes, truth. What is left to be done?'

'Seldon founded Second Foundation here. Here, as I said. I told no lie. The psychologists arrived and took control of the native population.'

'Of Tazenda?' The Mule plunged deeply into the flooding torture of the other's emotional upwellings – tearing at them brutally. 'It is Tazenda I have destroyed. You know what I want. Give it to me.'

'*Not* Tazenda. I *said* Second Foundationers might not be those apparently in power. Tazenda is the figurehead—' The words were almost unrecognizable, forming themselves against every atom of will of the Second Foundationer, 'Rossem—Rossem? *Rossem is the world*—'

The Mule loosed his grip and Channis dropped into a huddle of pain and torture.

'And you thought to fool me?' said the Mule, softly.

'You *were* fooled.' It was the last dying shed of resistance in Channis.

'But not long enough for you and yours. I am in communication with my Fleet. And after Tazenda can come Rossem. But first—'

Channis felt the excruciating darkness rise against him, and the automatic lift of his arm to his tortured eyes could not ward it off. It was a darkness that throttled, and as he felt his torn, wounded mind reeling backwards, backwards into the everlasting black – there was that final picture of the triumphant Mule – laughing matchstick – that long, fleshy nose quivering with laughter.

The sound faded away. The darkness embraced him lovingly.

It ended with a cracking sensation that was like the jagged glare of a lightning flash, and Channis came slowly to earth while sight returned painfully in blurry transmission through tear-drenched eyes.

His head ached unbearably, and it was only with a stab of agony that he could bring up a hand to it.

Obviously, he was alive. Softly, like feathers caught up in a eddy of air that had passed, his thoughts steadied and drifted to rest. He felt comfort suck in – from outside. Slowly, torturedly, he bent his neck – and relief was a sharp pang.

For the door was open; and the First Speaker stood just inside the threshold. He tried to speak, to shout, to warn – but his tongue froze and he knew that a part of the Mule's mighty mind still held him and clamped all speech within him.

He bent his neck once more. The Mule was still in the room. He was angry and hot-eyed. He laughed no longer, but his teeth were bared in a ferocious smile.

Channis felt the First Speaker's mental influence moving gently over his mind with a healing touch and then there was the numbing sensation as it came into contact with the Mule's defence for an instant of struggle and withdrew.

The Mule said gratingly, with a fury that was grotesque in his meagre body: 'Then another comes to greet me.' His agile mind reached its tendrils out of the room – out—

'You are alone,' he said.

And the First Speaker interrupted with an acquiescence: 'I am thoroughly alone. It is necessary that I be alone, since it was I who miscalculated your future five years ago. There would be a certain satisfaction to me in correcting that matter without aid. Unfortunately, I did not count on the strength of your Field of Emotional Repulsion that surrounded this place. It took me long to penetrate. I congratulate you upon the skill with which it was constructed.'

'Thank you for nothing,' came the hostile rejoinder. 'Bandy no compliments with me. Have you come to add your brain splinter to that of yonder cracked pillar of your realm?'

The First Speaker smiled: 'Why, the man you call Bail Channis performed his mission well, the more so since he was not your mental equal by far. I can see, of course, that you have mistreated him, yet it may be that we may restore him fully even yet. He is a brave man, sir. He volunteered for this mission, although we were able to predict mathematically the huge chance of damage to his mind – a more fearful alternative than that of mere physical crippling.'

Channis' mind pulsed futilely with what he wanted to say and couldn't; the warning he wished to shout and was unable to. He could only emit that continuous stream of fear – fear—

The Mule was calm. 'You know, of course, of the destruction of Tazenda.'

'I do. The assault by your fleet was foreseen.'

Grimly: 'Yes, so I suppose. But not prevented, eh?'

'No, not prevented.' The First Speaker's emotional symbology was plain. It was almost a self-horror; a complete self-disgust: 'And the fault is much more mine than yours. Who could have imagined your power five years ago. We suspected from the start – from the moment you captured Kalgan – that you had the powers of emotional control. That was not too surprising, First Citizen, as I can explain to you.

'Emotional contact such as you and I possess is not a very new development. Actually it is implicit in the human brain. Most humans can read emotion in a primitive manner by associating it pragmatically with facial expression, tone of voice and so on. A good many animals possess the faculty to a higher degree; they use the sense of smell to a good extent, and the emotions involved are, of course, less complex.

'Actually, humans are capable of much more, but the faculty of direct emotional contact tended to atrophy with the development of speech a million years back. It has been the great advance of our Second Foundation that this forgotten sense has been restored to at least some of its potentialities.

'But we are not born with its full use. A million years of decay is a formidable obstacle, and we must educate the sense, exercise it as we exercise our muscles. And there you have the main difference. *You* were born with it.

'So much we could calculate. We could also calculate the effect of such a sense upon a person in the world of men who did not possess it. The seeing man in the kingdom of the blind – We calculated the extent to which a megalomania would take control of you and we thought we were prepared. But for two factors we were not prepared.

'The first was the great extent of your sense. *We* can induce emotional contact only when in eyeshot, which is why we are more helpless against physical weapons than you might think. Sight plays such an enormous part. Not so with you. You are definitely known to have men under control, and, further, to have had intimate emotional contact with them when out of sight and out of earshot. That was discovered too late.

'Secondly, we did not know of your physical shortcomings, particularly the one that seemed so important to you, that you adopted the name of the Mule. We didn't foresee that you were not merely a mutant, but a sterile mutant and the added physic distortion due to your inferiority complex passed us by. We allowed only for a megalomania – not for an intensely psychopathic paranoia as well.

'It is myself that bears the responsibility for having missed all that, for I was the leader of the Second Foundation when you captured Kalgan. When you destroyed the First Foundation, we found out – but too late – and for that fault millions have died on Tazenda.'

'And you will correct things now?' The Mule's thin lips curled, his mind pulsing with hate: 'What will you do? Fatten me? Restore me to a masculine vigour? Take away from the past the long childhood in an alien environment. Do you regret *my* sufferings? Do you regret *my* unhappiness? I have no sorrow for what I did in my necessity. Let the Galaxy protect itself as best it can, since it stirred not a whit for my protection when I needed it.'

'Your emotions are, of course,' said the First Speaker, 'only the children of your background and are not to be condemned – merely changed. The destruction of Tazenda was unavoidable. The alternative would have been a much greater destruction generally throughout the Galaxy over a period of centuries. We did our best in our limited way. We withdrew as many men from Tazenda as we could. We decentralized the rest of the world. Unfortunately, our measures were of necessity far from adequate. It left many millions to die – do you not regret that?'

'Not at all – any more than I regret the hundred thousand that must die on Rossem in not more than six hours.'

'On Rossem?' said the First Speaker, quickly.

He turned to Channis who had forced himself into a half-sitting posture, and his mind exerted its force. Channis felt the duel of minds strain over him, and then there was a short snapping of the bond and the words came tumbling out of his mouth: 'Sir, I have failed completely. He forced it from me not ten minutes before your arrival. I could not resist him and I offer no excuses. He knows Tazenda is not the Second Foundation. He knows that Rossem is.'

And the bonds closed down upon him again.

The First Speaker frowned: 'I see. What is it you are planning to do?'

'Do you really wonder? Do you really find it difficult to penetrate the obvious? All this time that you have preached to me of the nature of emotional contact – all this time that you have been throwing words such as megalomania and paranoia at me, I have been working. I have been in contact with my Fleet and it has its orders. In six hours, unless I should for some reason counteract my orders, they are to bombard all of Rossem except this lone village and an area of a hundred square miles about it. They are to do a thorough job and are then to land here.

'You have six hours, and in six hours, you cannot beat down my mind, nor can you save the rest of Rossem.'

The Mule spread his hands and laughed again while the First Speaker seemed to find difficulty in absorbing this new state of affairs.

He said: 'The alternative?'

'Why should there even be an alternative? I can stand to gain no more by any alternative. Is it the lives of those on Rossem I'm to be chary of? Perhaps if you allow my ships to land and submit, all of you – all the men on the Second Foundation – to mental control sufficient to suit myself, I may countermand the bombardment orders. It may be worthwhile to put so many men of high intelligence under my control. But then again it would be a considerable effort and perhaps not worth it after all, so I'm not particularly eager to have you agree to it. What do you say, Second Foundationer? What weapon have you against my mind which is as strong as yours at least and against my ships which are stronger than anything you have ever dreamed of possessing?'

'What have I?' repeated the First Speaker, slowly: 'Why nothing – except a little grain – such a little grain of knowledge that even yet you do not possess.'

'Speak quickly,' laughed the Mule, 'speak inventively. For

squirm as you might, you won't squirm out of this.'

'Poor mutant,' said the First Speaker, 'I have nothing to squirm out of. Ask yourself – why was Bail Channis sent to Kalgan as a decoy – Bail Channis, who though young and brave is almost as much your mental inferior as is this sleeping officer of yours, this Han Pritcher. Why did not I go, or another of our leaders, who would be more your match?'

'Perhaps,' came the supremely confident reply, 'you were not sufficiently foolish, since perhaps none of you are my match.'

'The true reason is more logical. You knew Channis to be a Second Foundationer. He lacked the capacity to hide that from you. And you knew, too, that you were his superior, so you were not afraid to play his game and follow him as he wished you to in order to outwit him later. Had I gone to Kalgan, you would have killed me for I would have been a real danger, or had I avoided death by concealing my identity, I would yet have failed in persuading you to follow me into space. It was only known inferiority that lured you on. And had you remained on Kalgan, not all the force of the Second Foundation could have harmed you, surrounded as you were by your men, your machines, and your mental power.'

'My mental power is yet with me, squirmer,' said the Mule, 'and my men and machines are not far off.'

'Truly so, but you are not on Kalgan. You are here in the Kingdom of Tazenda, logically presented to you as the Second Foundation – very logically presented. It had to be so presented, for you are a wise man, First Citizen, and would follow only logic.'

'Correct, and it was a momentary victory for your side, but there was still time for me to worm the truth from your man, Channis, and still wisdom in me to realize that such a truth might exist.'

'And on our side, oh, not-quite-sufficiently-subtle one, was the realization that you might go one step further and so Bail Channis was prepared for you.'

'That he most certainly was not, for I stripped his brain clean as any plucked chicken. It quivered bare and open before me and when he said Rossem was the Second Foundation, it was basic truth for I had ground him so flat and smooth that not the smidgeon of a deceit could have any refuge in any microscopic crevice.'

'True enough. So much the better for our foresight. For I have told you already that Bail Channis was a volunteer. Do you know what sort of a volunteer? Before he left our Foundation for Kalgan and you, he submitted to emotional surgery of a drastic nature. Do you think it was sufficient to deceive you? Do you think Bail Channis, mentally untouched, could possibly deceive you? No, Bail Channis was himself deceived, of necessity and voluntarily. Down to the inner-most core of his mind, Bail Channis honestly believes that Rossem is the Seond Foundation.

'And for three years now, we of the Second Foundation have built up the appearance of that here in the Kingdom of Tazenda, in preparation and waiting for you. And we have succeeded, have we not? You penetrated to Tazenda, and beyond that, to Rossem – but past that, you could not go.'

The Mule was upon his feet: 'You dare tell me that Rossem also, is not the Second Foundation?'

Channis, from the floor, felt his bonds burst for good, under a stream of mental force on the part of the First Speaker and strained upright. He let out one long, incredulous cry: 'You mean Rossem is *not* the Second Foundation?'

The memories of life, the knowledge of his mind – everything whirled mistily about him in confusion.

The First Speaker smiled: 'You see, First Citizen, Channis is as upset as you are. Of course, Rossem is not the Second Foundation. Are we madmen then, to lead you, our greatest, most power-ful, most dangerous enemy to our own world. Oh, no!

'Let your Fleet bombard Rossem, First Citizen, if you must have it so. Let them destroy all they can. For at most they can kill only Channis and myself – and that will leave you in a situation improved not in the least.

'For the Second Foundation's Expedition to Rossem which has been here for three years and has functioned, temporarily, as Elders in this village, embarked yesterday and are returning to Kalgan. They will evade your Fleet, of course, and they will arrive in Kalgan at least a day before you can, which is why I tell you all this. Unless I countermand my orders, when you return, you will find a revolting Empire, a disintegrated realm, and only the men with you in your Fleet here will be loyal to you. They will be hopelessly outnumbered. And moreover, the men of the Second Foundation will be with your Home Fleet and will see to it that you reconvert no one. Your Empire is done, mutant.'

Slowly, the Mule bowed his head, as anger and despair cornered his mind completely, 'Yes. Too late— Too late— Now I see it.'

'Now you see it,' agreed the First Speaker, 'and now you don't.'

In the despair of that moment, when the Mule's mind lay open, the First Speaker – ready for that moment and pre-sure of its nature – entered quickly. It required a rather insignificant fraction of a second to consummate the change completely.

The Mule looked up and said: 'Then I shall return to Kalgan?'

'Certainly. How do you feel?'

'Excellently well.' His brow puckered: 'Who are you?'

'Does it matter?'

'Of course not.' He dismissed the matter, and touched Pritcher's shoulder: 'Wake up, Pritcher, we're going home.'

It was two hours later that Bail Channis felt strong enough to walk by himself. He said: 'He won't ever remember?'

'Never. He retains his mental powers and his Empire – but his motivations are now entirely different. The notion of a Second Foundation is a blank to him, and he is a man of peace. He will be a far happier man henceforward, too, for the few years of life left him by his maladjusted physique. And then, after he is dead, Seldon's Plan will go on – somehow.'

'And it is true,' urged Channis, 'it is true that Rossem is not the Second Foundation? I could swear – I tell you I *know* it is. I am not mad.'

'You are not mad, Channis, merely, as I have said, changed. Rossem is *not* the Second Foundation. Come! We, too, will return home.'


## LAST INTERLUDE

Bail Channis sat in the small white-tiled room and allowed his mind to relax. He was content to live in the present. There were the walls and the window and the grass outside. They had no names. They were just things. There was a bed and a chair and books that developed themselves idly on the screen at the foot of his bed. There was the nurse who brought him his food.

At first he had made efforts to piece together the scraps of things he had heard. Such as those two men talking together.

One had said: 'Complete aphasia now. It's cleaned out, and I think without damage. It will only be necessary to return the recording of his original brain-wave makeup.'

He remembered the sounds by rote, and for some reason they seemed peculiar sounds – as if they meant something. But why bother.

Better to watch the pretty changing colours on the screen at the foot of the thing he lay on.

And then someone entered and did things to him and for a long time, he slept.

And when that had passed, the bed was suddenly a bed and he knew he was in a hospital, and the words he remembered made sense.

He sat up: 'What's happening?'

The First Speaker was beside him, 'You're on the Second Foundation, and you have your mind back – your original mind.'

'Yes! *Yes!*' Channis came to the realization that he was *himself*, and there was incredible triumph and joy in that.

89

'And now tell me,' said the First Speaker, 'do you know where the Second Foundation is now?'

And the truth came flooding down in one enormous wave and Channis did not answer. Like Ebling Mis before him, he was conscious of only one vast, numbing surprise.

Until he finally nodded, and said: 'By the Stars of the Galaxy – now, I know.'

# Part II

## SEARCH BY THE FOUNDATION

# 7

# ARCADIA

DARELL, ARKADY *novelist, born 11, 5, 362 F.E., died 1, 7, 443 F.E. Although primarily a writer of fiction, Arkady Darell is best known for her biography of her grandmother, Bayta Darell. Based on first-hand information, it has for centuries served as a primary source of information concerning the Mule and his times ... Like 'Unkeyed Memories', her novel 'Time and Time and Over' is a stirring reflection of the brilliant Kalganian society of the early Interregnum, based, it is said, on a visit to Kalgan in her youth ...*

ENCYCLOPEDIA GALACTICA

Arcadia Darell declaimed firmly into the mouthpiece of her transcriber:

'The Future of Seldon's Plan, by A. Darell'

and then thought darkly that some day when she was a great writer, she would write all her masterpieces under the pseudonym of Arkady. Just Arkady. No last name at all.

'A. Darell' *would* be just the sort of thing that she would have to put on all her themes for her class in Composition and Rhetoric - so tasteless. All the other kids had to do it, too, except for Olynthus Dam, because the class laughed so when he did it the first time. And 'Arcadia' was a little girl's name, wished on her because her great grandmother had been called that; her parents just had no imagination *at all*.

Now that she was two days past fourteen, you'd think they'd recognize the simple fact of adulthood and call her Arkady. Her lips tightened as she thought of her father looking up from his book-viewer just long enough to say, 'But if you're going to pretend you're nineteen, Arcadia, what will you do when you're twenty-five and all the boys think you're thirty?'

From where she sprawled across the arms and into the

hollow of her own special armchair, she could see the mirror on her dresser. Her foot was a little in the way because her house slipper kept twirling about her big toe, so she pulled it in and sat with an unnatural straightness to her neck that she felt sure, somehow, lengthened it a full two inches into slim regality.

For a moment she considered her face thoughtfully – too fat. She opened her jaws half an inch behind closed lips, and caught the resultant trace of unnatural gauntness at every angle. She licked her lips with a quick touch of tongue and let them pout a bit in moist softness. Then she let her eyelids droop in a weary worldly way— Oh, golly if only her cheeks weren't that silly *pink*.

She tried putting her fingers to the outer corners of her eyes and tilting the lids to get that mysterious exotic languor of the women of the inner star systems, but her hands were in the way and she couldn't see her face very well.

Then she lifted her chin, caught herself at a half-profile, and with her eyes a little strained from looking out the corner and her neck muscles faintly aching, she said, in a voice one octave below its natural pitch, 'Really, father, if you think it makes a *particle* of difference to me what some silly old *boys* think, you just—'

And then she remembered that she still had the transmitter open in her hand and said, drearily, 'Oh, golly,' and shut it off.

The faintly violet paper with the peach margin line on the left had upon it the following:

## THE FUTURE OF SELDON'S PLAN

'Really, father, if you think it makes a particle of difference to me what some silly old boys think, you just

'Oh, golly.'

She pulled the sheet out of the machine with annoyance and another clicked neatly into place.

But her face smoothed out of its vexation, nevertheless, and her wide, little mouth stretched into a self-satisfied smile. She sniffed at the paper delicately. Just right. Just that proper touch of elegance and charm. And the penmanship was just the last word.

The machine had been delivered two days ago on her first adult birthday. She had said, 'But father, everybody – just *everybody* in the class who has the slightest pretensions to *being* anybody has one. Nobody but some old drips would use hand machines—'

The salesman had said, 'There is no other model as compact on the one hand and as adaptable on the other. It will spell and punctuate correctly according to the sense of the sentence. Naturally, it is a great aid to education since it encourages the user to employ careful enunciation and breathing in order to make sure of the correct spelling, to say nothing of demanding a proper and elegant delivery for correct punctuation.'

Even then her father had tried to get one geared for typeprint as if she were some dried-up, old-maid teacher.

But when it was delivered, it was the model she wanted – obtained perhaps with a little more wail and sniffle than quite went with the adulthood of fourteen – and copy was turned out in a charming and entirely feminine handwriting, with the most beautifully graceful capitals anyone ever saw.

Even the phrase, 'Oh, golly,' somehow breathed glamour when the Transcriber was done with it.

But just the same she had to get it right, so she sat up straight in her chair, placed her first draft before her in businesslike fashion, and began again, crisply and clearly; her abdomen flat, her chest lifted, and her breathing carefully controlled. She intoned, with dramatic fervor:

'The Future of Seldon's Plan.

'The Foundation's past history is, I am sure, well-known to all of us who have had the good fortune to be educated in our planet's efficient and well-staffed school system.

(There! That would start things off right with Miss Erlking, that mean old hag.)

That past history is largely the past history of the great plan of Hari Seldon. The two are one. But the question in the mind of most

95

people today is whether this Plan will continue in all its great wisdom, or whether it will be foully destroyed, or, perhaps, has been so destroyed already.

'To understand this, it may be best to pass quickly over some of the highlights of the Plan as it has been revealed to humanity thus far.

(This part was easy because she had taken Modern History the semester before.)

'In the days, nearly four centuries ago, when the First Galactic Empire was decaying into the paralysis that preceded final death, one man – the great Hari Seldon – foresaw the approaching end. Through the science of psychohistory, the intrissacies of whose mathematics has long since been forgotten.

(She paused in a trifle of doubt. She was sure that 'intricacies' was pronounced with soft *c's* but the spelling didn't look right. Oh, well, the machine couldn't very well be wrong—)

he and the men who worked with him are able to foretell the course of the great social and economic currents sweeping the Galaxy at the time. It was possible for them to realize that, left to itself, the Empire would break up, and thereafter there would be at least thirty thousand years of anarchic chaos prior to the establishment of a new Empire.

'It was too late to prevent the great Fall, but it was still possible, at least, to cut short the intermediate period of chaos. The Plan was, therefore, evolved whereby only a single millennium would separate the Second Empire from the First. We are completing the fourth century of that millennium, and many generations of men have lived and died while the Plan has continued its inexorable workings.

'Hari Seldon established two Foundations at the opposite ends of the Galaxy, in a manner and under such circumstances as would yield the best mathematical solution for his psychohistorical problem. In one of these, *our* Foundation, established here on Terminus, there was concentrated the physical science of the Empire, and through the possession of that science, the Foundation was able to withstand the attacks of the barbarous kingdoms which had broken away and become independent, out at the fringe of the Empire.

'The Foundation, indeed, was able to conquer in its turn these short-lived kingdoms by means of the leadership of a series of wise and heroic men like Salvor Hardin and Hober Mallow who were able to interpret the Plan intelligently and to guide our land through its

(She had written 'intricacies' here also, but decided not to risk it a second time.)

complications. All our planets still revere their memories although centuries have passed.

'Eventually, the Foundation established a commercial system which controlled a large portion of the Siwennian and Anacreonian sectors of the Galaxy, and even defeated the remnants of the old Empire under its last great general, Bel Riose. It seemed that nothing could stop the workings of Seldon's plan. Every crisis that Seldon had planned had come at its appropriate time and had been solved, and with each solution the Foundation had taken another giant stride toward Second Empire and peace.

'And then,

(Her breath came short at this point, and she hissed the words between her teeth, but the Transmitter simply wrote them, calmly and gracefully.)

with the last remnants of the dead First Empire gone and with only ineffectual warlords ruling over the splinters and remnants of the decayed colossus,

(She got *that* phrase out of a thriller on the video last week, but old Miss Erlking never listened to anything but symphonics and lectures, so *she'd* never know.)

there came the Mule.

'This strange man was not allowed for in the Plan. He was a mutant, whose birth could not have been predicted. He had the strange and mysterious power of controlling and manipulating human emotions, and in this manner could bend all men to his will. With breath-taking swiftness, he became a conqueror and Empire-builder, until, finally, he even defeated the Foundation itself.

'Yet he never obtained universal domination, since in his first overpowering lunge he was stopped by the wisdom and daring of a great woman

(Now there was that old problem again. Father *would* insist that she never bring up the fact that she was the grandchild of Bayta Darell. Everyone knew it and Bayta was just about the greatest woman there ever was and she *had* stopped the Mule singlehanded.)

in a manner the true story of which is known in its entirety to very few.

(There! If she had to read it to the class, that last could be said in a dark voice, and someone would be sure to ask what the true story was, and then – well, and then she couldn't *help* tell the truth if they asked her, could she? In her mind, she was already wordlessly whizzing through a hot and eloquent explanation to a stern and questioning paternal parent.)

'After five years of restricted rule, another change took place, the reasons for which are not known, and the Mule abandoned all plans for further conquest. His last five years were those of an enlightened despot.

'It is said by some that the change in the Mule was brought about by the intervention of the Second Foundation. However, no man has ever discovered the exact location of this other Foundation, nor knows its exact function, so that theory remains unproven.

'A whole generation has passed since the death of the Mule. What of the future, then, now that he has come and gone? He interrupted Seldon's Plan and seemed to have burst it to fragments, yet as soon as he died, the Foundation rose again, like a nova from the dead ashes of a dying star.

(She had made that up herself.)

Once again, the planet Terminus houses the centre of a commercial federation almost as great and as rich as before the conquest, and even more peaceful and democratic.

'Is this planned? Is Seldon's great dream still alive, and will a Second Galactic Empire yet be formed six hundred years from now? I, myself, believe so, because

(This was the important part. Miss Erlking always had those large, ugly red-pencil scrawls that went: 'But this is only descriptive. What are your personal reactions? Think! Express yourself! Penetrate your own soul!' Penetrate your own soul. A lot *she* knew about souls, with her lemon face that never smiled in its life—)

never at any time has the political situation been so favourable. The old Empire is completely dead and the period of the Mule's rule put an end to the era of warlords that preceded him. Most of the surrounding portions of the Galaxy are civilized and peaceful.

'Moreover the internal health of the Foundation is better than ever before. The despotic times of the pre-Conquest hereditary mayors have given way to the democratic elections of early times. There are no longer dissident worlds of independent Traders; no longer the injustices and dislocations that accompanied accumulations of great wealth in the hands of a few.

'There is no reason, therefore, to fear failure, unless it is true that the Second Foundation itself presents a danger. Those who think so have no evidence to back their claim, but merely vague fears and superstitions. I think that our confidence in ourselves, in our nation, and in Hari Seldon's great Plan should drive from our hearts and minds all uncertainties and

(Hm-m-m. This was awfully corny, but something like this was expected at the end.)

so I say—'

That is as far as 'The Future of Seldon's Plan' got, at that moment, because there was the gentlest little tap on the

99

window, and when Arcadia shot up to a balance on one arm of the chair, she found herself confronted by a smiling face beyond the glass, its even symmetry of feature interestingly accentuated by the short, vertical line of a finger before its lips.

With the slight pause necessary to assume an attitude of bepuzzlement, Arcadia dismounted from the armchair, walked to the couch that fronted the wide window that held the apparition and, kneeling upon it, stared out thoughtfully.

The smile upon the man's face faded quickly. While the fingers of one hand tightened whitely upon the sill, the other made a quick gesture. Arcadia obeyed calmly, and closed the latch that moved the lower third of the window smoothly into its socket in the wall, allowing the warm spring air to interfere with the conditioning within.

'You can't get in,' she said, with comfortable smugness. 'The windows are all screened, and keyed only to people who belong here. If you come in, all sorts of alarms will break loose.' A pause, then she added, 'You look sort of silly balancing on that ledge underneath the window. If you're not careful, you'll fall and break your neck and a lot of valuable flowers.'

'In that case,' said the man at the window, who had been thinking that very thing – with a slightly different arrangement of adjectives – 'will you shut off the screen and let me in?'

'No use in doing that,' said Arcadia. 'You're probably thinking of a different house, because I'm not the kind of girl who lets strange men into their ... her bedroom this time of night.' Her eyes, as she said it, took on a heavy-lidded sultriness – or an unreasonable facsimile thereof.

All traces of humour whatever had disappeared from the young stranger's face. He muttered, 'This is Dr Darell's house, isn't it?'

'Why should I tell you?'

'Oh, Galaxy – Goodbye—'

'If you jump off, young man, I will personally give the alarm.'

(This was intended as a refined and sophisticated thrust of

irony, since to Arcadia's enlightened eyes, the intruder was an obviously mature thirty, at least – quite elderly, in fact.)

Quite a pause. Then, tightly, he said, 'Well, now, look here, girlie, if you don't want me to stay, and don't want me to go, what *do* you want me to do?'

'You can come in, I suppose. Dr Darell *does* live here. I'll shut off the screen now.'

Warily, after a searching look, the young man poked his hand through the window, then hunched himself up and through it. He brushed at his knees with an angry, slapping gesture, and lifted a reddened face at her.

'You're quite sure that your character and reputation won't suffer when they find me here, are you?'

'Not as much as yours would, because just as soon as I hear footsteps outside, I'll just shout and yell and say you forced your way in here.'

'Yes?' he replied with heavy courtesy, 'And how do you intend to explain the shut-off protective screen?'

'Poof! That would be easy. There wasn't any there in the first place.'

The man's eyes were wide with chagrin. 'That was a bluff? How old are you, kid?'

'I consider that a very impertinent question, young man. And I am not accustomed to being addressed as "kid."'

'I don't wonder. You're probably the Mule's grandmother in disguise. Do you mind if I leave now before you arrange a lynching party with myself as star performer?'

'You had better not leave – because my father's expecting you.'

The man's look became a wary one, again. An eyebrow shot up as he said, lightly, 'Oh? Anyone with your father?'

'No.'

'Anyone called on him lately?'

'Only tradespeople – and you.'

'Anything unusual happen at all?'

101

'Only you.'

'Forget me, will you? No, don't forget me. Tell me, how did you know your father was expecting me?'

'Oh, that was easy. Last week, he received a Personal Capsule, keyed to him personally, with a self-oxidizing message, you know. He threw the capsule shell into the Trash Disinto, and yesterday, he gave Poli – that's our maid, you see – a month's vacation so she could visit her sister in Terminus City, and this afternoon, he made up the bed in the spare room. So I knew he expected somebody that I wasn't supposed to know anything about. Usually, he tells me everything.'

'Really! I'm surprised he has to. I should think you'd know everything before he tells you.'

'I usually do.' Then she laughed. She was beginning to feel very much at ease. The visitor was elderly, but very distinguished-looking with curly brown hair and very blue eyes. Maybe she could meet somebody like that again, sometimes, when she was old herself.

'And just how,' he asked, 'did you know it was *I* he expected?'

'Well, who else *could* it be? He was expecting somebody in so secrety a way, if you know what I mean – and then you come jumping around trying to sneak through windows, instead of walking through the front door, the way you would if you had any sense.' She remembered a favourite line, and used it promptly. 'Men are so stupid!'

'Pretty stuck on yourself, aren't you, kid? I mean, Miss. You could be wrong, you know. What if I told you that all this is a mystery to me and that as far as I know, your father is expecting someone else, not me.'

'Oh, I don't think so. I didn't ask you to come in, until after I saw you drop your briefcase.'

'My what?'

'Your briefcase, young man. I'm not blind. You didn't drop it by accident, because you looked down *first*, so as to make sure it would land right. Then you must have realized it would land just under the hedges and wouldn't be seen, so you dropped it and *didn't* look down afterwards. Now since you came to the window instead of the front door, it must mean that you were a little afraid to trust yourself in the house before investigating the place. And after you had a little trouble with me, you took care of your briefcase before taking care of yourself, which means that you consider whatever your briefcase has in it to be more valuable than your own safety, and *that* means as long as you're in here and the briefcase is out there and we know that it's out there, you're probably pretty helpless.'

She paused for a much-needed breath, and the man said, grittily, 'Except that I think I'll choke you just about medium dead and get out of here, *with* the briefcase.'

'Except, young man, that I happen to have a baseball bat under my bed, which I can reach in two seconds from where I'm sitting, and I'm very strong for a girl.'

Impasse. Finally, with a strained courtesy, the 'young man' said, 'Shall I introduce myself, since we're being so chummy? I'm Pelleas Anthor. And your name?'

'I'm Arca— Arkady Darell. Pleased to meet you.'

'And now, Arkady, would you be a good little girl and call your father?'

Arcadia bridled. 'I'm not a little girl. I think you're very rude – especially when you're asking a favour.'

Pelleas Anthor sighed. 'Very well. Would you be a good, kind, dear, little old lady, just chock full of lavender, and call your father?'

'That's not what I meant either, but I'll call him. Only not so I'll take my eyes off *you*, young man.' And she stamped on the floor.

There came the sound of hurrying footsteps in the hall, and the door was flung open.

'Arcadia—' There was a tiny explosion of exhaled air, and Dr Darell said, 'Who are you, sir?'

Pelleas sprang to his feet in what was quite obviously relief.

'Dr Toran Darell? I am Pelleas Anthor. You've received word about me, I think. At least, your daughter says you have.'

'My *daughter* says I have?' he bent a frowning glance at her which caromed harmlessly off the wide-eyed and impenetrable web of innocence with which she met the accusation.

Dr Darell said, finally: 'I *have* been expecting you. Would you mind coming down with me, please?' And he stopped as his eye caught a flicker of motion, which Arcadia caught simultaneously.

She scrambled towards her Transcriber, but it was quite useless, since her father was standing right next to it. He said, sweetly, 'You've left it going all this time, Arcadia.'

'Father,' she squeaked, in real anguish, 'it is very ungentlemanly to read another person's private correspondence, especially when it's talking correspondence.'

'Ah,' said her father, 'but "talking correspondence" with a strange man in your bedroom! As a father, Arcadia, I must protect you against evil.'

'Oh, golly – it was nothing like *that*.'

Pelleas laughed suddenly, 'Oh, but it was, Dr Darell. The young lady was going to accuse me of all sorts of things, and I must insist that you read it, if only to clear *my* name.'

'Oh—' Arcadia held back her tears with an effort. Her own father didn't even trust her. And that darned Transcriber— If that silly fool hadn't come gooping at the window, and making her forget to turn it off. And now her father would be making long, gentle speeches about what young ladies aren't supposed to do. There just wasn't anything they *were* supposed to do, it looked like, except choke and die, maybe.

'Arcadia,' said her father, gently, 'it strikes me that a young lady—'

She knew it. She knew it.

'— should not be quite so impertinent to men older than she is.'

'Well, what did he want to come peeping around my window for? A young lady has a right to privacy— Now I'll have to do my whole darned composition over.'

'It's not up to you to question his propriety in coming to your window. You should simply not have let him in. You should have called me instantly – especially if you thought I was expecting him.'

She said, peevishly, 'It's just as well if you didn't see him – stupid thing. He'll give the whole thing away if he keeps on going to windows, instead of doors.'

'Arcadia, nobody wants your opinion on matters you know nothing of.'

'I do, too. It's the Second Foundation, that's what it is.'

There was a silence. Even Arcadia felt a little nervous stirring in her abdomen.

Dr Darell said, softly, 'Where have you heard this?'

'Nowheres, but what else is there to be so secret about? And you don't have to worry that I'll tell anyone.'

'Mr Anthor,' said Dr Darell, 'I must apologize for all this.'

'Oh, that's all right,' came Anthor's rather hollow response. 'It's not your fault if she's sold herself to the forces of darkness. But do you mind if I ask her a question before we go. Miss Arcadia—'

'What do you want?'

'Why do you think it is stupid to go to windows instead of to doors?'

'Because you advertise what you're trying to hide, silly. If I have a secret, I don't put tape over my mouth and let everyone *know* I have a secret. I talk just as much as usual, only about something else. Didn't you ever read any of the sayings of Salvor Hardin? He was our first Mayor, you know.'

'Yes, I know.'

'Well, he used to say that only a lie that wasn't ashamed of itself could possibly succeed. He also said that nothing had to *be* true, but everything had to *sound* true. Well, when you come in through a window, it's a lie that's ashamed of itself and it doesn't sound true.'

'Then what would you have done?'

'If I had wanted to see my father on top secret business, I would have made his acquaintance openly and seen him about all sorts of strictly legitimate things. And then when everyone knew all about you and connected you with my father as a matter of course, you could be as top secret as you want and nobody would ever think of questioning it.'

Anthor looked at the girl strangely, then at Dr Darell. He said, 'Let's go. I have a briefcase I want to pick up in the garden. Wait! Just one last question. Arcadia, you don't really have a baseball bat under your bed, do you?'

'No! I don't.'

'Hah. I didn't think so.'

Dr Darell stopped at the door. 'Arcadia,' he said, 'when you rewrite your composition on the Seldon Plan, don't be unnecessarily mysterious about your grandmother. There is no necessity to mention that part at all.'

He and Pelleas descended the stairs in silence. Then the visitor asked in a strained voice, 'Do you mind, sir? How old is she?'

'Fourteen, day before yesterday.'

'*Fourteen*? Great Galaxy— Tell me, has she ever said she expects to marry some day?'

'No, she hasn't. Not to me.'

'Well, if she ever does, shoot him. The one she's going to marry, I mean.' He stared earnestly into the older man's eyes. 'I'm serious. Life could hold no greater horror than living with what she'll be like when she's twenty. I don't mean to offend you, of course.'

'You don't offend me. I think I know what you mean.'

Upstairs, the object of their tender analyses faced the Transcriber with revolted weariness and said, dully: 'Thefutureofseldonsplan.' The Transcriber with infinite aplomb, translated that into elegantly, complicated script capitals as:

'The Future of Seldon's Plan.'

# 8

# SELDON'S PLAN

MATHEMATICS *The synthesis of the calculus of n-variables and of n-dimensional geometry is the basis of what Seldon once called 'my little algebra of humanity'.* . . .

ENCYCLOPEDIA GALACTICA

Consider a room!

The location of the room is not in question at the moment. It is merely sufficient to say that in that room, more than anywhere, the Second Foundation existed.

It was a room which, through the centuries, had been the abode of pure science – yet it had none of the gadgets with which, through millenia of association, science has come to be considered equivalent. It was a science, instead, which dealt with mathematical concepts only, in a manner similar to the speculation of ancient, ancient races in the primitive, pre-historic days before technology had come to be; before Man had spread beyond a single, now-unknown world.

For one thing, there was in that room – protected by a mental science as yet unassailable by the combined physical might of the rest of the Galaxy – the Prime Radiant, which held in its vitals the Seldon Plan – complete.

For another, there was a man, too, in that room – The First Speaker.

He was the twelfth in the line of chief guardians of the Plan, and his title bore no deeper significance than the fact that at the gatherings of the leaders of the Second Foundation, he spoke first.

His predecessor had beaten the Mule, but the wreckage of that gigantic struggle still littered the path of the Plan— For twenty-five years, he, and his administration, had been trying to force a Galaxy of stubborn and stupid human beings back to the path— It was a terrible task.

The First Speaker looked up at the opening door. Even while, in the loneliness of the room, he considered his quarter century of effort, which now so slowly and inevitably approached its climax; even while he had been so engaged, his mind had been considering the newcomer with a gentle expectation. A youth, a student, one of those who might take over, eventually.

The young man stood uncertainly at the door, so that the First Speaker had to walk to him and lead him in, with a friendly hand upon the shoulder.

The Student smiled shyly, and the First Speaker responded by saying, 'First, I must tell you why you are here.'

They faced each other now, across the desk. Neither was speaking in any way that could be recognized as such by any man in the Galaxy who was not himself a member of the Second Foundation.

Speech, originally, was the device whereby Man learned, imperfectly, to transmit the thoughts and emotions of his mind. By setting up arbitrary sounds and combinations of sounds to represent certain mental nuances, he developed a method of communication – but one which in its clumsiness and thick-numbed inadequacy degenerated all the delicacy of the mind into gross and guttural signalling.

Down – down – the results can be followed; and all the suffering that humanity ever knew can be traced to the one fact that no man in the history of the Galaxy, until Hari Seldon, and very few men thereafter, could really understand one another. Every human being lived behind an impenetrable wall of choking mist within which no other but he existed. Occasionally there were the dim signals from deep within the cavern in which another man was located – so that each might grope toward the other. Yet because they did not know one another, and could not understand one another, and dared not trust one another, and felt from infancy the terrors and insecurity of that ultimate isolation – there was the hunted fear of man for man, the savage rapacity of man toward man.

Feet, for tens of thousands of years, had clogged and shuffled in the mud – and held down the minds which, for an equal time, had been fit for the companionship of the stars.

Grimly, Man had instinctively sought to circumvent the prison bars of ordinary speech. Semantics, symbolic logic, psychoanalysis – they had all been devices whereby speech could either be refined or by-passed.

Psychohistory had been the development of mental science, the final mathematicization thereof, rather, which had finally succeeded. Through the development of the mathematics necessary to understand the facts of neural physiology and the electro-chemistry of the nervous system, which themselves had to be, *had* to be, traced down to nuclear forces, it first became possible to truly develop psychology. And through the generalization of psychological knowledge from the individual to the group, sociology was also mathematicized.

The larger groups; the billions that occupied planets; the trillions that occupied Sectors; the quadrillions that occupied the whole Galaxy, became, not simply human beings, but gigantic forces amenable to statistical treatment – so that to Hari Seldon, the future became clear and inevitable, and the Plan could be set up.

The same basic developments of mental science that had brought about the development of the Seldon Plan, thus made it also unnecessary for the First Speaker to use words in addressing the Student.

Every reaction to a stimulus, however slight, was completely indicative of all the trifling changes, of all the flickering currents that went on in another's mind. The First Speaker could not sense the emotional content of the Student's instinctively, as the Mule would have been able to do – since the Mule was a mutant with powers not ever likely to become completely comprehensible to any ordinary man, even a Second Foundationer – rather he deduced them, as the result of intensive training.

Since, however, it is inherently impossible in a society based on speech to indicate truly the method of communication of Second Foundationers among themselves, the whole matter will be hereafter ignored. The First Speaker will be represented as speaking in ordinary fashion, and if the translation is not always entirely valid, it is at least the best that can be done under the circumstances.

It will be pretended, therefore, that the First Speaker *did* actually say, 'First, I must tell you why you are here,' instead of smiling *just* so and lifting a finger *exactly* thus.

The First Speaker said, 'You have studied mental science hard and well for most of your life. You have absorbed all your teachers could give you. It is time for you and a few others like yourself to begin your apprenticeship for Speakerhood.'

Agitation from the other side of the desk.

'No – now you must take this phlegmatically. You had hoped you would qualify. You had feared you would not. Actually, both hope and fear are weaknesses. You *knew* you would qualify and you hesitate to admit the fact because such knowledge might stamp you as cocksure and therefore unfit. Nonsense! The most helplessly stupid man is he who is not aware that he is wise. It is part of your qualification that you *knew* you would qualify.'

Relaxation on the other side of the desk.

'Exactly. Now you feel better and your guard is down. You are fitter to concentrate and fitter to understand. Remember, to be truly effective, it is not necessary to hold the mind under a tight, controlling barrier which to the intelligent probe is as informative as a naked mentality. Rather, one should cultivate an innocence, an awareness of self, and an unselfconsciousness of self which leaves one nothing to hide. My mind is open to you. Let this be so for both of us.'

He went on. 'It is not an easy thing to be a Speaker. It is not an easy thing to be a Psychohistorian in the first place; and not even the best Psychohistorian need necessarily qualify to be a Speaker. There is a distinction here. A Speaker must not only be aware of the mathematical intricacies of the Seldon Plan; he must have a sympathy for it and for its ends. He must *love* the Plan; to him it must be life and breath. More than that, it must even be as a living friend.

'Do you know what this is?'

The First Speaker's hand hovered gently over the black, shining cube in the middle of the desk. It was featureless.

'No, Speaker, I do not.'

'You have heard of the Prime Radiant?

'This?' – Astonishment.

'You expected something more noble and awe-inspiring? Well, that is natural. It was created in the days of the Empire, by men of Seldon's time. For nearly four hundred years, it has served our needs perfectly, without requiring repairs or adjustment. And fortunately so, since none of the Second Foundation is qualified to handle it in any technical fashion.' He smiled gently. 'Those of the First Foundation might be able to duplicate this, but they must never know, of course.'

He depressed a lever on his side of the desk and the room was in darkness. But only for a moment, since with a gradually livening flush, the two long walls of the room glowed to life. First, a pearly white, unrelieved, then a trace of faint darkness here and there, and finally, the fine neatly printed equations in black, with an occasional red hairline that wavered through the darker forest like a staggering rillet.

'Come, my boy, step here before the wall. You will not cast a shadow. This light does not radiate from the Radiant in an ordinary manner. To tell you the truth, I do not know even faintly by what medium this effect is produced, but you will not cast a shadow. I know that.'

They stood together in the light. Each wall was thirty feet long, and ten high. The writing was small and covered every inch.

'This is not the whole Plan,' said the First Speaker. 'To get it all upon both walls, the individual equations would have to be reduced to microscopic size – but that is not necessary. What you now see represents the main portions of the Plan till now. You have learned about this, have you not?'

'Yes, Speaker, I have.'

'Do you recognize any portion.'

A slow silence. The student pointed a finger and as he did so, the line of equation marched down the wall, until the single series of functions he had thought of – one could scarcely consider the quick, generalized gesture of the finger to have been sufficiently precise – was at eye-level.

The First Speaker laughed softly, 'You will find the Prime Radiant to be attuned to your mind. You may expect more surprises from the little gadget. What were you about to say about the equation you have chosen?'

'It,' faltered the Student, 'is a Rigellian integral, using a planetary distribution of a bias indicating the presence of two chief economic classes on the planet, or maybe a Sector, plus an unstable emotional pattern.'

'And what does it signify?'

'It represents the limit of tension, since we have here' – he pointed, and again the equations veered – 'a converging series.'

'Good,' said the First Speaker. 'And tell me, what do you think of all this. A finished work of art, is it not?'

'Definitely!'

'Wrong! It is not.' This, with sharpness. 'It is the first lesson you must unlearn. The Seldon Plan is neither complete nor correct. Instead, it is merely the best that could be done at the time. Over a dozen generations of men have pored over these equations, worked at them, taken them apart to the last decimal place, and put them together again. They've done more than that. They've watched nearly four hundred years pass and against the predictions and equations, they've checked reality, and they have learned.

'They have learned more than Seldon ever knew, and if with the accumulated knowledge of the centuries we could repeat Seldon's work, we could do a better job. Is that perfectly clear to you?'

The Student appeared a little shocked.

'Before you obtain your Speakerhood,' continued the First Speaker, 'you yourself will have to make an original contribution to the Plan. It is not such great blasphemy. Every red mark you see on the wall is the contribution of a man among us who lived since Seldon. Why ... why—' He looked upward, 'There!'

The whole wall seemed to whirl down upon him.

'This,' he said, 'is mine.' A fine red line encircled two forking arrows and included six square feet of deductions along each path. Between the two were a series of equations in red.

'It does not,' said the Speaker, 'seem to be much. It is at a point in the Plan which we will not reach yet for a time as long as that which has already passed. It is at the period of coalescence, when the Second Empire that is to be is in the grip of rival personalities who will threaten to pull it apart if the fight is too even, or clamp it into rigidity, if the fight is too uneven. Both possibilities are considered here, followed, and the method of avoiding either indicated.

'Yet it is all a matter of probabilities and a third course can exist. It is one of comparatively low likelihood – twelve point six four percent, to be exact – but even smaller chances have *already* come to pass and the Plan is only forty percent complete. This third probability consists of a possible compromise between two or more of the conflicting personalities being considered. This, I showed, would first freeze the Second Empire into an unprofitable mold, and then, eventually, inflict more damage through civil wars than would have taken place had a compromise never been made in the first place. Fortunately, that could be prevented, too. And that was my contribution.'

'If I may interrupt, Speaker— How is a change made?'

'Through the agency of the Radiant. You will find in your own case, for instance, that your mathematics will be checked rigorously by five different boards; and that you will be required to defend it against a concerted and merciless attack. Two years will then pass, and your development will be reviewed again. It has happened more than once that a seemingly perfect piece of work has uncovered its fallacies only after an induction period of months or years. Sometimes, the contributor himself discovers the flaw.

'If, after two years, another examination, not less detailed than the first, still passes it, and – better still – if in the interim the young scientist has brought to light additional details, subsidiary evidence, the contribution will be added to the Plan. It was the climax of my career; it will be the climax of yours.

'The Prime Radiant can be adjusted to your mind, and all corrections and additions can be made through mental rapport. There will be nothing to indicate that the correction or addition is yours. In all the history of the Plan there has been no personalization. It is rather a creation of all of us together. Do you understand?'

'Yes, Speaker!'

'Then, enough of that.' A stride to the Prime Radiant, and the walls were blank again save for the ordinary room-lighting region along the upper borders. 'Sit down here at my desk, and let me talk to you. It is enough for a Psychohistorian, as such, to know his Biostatistics and his Neurochemical Electro-mathematics. Some know nothing else and are fit only to be statistical technicians. But a Speaker must be able to discuss the Plan without mathematics. If not the Plan itself, at least its philosophy and its aims.

'First of all, what is the aim of the Plan? Please tell me in your own words – and don't grope for fine sentiment. You won't be judged on polish and suavity, I assure you.'

It was the Student's first chance at more than a bisyllable, and he hesitated before plunging into the expectant space cleared away for him. He said, diffidently: 'As a result of what I have learned, I believe that it is the intention of the Plan to establish a human civilization based on an orientation entirely different from anything that ever before existed. An orientation which, according to the findings of Psychochemistry, could never *spontaneously* come into being—'

'Stop!' The First Speaker was insistent. 'You must not say "never." That is a lazy slurring over of the facts. Actually, Psychohistory predicts only probabilities. A particular event may be infinitesimally probable, but the probability is always greater than zero.'

'Yes, Speaker. The orientation desired, if I may correct myself, then, is well known to possess no significant probability of spontaneously coming to pass.'

'Better. What is the orientation?'

'It is that of a civilization based on mental science. In all the known history of Mankind, advances have been made primarily in physical technology; in the capacity of handling the inanimate world about Man. Control of self and society has been left to chance or to the vague gropings of intuitive ethical systems based on inspiration and emotion. As a result, no culture of greater stability than about fifty-five percent has ever existed, and these only as the result of great human misery.'

'And why is the orientation we speak of a non-spontaneous one?'

'Because a large minority of human beings are mentally equipped to take part in the advance of physical science, and all receive the crude and visible benefits thereof. Only an insignificant minority, however, are inherently able to lead Man through the greater involvements of Mental Science; and the benefits derived therefrom, while longer lasting, are more subtle and less apparent. Furthermore, since such an orientation would lead to the development of a benevolent dictatorship of the mentally best – virtually a higher subdivision of Man – it would be resented and could not be stable without the application of a force which would depress the rest of Mankind to brute level. Such a development is repugnant to us and must be avoided.'

'What, then, is the solution?'

'The solution is the Seldon Plan. Conditions have been so arranged and so maintained that in a millennium from its beginnings – six hundred years from now, a Second Galactic

Empire will have been established in which Mankind will be ready for the leadership of Mental Science. In that same interval, the Second Foundation, in its development, will have brought forth a group of Psychologists ready to assume leadership. Or, as I have myself often thought, the First Foundation supplies the physical framework of a single political unit, and the Second Foundation supplies the mental framework of a ready-made ruling class.'

'I see. Fairly adequate. Do you think that *any* Second Empire, even if formed in the time set by Seldon, would do as a fulfilment of his Plan?'

'No, Speaker, I do not. There are several possible Second Empires that may be formed in the period of time stretching from nine hundred to seventeen hundred years after the inception of the Plan, but only one of these is *the* Second Empire.'

'And in view of all this, why is it necessary that the existence of the Second Foundation be hidden – above all, from the First Foundation?'

The Student probed for a hidden meaning to the question and failed to find it. He was troubled in his answer, 'For the same reason that the details of the Plan as a whole must be hidden from Mankind in general. The laws of Psychohistory are statistical in nature and are rendered invalid if the actions of individual men are not random in nature. If a sizable group of human beings learned of key details of the Plan, their actions would be governed by that knowledge and would no longer be random in the meaning of the axioms of Psychohistory. In other words, they would no longer be perfectly predictable. Your pardon, Speaker, but I feel that the answer is not satisfactory.'

'It is well that you do. Your answer is quite incomplete. It is the Second Foundation itself which must be hidden, not simply the Plan. The Second Empire is not yet formed. We have still a society which would resent a ruling class of psychologists, and which would fear its development and fight against it. Do you understand that?'

'Yes, Speaker, I do. The point has never been stressed—'

'Don't minimize. It has never been made – in the classroom, though you should be capable of deducing it yourself. This and many other points we will make now and in the near future during your apprenticeship. You will see me again in a week. By that time, I would like to have comments from you as to a certain problem which I now set before you. I don't want complete and rigorous mathematical treatment. That would take a year for an expert, and not a week for you. But I do want an indication as to trends and directions—

'You have here a fork in the Plan at a period in time of about half a century ago. The necessary details are included. You will note that the path followed by the assumed reality diverges from all the plotted predictions; its probability being under one percent. You will estimate for how long the divergence may continue before it becomes uncorrectable. Estimate also the probable end if uncorrected, and a reasonable method of correction.'

The Student flipped the Viewer at random and looked stonily at the passages presented on the tiny, built-in screen.

He said: 'Why this particular problem, Speaker? It obviously has significance other than purely academic.'

'Thank you, my boy. You are as quick as I had expected. The problem is not suppositious. Nearly half a century ago, the Mule burst into Galactic history and for ten years was the largest single fact in the universe. He was unprovided for; uncalculated for. He bent the Plan seriously, but not fatally.

'To stop him before he *did* become fatal, however, we were forced to take active part against him. We revealed our existence, and infinitely worse, a portion of our power. The First Foundation has learned of us, and their actions are now predicated on that knowledge. Observe in the problem presented. Here. And here.

'Naturally, you will not speak of this to anyone.'

There was an appalled pause, as realization seeped into the Student. He said: 'Then the Seldon Plan has failed!'

'Not yet. It merely *may* have failed. The probabilities of success are *still* twenty-one point four percent, as of the last assessment.'

117

# 9

# THE CONSPIRATORS

For Mr Darell and Pelleas Anthor, the evenings passed in friendly intercourse; the days in pleasant unimportance. It might have been an ordinary visit. Dr Darell introduced the young man as a cousin from across space, and interest was dulled by the cliché.

Somehow, however, among the small talk, a name might be mentioned. There would be an easy thoughtfulness. Dr Darell might say, 'No,' or he might say, 'Yes.' A call on the open Communiwave issued a casual invitation, 'Want you to meet my cousin.'

And Arcadia's preparations proceeded in their own manner. In fact, her actions might be considered the least straightforward of all.

For instance, she induced Olynthus Dam at school to donate to her a home-built, self-contained sound receiver by methods which indicated a future for her that promised peril to all males with whom she might come into contact. To avoid details, she merely exhibited such an interest in Olynthus' self-publicized hobby – he had a home workshop – combined with such a well-modulated transfer of this interest to Olynthus' own pudgy features, that the unfortunate youth found himself: 1) discoursing at great and animated length upon the principles of the hyperwave motor; 2) becoming dizyingly aware of the great, absorbed eyes that rested so lightly upon his; and 3) forcing into her willing hands his own greatest creation, the aforesaid sound-receiver.

Arcadia cultivated Olynthus in diminishing degree thereafter for just long enough to remove all suspicion that the sound-receiver had been the cause of the friendship. For months afterwards, Olynthus felt the memory of that short period in his life over and over again with the tendrils of his mind; until finally, for lack of further addition, he gave up and let it slip away.

When the seventh evening came, and five men sat in the Darell living room with food within and tobacco without, Arcadia's desk upstairs was occupied by this quite unrecognizable home-product of Olynthus' ingenuity.

Five men then. Dr Darell, of course, with greying hair and meticulous clothing, looking somewhat older than his forty-two years. Pelleas Anthor, serious and quick-eyed at the moment, looking young and unsure of himself. And the three new men: Jole Turbor, visicastor, bulky and plump-lipped; Dr Elvett Semic, professor-emeritus of physics at the University, scrawny and wrinkled, his clothes only half-filled; Homir Munn, librarian, lanky and terribly ill-at-ease.

Dr Darell spoke easily, in a normal, matter-of-fact tone: 'This gathering has been arranged, gentlemen, for a trifle more than merely social reasons. You may have guessed this. Since you have been deliberately chosen because of your backgrounds, you may also guess the danger involved. I won't minimize it, but I will point out that we are all condemned men, in any case.

'You will notice that none of you have been invited with any attempt at secrecy. None of you have been asked to come here unseen. The windows are not adjusted to non-insight. No screen of any sort is about the room. We have only to attract the attention of the enemy to be ruined; and the best way to attract that attention is to assume a false and theatrical secrecy.

(*Hah*, thought Arcadia, bending over the voices coming – a bit screechily – out of the little box.)

'Do you understand that?'

Elvett Semic twitched his lower lip and bared his teeth in the screwup, wrinkled gesture that preceded his every sentence. 'Oh, get on with it. Tell us about the youngster.'

Dr Darell said, 'Pelleas Anthor is his name. He was a student of my old colleague, Kleise, who died last year. Kleise sent me his brain-pattern to the fifth sublevel before he died, which pattern has been now checked against that of the man before you. You know, of course, that a brain-pattern cannot be duplicated that far, even by men of the Science of Psychology.

If you don't know that, you'll have to take my word for it.'

Turbor said, purse-lipped, 'We might as well make a beginning somewheres. We'll take your word for it, especially since you're the greatest electroneurologist in the Galaxy now that Kleise is dead. At least, that is the way I've described you in my visicast comment, and I even believe it myself. How old are you, Anthor?'

'Twenty-nine, Mr Turbor.'

'Hm-m-m. And are you an electroneurologist, too? A great one?'

'Just a student of the science. But I work hard, and I've had the benefit of Kleise's training.'

Munn broke in. He had a slight stammer at periods of tension. 'I ... I wish you'd g ... get started. I think everyone's t ... talking too much.'

Dr Darell lifted an eyebrow in Munn's direction. 'You're right, Homir. Take over, Pelleas.'

'Not for a while,' said Pelleas Anthor, slowly, 'because before we can get started – although I appreciate Mr Munn's sentiment – I must request brain-wave data.'

Darell frowned. 'What is this, Anthor? What brain-wave data do you refer to?'

'The patterns of all of you. You have taken mine, Dr Darell. I must take yours and those of the rest of you. And I must take the measurements myself.'

Turbor said, 'There is no reason for him to trust us, Darell. The young man is within his rights.'

'Thank you,' said Anthor. 'If you'll lead the way to your laboratory then, Dr Darell, we'll proceed. I took the liberty this morning of checking your apparatus.'

The science of electroencephalography was at once new and old. It was old in the sense that the knowledge of the micro-currents generated by nerve cells of living beings belonged to that immense category of human knowledge whose origin was completely lost. It was knowledge that stretched back as far as the earliest remnants of human history—

And yet it was new, too. The fact of the existence of microcurrents slumbered through the tens of thousands of years of Galactic Empire as one of those vivid and whimsical, but quite useless, items of human knowledge. Some had attempted to form classifications of waves into waking and sleeping, calm and excited, well and ill – but even the broadest conceptions had had their hordes of vitiating exceptions.

Others had tried to show the existence of brain-wave groups, analogous to the well-known blood groups, and to show that external environment was the defining factor. These were the race-minded people who claimed that Man could be divided into subspecies. But such a philosophy could make no headway against the overwhelming ecumenical drive involved in the fact of Galactic Empire – one political unit covering twenty million stellar systems, involving all of Man from the central world of Trantor – now a gorgeous and impossible memory of the great past – to the loneliest asteroid on the periphery.

And then again, in a society given over, as that of the First Empire was, to the physical sciences and inanimate technology, there was a vague but mighty sociological *push* away from the study of the mind. It was less respectable because less immediately useful; and it was poorly financed since it was less profitable.

After the disintegration of the First Empire, there came the fragmentation of organized science, back, back – past even the fundamentals of atomic power into the chemical power of coal and oil. The one exception to this, of course, was the First Foundation where the spark of science, revitalized and grown more intense was maintained and fed to flame. Yet there, too, it was the physical that ruled, and the brain, except for surgery, was neglected ground.

Hari Seldon was the first to express what afterwards came to be accepted as truth.

'Neural microcurrents,' he once said, 'carry within them the spark of every varying impulse and response, conscious and unconscious. The brain-waves recorded on neatly squared paper in trembling peaks and troughs are the mirrors of the combined thought-pulses of billions of cells. Theoretically, analysis should reveal the thoughts and emotions of the subject, to the last and least. Differences should be detected that are due not only to gross physical defects, inherited or acquired, but also to shifting states of emotion, to advancing education and experience, even to something as subtle as a change in the subject's philosophy of life.'

But even Seldon could approach no further than speculation.

And now for fifty years, the men of the First Foundation had been tearing at that incredibly vast and complicated storehouse of new knowledge. The approach, naturally, was made through new techniques – as, for example, the use of electrodes at skull suture by a newly-developed means which enabled contact to be made directly with the grey cells, without even the necessity of shaving a patch of skull. And then there was a recording device which automatically recorded the brain-wave data as an overall total, and as separate functions of six independent variables.

What was most significant, perhaps, was the growing respect in which encephalography and the encephalographer were held. Kleise, the greatest of them, sat at scientific conventions on an equal basis with the physicist. Dr Darell, though no longer active in the science, was known for his brilliant advances in encephalographic analysis almost as much as for the fact that he was the son of Bayta Darell, the great heroine of the past generation.

And so now, Dr Darell sat in his own chair, with the delicate touch of the feathery electrodes scarcely hinting at pressure upon his skull, while the vacuum-incased needles wavered to and fro. His back was to the recorder – otherwise, as was well known, the sight of the moving curves induced an unconscious effort to control them, with noticeable results – but he knew that the central dial was expressing the strongly rhythmic and little-varying Sigma curve, which was to be expected of his own powerful and disciplined mind. It would be strengthened and purified in the subsidiary dial dealing with the Cerebellar wave. There would be the sharp, near-discontinuous leaps from the frontal lobe, and the subdued shakiness from the subsurface regions with its narrow range of frequencies—

He knew his own brain-wave pattern much as an artist might be perfectly aware of the colour of his eyes.

Pelleas Anthor made no comment when Darell rose from the reclining chair. The young man abstracted the seven recordings, glanced at them with the quick, all-embracing eyes of one who knows exactly what tiny facet of near-nothingness is being looked for.

'If you don't mind, Dr Semic.'

Semic's age-yellowed face was serious. Electroencephalography was a science of his old age of which he knew little; an upstart that he faintly resented. He knew that he was old and that his wave-pattern would show it. The wrinkles on his face showed it, the stoop in his walk, the shaking of his hand – but *they* spoke only of his body. The brain-wave patterns might show that his mind was old, too. An embarrassing and unwarranted invasion of a man's last protecting stronghold, his own mind.

The electrodes were adjusted. The process did not hurt, of course, from beginning to end. There was just that tiny tingle, far below the threshold of sensation.

And then came Turbor, who sat quietly and unemotionally through the fifteen minute process, and Munn, who jerked at the first touch of the electrodes, and then spent the session rolling his eyes as though he wished he could turn them backwards and watch through a hole in his occiput.

'And now—' said Darell, when all was done.

'And now,' said Anthor, apologetically, 'there is one more person in the house.'

Darell, frowning, said: 'My daughter?'

'Yes. I suggested that she stay home tonight, if you'll remember.'

'For encephalographical analysis? What in the Galaxy for?'

'I cannot proceed without it.'

Darell shrugged and climbed the stairs. Arcadia, amply

warned, had the sound-receiver off when he entered; then followed him down with mild obedience. It was the first time in her life – except for the taking of her basic mind pattern as an infant, for identification and registration purposes – that she found herself under the electrodes.

'May I see,' she asked, when it was over, holding out her hand.

Dr Darell said, 'You would not understand, Arcadia. Isn't it time for you to go to bed?'

'Yes, father,' she said, demurely. 'Good night, all.'

She ran up the stairs and plumped into bed with a minimum of basic preparation. With Olynthus' sound-receiver propped beside her pillow, she felt like a character out of a book-film, and hugged every moment of it close to her chest in an ecstasy of 'spy-stuff.'

The first words she heard were Anthor's and they were: 'The analyses, gentlemen, are all satisfactory. The child's as well.'

Child, she thought disgustedly, and bristled at Anthor in the darkness.


Anthor had opened his briefcase now, and out of it, he took several dozen brain-wave records. They were not originals. Nor had the briefcase been fitted with an ordinary lock. Had the key been held in any hand other than his own, the contents thereof would have silently and instantly oxidized to an indecipherable ash. Once removed from the briefcase, the records did so anyway after half an hour.

But during their short lifetime, Anthor spoke quickly. 'I have the records here of several minor government officials at Anacreon. This is a psychologist at Locris University; this an industrialist at Siwenna. The rest are as you see.'

They crowded closely. To all but Darell, they were so many quivers on parchment. To Darell, they shouted with a million tongues.

Anthor pointed lightly, 'I call your attention, Dr Darell, to the plateau region among the secondary Tauian waves in the frontal lobe, which is what all these records have in common. Would you use my Analytical Rule, sir, to check my statement?'

The Analytical Rule might be considered a distant relation – as a skyscraper is to a shack – of that kindergarten toy, the logarithmic Slide Rule. Darell used it with the wristflip of long practice. He made freehand drawings of the result and, as Anthor stated, there were featureless plateaus in frontal lobe regions where strong swings should have been expected.

'How would you interpret that Dr Darell?' asked Anthor.

'I'm not sure. Offhand, I don't see how it's possible. Even in cases of amnesia, there is suppression, but not removal. Drastic brain surgery, perhaps?'

'Oh, something's been cut out,' cried Anthor, impatiently, 'yes! Not in the physical sense, however. You know, the Mule could have done just that. He could have suppressed completely all capacity for a certain emotion or attitude of mind, and leave nothing but just such a flatness. Or else—'

'Or else the Second Foundation could have done it. Is that it?' asked Turbor, with a slow smile.

There was no real need to answer that thoroughly rhetorical question.

'What made you suspicious, Mr Anthor?' asked Munn.

'It wasn't I. It was Dr Kleise. He collected brain wave patterns, much as the Planetary Police do, but along different lines. He specialized in intellectuals, government officials and business leaders. You see, it's quite obvious that if the Second Foundation is directing the historical course of the Galaxy – of us – they must do it subtly and in as minimal a fashion as possible. If they work through minds, as they must, it is the minds of people with influence; culturally, industrially, or politically. And with those he concerned himself.'

'Yes,' objected Munn, 'but is there corroboration? How do these people act – I mean the ones with the plateau. Maybe it's all a perfectly normal phenomenon.' He looked hopelessly at the others out of his, somehow, childlike blue eyes, but met no encouraging return.

'I leave that to Dr Darell,' said Anthor. 'Ask him how many times he's seen this phenomenon in his general studies, or in reported cases in the literature over the past generation. Then ask him the chances of it being discovered in almost one out of every thousand cases among the categories Dr Kleise studies.'

'I suppose that there is no doubt,' said Darell, thoughtfully, 'that these are artificial mentalities. They have been tampered with. In a way, I have suspected this—'

'I know that, Dr Darell,' said Anthor. 'I also know you once worked with Dr Kleise. I would like to know why you stopped.'

There wasn't actually hostility in his question. Perhaps nothing more than caution; but, at any rate, it resulted in a long pause. Darell looked from one to another of his guests, then said brusquely, 'Because there was no point to Kleise's battle. He was competing with an adversary too strong for him. He was detecting what we – he and I – knew he would detect – that we were not our own masters. *And I didn't want to know!* I had my self-respect. I liked to think that our Foundation was captain of its collective soul; that our forefathers had not quite fought and died for nothing. I thought it would be most simple to turn my face away as long as I was not quite sure. I didn't need my position since the Government pension awarded to my mother's family in perpetuity would take care of my uncomplicated needs. My home laboratory would suffice to keep boredom away, and life would some day end— Then Kleise died—'

Semic showed his teeth and said: 'This fellow Kleise; I don't know him. How did he die?'

Anthor cut in: 'He *died*. He thought he would. He told me half a year before that he was getting too close—'

'Now *we're* too c . . . close, too, aren't we?' suggested Munn, dry-mouthed, as his Adam's apple jiggled.

'Yes,' said Anthor, flatly, 'but we were, anyway – all of us. It's why you've all been chosen. I'm Kleise's student. Dr Darell was his colleague. Jole Turbor has been denouncing our blind faith in the saving hand of the Second Foundation on the air, until the government shut him off – through the agency, I might mention, of a powerful financier whose brain shows what Kleise used to call the Tamper Plateau. Homir Munn has the largest home collection of Muliana – if I may use the phrase to signify collected data concerning the Mule – in existence, and has published some papers containing speculation on the nature and function of the Second Foundation. Dr Semic has contributed as much as anyone to the mathematics of encephalographic analysis, though I don't believe he realized that his mathematics could be so applied.'

Semic opened his eyes wide and chuckled gaspingly, 'No, young fellow. I was analyzing intranuclear motions – the n-body problem, you know. I'm lost in encephalography.'

'Then we know where we stand. The government can, of course, do nothing about the matter. Whether the mayor or anyone in his administration is aware of the seriousness of the situation, I don't know. But this I do know – we five have nothing to lose and stand to gain much. With every increase in our knowledge, we can widen ourselves in safe directions. We are but a beginning, you understand.'

'How widespread,' put in Turbor, 'is this Second Foundation infiltration?'

'I don't know. There's a flat answer. All the infiltrations we have discovered were on the outer fringes of the nation. The capital world may yet be clean, though even that is not certain – else I would not have tested you. You were particularly suspicious, Dr Darell, since you abandoned research with Kleise. Kleise never forgave you, you know. I thought that perhaps the Second Foundation had corrupted you, but Kleise always insisted that you were a coward. You'll forgive me, Dr Darell, if I explain this to make my own position clear. I, personally, think I understand your attitude, and, if it was cowardice, I consider it venial.'

Darell drew a breath before replying. 'I ran away! Call it what you wish. I tried to maintain our friendship, however, yet he never wrote nor called me until the day he sent me your brain-wave data, and that was scarcely a week before he died—'

'If you don't mind,' interrupted Homir Munn, with a flash of nervous eloquence, 'I d ... don't see what you think you're doing. We're a p ... poor bunch of conspirators, if we're just going to talk and talk and t ... talk. And I don't see what else we can do, anyway. This is v ... very childish. B ... brain-waves and mumbo jumbo and all that. Is there just one thing you intend to *do*?'

Pelleas Anthor's eyes were bright, 'Yes, there is. We need more information on the Second Foundation. It's the prime necessity. The Mule spent the first five years of his rule in just that quest for information and failed – or so we have all been led to believe. But then he stopped looking! Why? Because he failed? Or because he succeeded?'

'M ... more talk,' said Munn, bitterly. 'How are we ever to know?'

'If you'll listen to me— The Mule's capital was on Kalgan. Kalgan was not part of the Foundation's commercial sphere of influence before the Mule and it is not part of it now. Kalgan is ruled, at the moment, by the man, Stettin, unless there's another palace revolution by tomorrow. Stettin calls himself First Citizen and considers himself the successor of the Mule. If there is any tradition in that world, it rests with the super-humanity and greatness of the Mule – a tradition almost superstitious in intensity. As a result, the Mule's old palace is maintained as a shrine. No unauthorized person may enter; nothing within has ever been touched.'

'Well?'

'Well, why is that so? At times like these, nothing happens without a reason. What if it is not superstition only that makes the Mule's palace inviolate? What if the Second Foundation has so arranged matters? In short what if the results of the Mule's five-year search are within —'

'Oh, p ... poppycock.'

'Why not?' demanded Anthor. 'Throughout its history the Second Foundation has hidden itself and interfered in Galactic affairs in minimal fashion only. I know that to us it would seem more logical to destroy the Palace or, at the least, to remove the data. But you must consider the psychology of these master psychologists. They are Seldons; they are Mules and they work by indirection, through the mind. They would never destroy

128

or remove when they could achieve their ends by creating a state of mind. Eh?'

No immediate answer, and Anthor continued, 'And you, Munn, are just the one to get the information we need.'

'*I?*' It was an astounded yell. Munn looked from one to the other rapidly, 'I can't do such a thing. I'm no man of action; no hero of any teleview. I'm a librarian. If I can help you that way, all right, and I'll risk the Second Foundation, but I'm not going out into space on any qu...quixotic thing like that.'

'Now, look,' said Anthor, patiently, 'Dr Darell and I have both agreed that you're the man. It's the only way to do it naturally. You say you're a librarian. Fine! What is your main field of interest? Muliana! You already have the greatest collection of material on the Mule in the Galaxy. It is natural for you to want more; more natural for you than for anyone else. *You* could request entrance to the Kalgan palace without arousing suspicion of ulterior motives. You might be refused but you would not be suspected. What's more, you have a one-man cruiser. You're known to have visited foreign planets during your annual vacation. You've even been on Kalgan before. Don't you understand that you need only act as you always have?'

'But I can't just say, "W...won't you kindly let me in to your most sacred shrine, M...Mr First Citizen?"'

'Why not?'

'Because, by the Galaxy, he won't let me!'

'All right, then. So he won't. Then you'll come home and we'll think of something else.'

Munn looked about in helpless rebellion. He felt himself being talked into something he hated. No one offered to help him extricate himself.

So in the end two decisions were made in Dr Darell's house. The first was a reluctant one of agreement on the part of Munn to take off into space as soon as his summer vacation began.

The other was a highly unauthorized decision on the part of a thoroughly unofficial member of the gathering, made as she clicked off a sound-receiver and composed herself for a belated sleep. This second decision does not concern us just yet.

# 10

## APPROACHING CRISIS

A week had passed on the Second Foundation, and the First Speaker was smiling once again upon the Student.

'You must have brought me interesting results, or you would not be so filled with anger.'

The Student put his hand upon the sheaf of calculating paper he had brought with him and said, 'Are you sure that the problem is a factual one?'

'The premises are true. I have distorted nothing.'

'Then I *must* accept the results, and I do not want to.'

'Naturally. But what have your wants to do with it? Well, tell me what disturbs you so. No, no, put your derivations to one side. I will subject them to analysis afterwards. Meanwhile, *talk* to me. Let me judge your understanding.'

'Well, then, Speaker— It becomes very apparent that a gross overall change in the basic psychology of the First Foundation has taken place. As long as they knew of the existence of a Seldon Plan, without knowing any of the details thereof, they were confident but uncertain. They knew they would succeed, but they didn't know when or how. There was, therefore, a continuous atmosphere of tension and strain – which was what Seldon desired. The First Foundation, in other words, could be counted upon to work at maximum potential.'

'A doubtful metaphor,' said the First Speaker, 'but I understand you.'

'But now, Speaker, they know of the existence of a Second Foundation in what amounts to detail, rather merely than as an ancient and vague statement of Seldon's. They have an inkling as to its function as the guardian of the Plan. They know that an agency exists which watches their every step and will not let them fall. So they abandon their purposeful stride and allow

130

themselves to be carried upon a litter. Another metaphor, I'm afraid.'

'Nevertheless, go on.'

'And that very abandonment of effort; that growing inertia; that lapse into softness and into a decadent and hedonistic culture, means the ruin of the Plan. They *must* be self-propelled.'

'Is that all?'

'No, there is more. The majority reaction is as described. But a great probability exists for a minority reaction. Knowledge of our guardianship and our control will rouse among a few, not complacency, but hostility. This follows from Korillov's Theorem—'

'Yes, yes. I know the theorem.'

'I'm sorry, Speaker. It is difficult to avoid mathematics. In any case, the effect is that not only is the Foundation's effort diluted, but part of it is turned against us, actively against us.'

'And is *that* all?'

'There remains one other factor of which the probability is moderately low—'

'Very good. What is that?'

'While the energies of the First Foundation were directed only to Empire; while their only enemies were huge and outmoded hulks that remained from the shambles of the past, they were obviously concerned only with the physical sciences. With *us* forming a new, large part of their environment, a change in view may well be imposed on them. They may try to become psychologists—'

'That change,' said the First Speaker, coolly, '*has* already taken place.'

The Student's lips compressed themselves into a pale line. 'Then all is over. It is the basic incompatibility with the Plan. Speaker, would I have known of this if I had lived – outside?'

The First Speaker spoke seriously, 'You feel humiliated, my young man, because, thinking you understood so much so well, you suddenly find that many very apparent things were unknown to you. Thinking you were one of the Lords of the Galaxy, you suddenly find that you stand near to destruction. Naturally, you will resent the ivory tower in which you lived; the seclusion in which you were educated; the theories on which you were reared.

'I once had that feeling. It is normal. Yet it was necessary that in your formative years you have no direct contact with the Galaxy; that you remain *here*, where all knowledge is filtered to you, and your mind carefully sharpened. We could have shown you this ... this part-failure of the Plan earlier and spared you the shock now, but you would not have understood the significance properly, as you now will. Then you find no solution at all to the problem?'

The Student shook his head and said hopelessly, 'None!'

'Well, it is not surprising. Listen to me, young man. A course of action exists and has been followed for over a decade. It is not a usual course, but one that we have been forced into against our will. It involves low probabilities, dangerous assumptions — We have even been forced to deal with individual reactions at times, because that was the only possible way, and you know that Psychostatistics by its very nature has no meaning when applied to less than planetary numbers.'

'Are we succeeding?' gasped the Student.

'There's no way of telling yet. We have kept the situation stable so far – but for the first time in the history of the Plan, it is possible for the unexpected actions of a single individual to destroy it. We have adjusted a minimum number of outsiders to a needful state of mind; we have our agents – but their paths are planned. They dare not improvise. That should be obvious to you. And I will not conceal the worst – if we are discovered, here, on this world, it will not only be the Plan that is destroyed, but ourselves, our physical selves. So you see, our solution is not very good.'

'But the little you have described does not sound like a solution at all, but like a desperate guess.'

'No. Let us say, an intelligent guess.'

'When is the crisis, Speaker? When will we know whether we have succeeded or not?'

'Well within the year, no doubt.'

The Student considered that, then nodded his head. He shook hands with the Speaker. 'Well, it's good to know.'

He turned on his heel and left.

The First Speaker looked out silently as the window gained transparency. Past the giant structures to the quiet, crowding stars.

A year would pass quickly. Would any of them, any of Seldon's heritage, be alive at its end?

# 11

## STOWAWAY

It was a little over a month before the summer could be said to have started. Started, that is, to the extent that Homir Munn had written his final financial report of the fiscal year, seen to it that the substitute librarian supplied by the Government was sufficiently aware of the subtleties of the post – last year's man had been quite unsatisfactory – and arranged to have his little cruiser the *Unimara* – named after a tender and mysterious episode of twenty years past – taken out of its winter cobwebbery.

He left Terminus in a sullen distemper. No one was at the port to see him off. That would not have been natural since no one ever had in the past. He knew very well that it was important to have this trip in no way different from any he had made in the past, yet he felt drenched in a vague resentment. He, Homir Munn, was risking his neck in derring-doery of the most outrageous sort, and yet he left alone.

At least, so he thought.

And it was because he thought wrongly, that the following day was one of confusion, both on the *Unimara* and in Dr Darell's suburban home.

It hit Dr Darell's home first, in point of time, through the medium of Poli, the maid, whose month's vacation was now quite a thing of the past. She flew down the stairs in a flurry and stutter.

The good doctor met her and she tried vainly to put emotion into words but ended by thrusting a sheet of paper and a cubical object at him.

He took them unwillingly and said: 'What's wrong, Poli?'

'She's *gone*, doctor.'

'Who's gone?'

134

'Arcadia!'

'What do you mean, gone? Gone where? What are you talking about?'

And she stamped her foot: '*I* don't know. She's gone, and there's a suitcase and some clothes gone with her and there's that letter. Why don't you read it, instead of just standing there? Oh, you *men*!'

Dr Darell shrugged and opened the envelope. The letter was not long, and except for the angular signature, 'Arkady,' was in the ornate and flowing handwriting of Arcadia's transcriber.

Dear Father:

It would have been simply too heartbreaking to say good-bye to you in person. I might have cried like a little girl and you would have been ashamed of me. So I'm writting a letter instead to tell you how much I'll miss you, even while I'm having this perfectly wonderful summer vacation with Uncle Homir. I'll take good care of myself and it won't be long before I'm home again. Meanwhile, I'm leaving you something that's all my own. You can have it now.

Your loving daughter,

Arkady.

He read it through several times with an expression that grew blanker each time. He said stiffly, 'Have you read this, Poli?'

Poli was instantly on the defensive. 'I certainly can't be blamed for that, doctor. The envelope has "Poli" written on the outside, and I had no way of telling there was a letter for you on the inside. I'm no snoop, doctor, and in the years I've been with—'

Darell held up a placating hand, 'Very well, Poli. It's not important. I just wanted to make sure you understood what had happened.'

He was considering rapidly. It was no use telling her to forget the matter. With regard to the enemy, 'forget' was a meaningless word; and the advice, insofar as it made the matter more important, would have had an opposite effect.

He said instead, 'She's a queer little girl, you know. Very romantic. Ever since we arranged to have her go off on a space trip this summer, she's been quite excited.'

'And just why has no one told *me* about this space trip?'

'It was arranged while you were away, and we forgot it. It's nothing more complicated than that.'

Poli's original emotions now concentrated themselves into a single, overwhelming indignation, 'Simple, is it? The poor chick has gone off with one suitcase, without a decent stitch of clothes to her, and alone at that. How long will she be away?'

'Now I won't have you worrying about it, Poli. There will be plenty of clothes for her on the ship. It's all been arranged. Will you tell Mr Anthor that I want to see him? Oh, and first – is this the object that Arcadia has left for me?' He turned it over in his hand.

Poli tossed her head. 'I'm sure I don't know. The letter was on top of it and that's every bit I can tell you. Forget to tell me, indeed. If her mother were alive—'

Darell waved her away. 'Please call Mr Anthor.'


Another's viewpoint on the matter differed radically from that of Arcadia's father. He punctuated his initial remarks with clenched fists and torn hair, and from there, passed on to bitterness.

'Great Space, what are you waiting for? What are we both waiting for? Get the spaceport on the viewer and have them contact the *Unimara*.'

'Softly, Pelleas, she's *my* daughter.'

'But it's not your Galaxy.'

'Now, wait. She's an intelligent girl, Pelleas, and she's thought this thing out carefully. We had better follow her thoughts while this thing is fresh. Do you know what this thing is?'

'No. Why should it matter what it is?'

'Because it's a sound-receiver.'

'That thing?'

'It's homemade, but it will work. I've tested it. Don't you see? It's her way of telling us that she's been a party to our conversations of policy. She knows where Homir Munn is going and why. She's decided it would be exciting to go along.'

'Oh, Great Space,' groaned the younger man. 'Another mind for the Second Foundation to pick.'

'Except that there's no reason why the Second Foundation should, *a priori*, suspect a fourteen-year-old girl of being a danger – *unless* we do anything to attract attention to her, such as calling back a ship out of space for no reason other than to take her off. Do you forget with whom we're dealing? How narrow the margin is that separates us from discovery? How helpless we are thereafter?'

'But we can't have everything depend on an insane child.'

'She's not insane, and we have no choice. She need not have written the letter, but she did it to keep us from going to the police after a lost child. Her letter suggests that we convert the entire matter into a friendly offer on the part of Munn to take an old friend's daughter off for a short vacation. And why not? He's been my friend for nearly twenty years. He's known her since she was three, when I brought her back from Trantor. It's a perfectly natural thing, and, in fact, ought to decrease suspicion. A spy does not carry a fourteen-year-old niece about with him.'

'So. And what will Munn do when he finds her?'

Dr Darell heaved his eyebrows once. 'I can't say – but I presume she'll handle him.'

But the house was somehow very lonely at night and Dr Darell found that fate of the Galaxy made remarkably little difference while his daughter's mad little life was in danger.

The excitement on the *Unimara*, if involving fewer people, was considerably more intense.

In the luggage compartment, Arcadia found herself, in the first place, aided by experience, and in the second, hampered by the reverse.

137

Thus, she met the initial acceleration with equanimity and the more subtle nausea that accompanied the inside-outness of the first jump through hyperspace with stoicism. Both had been experienced on space hops before, and she was tensed for them. She knew also that luggage compartments were included in the ship's ventilation system and that they could even be bathed in wall-light. This last, however, she excluded as being too unconscionably unromantic. She remained in the dark, as a conspirator should, breathing very softly, and listening to the little miscellany of noises that surrounded Homir Munn.

They were undistinguished noises, the kind made by a man alone. The shuffling of shoes, the rustle of fabric against metal, the soughing of an upholstered chair seat retreating under weight, the sharp click of a control unit, or the soft slap of a palm over a photoelectric cell.

Yet, eventually, it was the lack of experience that caught up with Arcadia. In the book films and on the videos, the stowaway seemed to have such an infinite capacity for obscuring. Of course, there was always the danger of dislodging something which would fall with a crash, or of sneezing – in videos you were almost sure to sneeze; it was an accepted matter. She knew all this, and was careful. There was also the realization that thirst and hunger might be encountered. For this, she was prepared with ration cans out of the pantry. But yet things remained that the films never mentioned, and it dawned upon Arcadia with a shock that, despite the best intentions in the world, she could stay hidden in the closet for only a limited time.

And on a one-man sports-cruiser, such as the *Unimara*, living space consisted, essentially, of a single room, so that there wasn't even the risky possibility of sneaking out of the compartment while Munn was engaged elsewhere.

She waited frantically for the sounds of sleep to arise. If only she knew whether he snored. At least she knew where the bunk was and she could recognize the rolling protest of one when she heard it. There was a long breath and then a yawn. She waited through a gathering silence, punctuated by the bunk's soft protest against a changed position or a shifted leg.

The door of the luggage compartment opened easily at the pressure of her finger, and her craning neck—

There was a definite human sound that broke off sharply.

Arcadia solidified. Silence! Still silence!

She tried to poke her eyes outside the door without moving her head and failed. The head followed the eyes.

Homir Munn was awake, of course – reading in bed, bathed in the soft, unspreading bed light, staring into the darkness with wide eyes, and groping one hand stealthily under the pillow.

Arcadia's head moved sharply back of itself. Then, the light went out entirely and Munn's voice said with shaky sharpness, 'I've got a blaster, and I'm shooting, by the Galaxy—'

And Arcadia wailed, 'It's only me. Don't shoot.'

Remarkable what a fragile flower romance is. A gun with a nervous operator behind it can spoil the whole thing.

The light was back on – all over the ship – and Munn was sitting up in bed. The somewhat grizzled hair on his thin chest and the sparse one-day growth on his chin lent him an entirely fallacious appearance of disreputability.

Arcadia stepped out, yanking at her metallene jacket which was supposed to be guaranteed wrinkleproof.

After a wild moment in which he almost jumped out of bed, but remembered, and instead yanked the sheet up to his shoulders, Munn gargled, 'W ... wha ... what—'

He was completely incomprehensible.

Arcadia said meekly, 'Would you excuse me for a minute? I've got to wash my hands.' She knew the geography of the vessel, and slipped away quickly. When she returned, with her courage oozing back, Homir Munn was standing before her with a faded bathrobe on the outside and a brilliant fury on the inside.

'What the black holes of Space are you d ... doing aboard this ship? H ... how did you get on here? What do you th ... think I'm supposed to do with you? What's going *on* here?'

He might have asked questions indefinitely, but Arcadia interrupted sweetly, 'I just wanted to come along, Uncle Homir.'

'Why? I'm not going anywhere!'

'You're going to Kalgan for information about the Second Foundation.'

And Munn let out a wild howl and collapsed completely. For one horrified moment, Arcadia thought he would have hysterics or beat his head against the wall. He was still holding the blaster and her stomach grew ice-cold as she watched it.

'Watch out—Take it easy—' was all she could think of to say.

But he struggled back to relative normality and threw the blaster on the bunk with such a force that should have set it off and blown a hole through the ship's hull.

'How did you get on?' he asked slowly, as though gripping each word with his teeth very carefully to prevent it from trembling before letting it out.

'It was easy. I just came into the hangar with my suitcase, and said, "Mr Munn's baggage!" and the man in charge just waved his thumb without even looking up.'

'I'll have to take you back, you know,' said Homir, and there was a sudden wild glee within him at the thought. By Space, this wasn't his fault.

'You can't, said Arcadia, calmly, 'it would attract attention.'

'What?'

'*You* know. The whole purpose of *your* going to Kalgan was because it was natural for you to go and ask for permission to look into the Mule's records. And you've got to be so natural that you're to attract no attention at all. If you go back with a girl stowaway, it might even get into the tele-news reports.'

'Where did you g ... get those notions about Kalgan? These ... uh ... childish—' He was far too flippant for conviction, of course, even to one who knew less than did Arcadia.

'I heard,' she couldn't avoid pride completely, 'with a

sound-recorder. I know all about it – so you've *got* to let me come along.'

'What about your father?' He played a quick trump. 'For all he knows, you're kidnapped ... dead.'

'I left a note,' she said, overtrumping, 'and he probably knows he mustn't make a fuss, or anything. You'll probably get a spacegram from him.'

To Munn the only explanation was sorcery, because the receiving signal sounded wildly two seconds after she finished.

She said: 'That's my father, I bet,' and it was.

The message wasn't long and it was addressed to Arcadia. It said: 'Thank you for your lovely present, which I'm sure you put to good use. Have a good time.'

'You see, she said, 'that's instructions.'

Homir grew used to her. After a while, he was glad she was there. Eventually, he wondered how he would have made it without her. She prattled! She was excited! Most of all, she was completely unconcerned. She knew the Second Foundation was the enemy, yet it didn't bother her. She knew that on Kalgan, he was to deal with a hostile officialdom, but she could hardly wait.

Maybe it came of being fourteen.

At any rate, the week-long trip now meant conversation rather than introspection. To be sure, it wasn't a very enlightening conversation, since it concerned, almost entirely, the girl's notions on the subject of how best to treat the Lord of Kalgan. Amusing and nonsensical, and yet delivered with weighty deliberation.

Homir found himself actually capable of smiling as he listened and wondered out of just which gem of historical fiction she got her twisted notion of the great universe.

It was the evening before the last jump. Kalgan was a bright star in the scarcely-twinkling emptiness of the outer reaches of the Galaxy. The ship's telescope made it a sparkling blob of barely-perceptible diameter.

Arcadia sat cross-legged in the good chair. She was wearing a pair of slacks and a none-too-roomy shirt that belonged to Homir. Her own more feminine wardrobe had been washed and ironed for the landing.

She said, 'I'm going to write historical novels, you know.' She was quite happy about the trip. Uncle Homir didn't the least mind listening to her and it made conversation so much more pleasant when you could talk to a really intelligent person who was serious about what you said.

She continued: 'I've read books and books about all the great men of Foundation history. You know, like Seldon, Hardin, Mallow, Devers and all the rest. I've even read most of what you've written about the Mule, except that it isn't much fun to read those parts where the Foundation loses. Wouldn't you rather read a history where they skipped the silly, tragic parts?'

'Yes, I would,' Munn assured her, gravely. 'But it wouldn't be a fair history, would it, Arkady? You'd never get academic respect, unless you give the whole story.'

'Oh, poof. Who cares about academic respect?' She found him delightful. He hadn't missed calling her Arkady for days. 'My novels are going to be interesting and are going to sell and be famous. What's the use of writing books unless you sell them and become well-known? I don't want just some old professors to know me. It's got to be everybody.'

Her eyes darkened with pleasure at the thought and she wriggled into a more comfortable position. 'In fact, as soon as I can get father to let me, I'm going to visit Trantor, so's I can get background material on the First Empire, you know. I was born on Trantor; did you know that?'

He did, but he said, 'You were?' and put just the right amount of amazement into his voice. He was rewarded with something between a beam and a simper.

'Uh-huh. My grandmother ... you know, Bayta Darell, you've heard of *her* ... was on Trantor once with my grandfather. In fact, that's where they stopped the Mule, when

142

all the Galaxy was at his feet; and my father and mother went there also when they were first married. I was born there. I even lived there till mother died, only I was just three then, and I don't remember much about it. Were you ever on Trantor, Uncle Homir?'

'No, can't say I was.' He leaned back against the cold bulkhead and listened idly. Kalgan was very close, and he felt his uneasiness flooding back.

'Isn't it just the most *romantic* world? My father says that under Stannel V, it had more people than any *ten* worlds nowadays. He says it was just one big world of metals – one big city – that was the capital of all the Galaxy. He's shown me pictures that he took on Trantor. It's all in ruins now, but it's still stu*pen*dous. I'd just *love* to see it again. In fact ... Homir!'

'Yes?'

'Why don't we go there, when we're finished with Kalgan?'

Some of the fright hurtled back into his face. 'What? Now don't start on that. This is business, not pleasure. Remember that.'

'But it *is* business,' she squeaked. 'There might be incredible amounts of information on Trantor. Don't you think so?'

'No, I don't.' He scrambled to his feet. 'Now untangle yourself from the computer. We've got to make the last jump, and then you turn in.' One good thing about landing, anyway; he was about fed up with trying to sleep on an overcoat on the metal floor.

The calculations were not difficult. The 'Space Route Handbook' was quite explicit on the Foundation-Kalgan route. There was the momentary twitch of the timeless passage through hyperspace and the final light-year dropped away.

The sun of Kalgan was a sun now – large, bright, and yellow-white; invisible behind the portholes that had automatically closed on the sunlit side.

Kalgan was only a night's sleep away.

# 12

## LORD

Of all the worlds of the Galaxy, Kalgan undoubtedly had the most unique history. That of the planet Terminus, for instance, was that of an almost uninterrupted rise. That of Trantor, once capital of the Galaxy, was that of an almost uninterrupted fall. But Kalgan—

Kalgan first gained fame as the pleasure world of the Galaxy two centuries before the birth of Hari Seldon. It was a pleasure world in the sense that it made an industry – and an immensely profitable one, at that – out of amusement.

And it was a stable industry. It was the most stable industry in the Galaxy. When all the Galaxy perished as a civilization, little by little, scarcely a feather's weight of catastrophe fell upon Kalgan. No matter how the economy and sociology of the neighbouring sectors of the Galaxy changed, there was always an elite; and it is always the characteristic of an elite that it possesses leisure as *the* great reward of its elite-hood.

Kalgan was at the service, therefore, successively – and successfully of the effete and perfumed dandies of the Imperial Court with their sparkling and libidinous ladies; of the rough and raucous warlords who ruled in iron the worlds they had gained in blood, with their unbridled and lascivious wenches; of the plump and luxurious businessmen of the Foundation, with their lush and flagitious mistresses.

It was quite undiscriminating, since they all had money. And since Kalgan serviced all and barred none; since its commodity was in unfailing demand; since it had the wisdom to interfere in no world's politics, to stand on no one's legitimacy, it prospered when nothing else did, and remained fat when all grew thin.

That is, until the Mule. Then, somehow, it fell, too, before a conqueror who was impervious to amusement, or to anything but conquest. To him all planets were alike, even Kalgan.

So for a decade, Kalgan found itself in the strange role of Galactic metropolis; mistress of the greatest Empire since the end of the Galactic Empire itself.

And then, with the death of the Mule, as sudden as the zoom, came the drop. The Foundation broke away. With it and after it, much of the rest of the Mule's dominions. Fifty years later there was left only the bewildering memory of that short space of power, like an opium dream. Kalgan never quite recovered. It could never return to the unconcerned pleasure world it had been, for the spell of power never quite released its hold. It lived instead under a succession of men whom the Foundation called the Lords of Kalgan, but who styled themselves First Citizen of the Galaxy, in imitation of the Mule's only title, and who maintained the fiction that they were conquerors too.

The current Lord of Kalgan had held that position for five months. He had gained it originally by virtue of his position at the head of the Kalganian navy, and through a lamentable lack of caution on the part of the previous lord. Yet no one on Kalgan was quite stupid enough to go into the question of legitimacy too long or too closely. These things happened, and are best accepted.

Yet that sort of survival of the fittest, in addition to putting a premium on bloodiness and evil, occasionally allowed capability to come to the fore as well. Lord Stettin was competent enough and not easy to manage.

Not easy for his eminence, the First Minister, who, with fine impartiality, had served the last lord as well as the present; and who would, if he lived long enough, serve the next as honestly.

Not easy for the Lady Callia, who was Stettin's more than friend, yet less than wife.

In Lord Stettin's private apartments the three were alone that evening. The First Citizen, bulky and glistening in the admiral's uniform that he affected, scowled from out the unupholstered chair in which he sat stiffly as the plastic of which is was composed. His First Minister, Lev Meirus, faced him with a far-off unconcern, his long, nervous fingers stroking absently and rhythmically the deep line that curved from hooked nose along gaunt and sunken cheek to the point, nearly, of the grey-bearded chin. The Lady Callia disposed of herself gracefully on the deeply furred covering of a foamite couch, her full lips trembling a bit in an unheeded pout.

'Sir,' said Meirus – it was the only title adhering to a lord who was styled only First Citizen, 'you lack a certain view of the continuity of history. Your own life, with its tremendous revolutions, leads you to think of the course of civilization as something equally amenable to sudden change. But it is not.'

'The Mule showed otherwise.'

'But who can follow in his footsteps. He was more than man, remember. And he, too, was not entirely successful.'

'Poochie,' whimpered the Lady Callia, suddenly, and then shrank into herself at the furious gesture from the First Citizen.

Lord Stettin said, harshly, 'Do not interrupt, Callia. Meirus, I am tired of inaction. My predecessor spent his life polishing the navy into a finely-tuned instrument that has not its equal in the Galaxy. And he died with the magnificent machine lying idle. Am I to continue that? I, an Admiral of the Navy?

'How long before the machine rusts? At present, it is a drain on the Treasury and returns nothing. Its officers long for dominion, its men for loot. All Kalgan desires the return of Empire and glory. Are you capable of understanding that?'

'These are but words that you use, but I grasp your meaning. Dominion, loot, glory – pleasant when they are obtained, but the process of obtaining them is often risky and always unpleasant. The first fine flush may not last. And in all history, it has never been wise to attack the Foundation. Even the Mule would have been wiser to refrain—'

There were tears in the Lady Callia's blue, empty eyes. Of

late, Poochie scarcely saw her, and now, when he had promised the evening to her, this horrible, thin, grey man, who always looked through her rather than at her, had forced his way in. And Poochie *let* him. She dared not say anything; was frightened even of the sob that forced its way out.

But Stettin was speaking now in the voice she hated, hard and impatient. He was saying: 'You're a slave to the far past. The Foundation is greater in volume and population, but they are loosely knit and will fall apart at a blow. What holds them together these days is merely inertia; an inertia I am strong enough to smash. You are hypnotized by the old days when only the Foundation had atomic power. They were able to dodge the last hammer blows of the dying Empire and then faced only the unbrained anarchy of the warlords who would counter the Foundation's atomic vessels only with hulks and relics.

'But the Mule, my dear Meirus, has changed that. He spread the knowledge, that the Foundation had hoarded to itself, through half the Galaxy and the monopoly in science is gone forever. We can match them.'

'And the Second Foundation?' questioned Meirus, coolly.

'And the Second Foundation?' repeated Stettin as coolly. 'Do *you* know its intentions? It took ten years to stop the Mule, if, indeed, it was the factor, which some doubt. Are you unaware that a good many of the Foundation's psychologists and sociologists are of the opinion that the Seldon Plan has been completely disrupted since the days of the Mule? If the Plan has gone, then a vacuum exists which I may fill as well as the next man.'

'Our knowledge of these matters is not great enough to warrant the gamble.'

'*Our* knowledge, perhaps, but we have a Foundation visitor on the planet. Did you know that? A Homir Munn – who, I understand, has written articles on the Mule, and has expressed exactly the opinion, that the Seldon Plan no longer exists.'

The First Minister nodded, 'I have heard of him, or at least of his writings. What does he desire?'

'He asks permission to enter the Mule's palace.'

'Indeed? It would be wise to refuse. It is never advisable to disturb the superstitions with which a planet is held.'

'I will consider that – and we will speak again.'

Meirus bowed himself out.

Lady Callia said tearfully, 'Are you angry with me, Poochie?'

Stettin turned on her savagely. 'Have I not told you before never to call me by that ridiculous name in the presence of others?'

'You *used* to like it.'

'Well, I don't any more, and it is not to happen again.'

He stared at her darkly. It was a mystery to him that he tolerated her these days. She was a soft, empty-headed thing, comfortable to the touch, with a pliable affection that was a convenient facet to a hard life. Yet, even that affection was becoming wearisome. She dreamed of marriage, of being First Lady.

Ridiculous!

She was all very well when he had been an admiral only – but now as First Citizen and future conqueror, he needed more. He needed heirs who could unite his future dominions, something the Mule had never had, which was why his Empire did not survive his strange nonhuman life. He, Stettin, needed someone of the great historic families of the Foundation with whom he could fuse dynasties.

He wondered testily why he did not rid himself of Callia now. It would be no trouble. She would whine a bit— He dismissed the thought. She had her points, occasionally.

Callia was cheering up now. The influence of Graybeard was gone and her Poochie's granite face was softening now. She lifted herself in a single, fluid motion and melted toward him.

'You're not going to scold me, are you?'

'No.' He patted her absently. 'Now just sit quietly for a while, will you? I want to think.'

'About the man from the Foundation?'

'Yes.'

'Poochie?' This was a pause.

'What?'

'Poochie, the man has a little girl with him, you said. Remember? Could I see her when she comes? I never—'

'Now what do you think I want him to bring his brat with him for? Is my audience room to be a grammar school? Enough of your nonsense, Callia.'

'But I'll take care of her, Poochie. You won't even have to bother with her. It's just that I hardly ever see children, and you know how I love them.'

He looked at her sardonically. She never tired of this approach. She loved children; i.e. *his* children; i.e. his *legitimate* children; i.e. marriage. He laughed.

'This particular little piece,' he said, 'is a great girl of fourteen or fifteen. She's probably as tall as you are.'

Callia looked crushed. 'Well, could I, anyway? She could tell me about the Foundation? I've always wanted to go there, you know. My grandfather was a Foundation man. Won't you take me there, sometime, Poochie?'

Stettin smiled at the thought. Perhaps he would, as conqueror. The good nature that the thought supplied him with made itself felt in his words, 'I will, I will. And you can see the girl and talk Foundation to her all you want. But not near me, understand.'

'I won't bother you, honestly. I'll have her in my own rooms.' She was happy again. It was not very often these days that she was allowed to have her way. She put her arms about his neck and after the slightest hesitation, she felt its tendons relax and the large head come softly down upon her shoulder.

# 13

## LADY

Arcadia felt triumphant. How life had changed since Pelleas Anthor had stuck his silly face up against her window – and all because she had the vision and courage to do what needed to be done.

Here she was on Kalgan. She had been to the great Central Theatre – the largest in the Galaxy – and seen *in person* some of the singing stars who were famous even in the distant Foundation. She had shopped all on her own along the Flowered Path, fashion centre of the gayest world in Space. And she had made her own selections because Homir just didn't know anything about it at all. The saleswoman raised no objections at all to long, shiny dresses with those vertical sweeps that made her look so tall – and Foundation money went a long, long way. Homir had given her a ten-credit bill and when she changed it to Kalganian 'Kalganids,' it made a terribly thick sheaf.

She had even had her hair redone – sort of half-short in back, with two glistening curls over each temple. And it was treated so that it looked goldier than ever; it just *shone*.

But *this*; this was best of all. To be sure, the Palace of Lord Stettin wasn't as grand and lavish as the theatres, or as mysterious and historical as the old palace of the Mule – of which, so far they had only glimpsed the lonely towers in their air flight across the planet – but, imagine, a real Lord. She was rapt in the glory of it.

And not only that. She was actually face to face with his Mistress. Arcadia capitalized the word in her mind, because she knew the role such women had played in history; knew their glamour and power. In fact, she had often thought of being an all-powerful and glittering creature, herself, but somehow mistresses weren't in fashion at the Foundation just then and besides, her father probably wouldn't let her, if it came to that.

Of course, the Lady Callia didn't come up to Arcadia's notion of the part. For one thing, she was rather plump, and didn't look at all wicked and dangerous. Just sort of faded and nearsighted. Her voice was high, too, instead of throaty, and—

Callia said, 'Would you like more tea, child?'

'I'll have another cup, thank you, your grace,' – or was it your highness?

Arcadia continued with a connoisseur's condescension, 'Those are lovely pearls you are wearing, my lady.' (On the whole, 'my lady' seemed best.)

'Oh? Do you think so?' Callia seemed vaguely pleased. She removed them and let them swing milkily to and fro. 'Would you like them? You can have them, if you like.'

'Oh, my— You really mean—' She found them in her hand, then, repelling them mournfully, she said, 'Father wouldn't like it.'

'He wouldn't like the pearls? But they're quite nice pearls.'

'He wouldn't like my taking them, I mean. You're not supposed to take expensive presents from other people, he says.'

'You aren't? But ... I mean, this was a present to me from Poo ... from the First Citizen. Was that wrong, do you suppose?'

Arcadia reddened. 'I didn't mean—'

But Callia had tired of the subject. She let the pearls slide to the ground and said, 'You were going to tell me about the Foundation. Please do so right now.'

And Arcadia was suddenly at a loss. What does one say about a world dull to tears. To her, the Foundation was a suburban town, a comfortable house, the annoying necessities of education, the uninteresting eternities of a quiet life. She said, uncertainly, 'It's just like you view in the book-films, I suppose.'

'Oh, do you view book-films? They give me such a headache when I try. But do you know I always love video stories about your Traders – such big, savage men. It's always so exciting. Is your friend, Mr Munn, one of them? He doesn't seem nearly savage enough. Most of the Traders had beards and big bass voices, and were so domineering with women – don't you think so?'

Arcadia smiled, glassily. 'That's just part of history, my lady. I mean, when the Foundation was young, the Traders were the pioneers pushing back the frontiers and bringing civilization to the rest of the Galaxy. We learned all about that in school. But that time has passed. We don't have Traders any more; just corporations and things.'

'Really? What a shame. Then what does Mr Munn do? I mean, if he's not a Trader.'

'Uncle Homir's a librarian.'

Callia put a hand to her lips and tittered. 'You mean he takes care of book-films. Oh, my! It seems like such a silly thing for a grown man to do.'

'He's a very good librarian, my lady. It is an occupation that is very highly regarded at the Foundation.' She put down the little, iridescent teacup upon the milky-metalled table surface.

Her hostess was all concern. 'But my dear child. I'm sure I didn't mean to offend you. He must be a very *intelligent* man. I could see it in his eyes as soon as I looked at him. They were so ... so *intelligent*. And he must be brave, too, to want to see the Mule's palace.'

'Brave?' Arcadia's internal awareness twitched. This was what she was waiting for. Intrigue! Intrigue! With great indifference, she asked, staring idly at her thumbtip: 'Why must one be brave to wish to see the Mule's palace?'

'Didn't you know?' Her eyes were round, and her voice sank. 'There's a curse on it. When he died, the Mule directed that no one ever enter it until the Empire of the Galaxy is established. Nobody on Kalgan would dare even to enter the grounds.'

Arcadia absorbed that. 'But that's superstition—'

'Don't say that,' Callia was distressed. 'Poochie always says that. He says it's useful to say it isn't though, in order to maintain his hold over the people. But I notice he's never gone in himself. And neither did Thallos, who was First Citizen before Poochie.' A thought struck her and she was all curiosity again: 'But why does Mr Munn want to see the Palace?'

And it was here that Arcadia's careful plan could be put into action. She knew well from the books she had read that a ruler's mistress was the real power behind the throne, that she was the very well-spring of influence. Therefore, if Uncle Homir failed with Lord Stettin – and she was sure he would – she must retrieve that failure with Lady Callia. To be sure, Lady Callia was something of a puzzle. She didn't seem at *all* bright. But, well, all history proved—

She said, 'There's a reason, my lady – but will you keep it in confidence?'

'Cross my heart,' said Callia, making the appropriate gesture on the soft, billowing whiteness of her breast.

Arcadia's thoughts kept a sentence ahead of her words. 'Uncle Homir is a great authority on the Mule, you know. He's written books and books about it, and he thinks that all of Galactic history has been changed since the Mule conquered the Foundation.'

'Oh, my.'

'He thinks the Seldon Plan—'

Callia clapped her hands. 'I know about the Seldon Plan. The videos about the Traders were always all about the Seldon Plan. It was supposed to arrange to have the Foundation win all the time. Science had something to do with it, though I could never quite see how. I always get so restless when I have to listen to explanations. But you go right ahead, my dear. It's different when you explain. You make everything seem so clear.'

Arcadia continued, 'Well, don't you see then that when the Foundation was defeated by the Mule, the Seldon Plan didn't work and it hasn't worked since. So who will form the Second Empire?'

'The Second Empire?'

'Yes, one must be formed some day, but how? That's the problem, you see. And there's the Second Foundation.'

'The *Second* Foundation?' She was quite completely lost.

'Yes, they're the planners of history that are following in the footsteps of Seldon. They stopped the Mule because he was premature, but now, they may be supporting Kalgan.'

'Why?'

'Because Kalgan may now offer the best chance of being the nucleus for a new Empire.'

Dimly, Lady Callia seemed to grasp that. 'You mean *Poochie* is going to make a new Empire.'

'We can't tell for sure. Uncle Homir thinks so, but he'll have to see the Mule's records to find out.'

'It's all very complicated,' said Lady Callia, doubtfully.

Arcadia gave up. She had done her best.

Lord Stettin was in a more-or-less savage humour. The session with the milksop from the Foundation had been quite unrewarding. It had been worse; it had been embarrassing. To be absolute ruler of twenty-seven worlds, master of the Galaxy's greatest military machine, owner of the universe's most vaulting ambition – and left to argue nonsense with an antiquarian.

Damnation!

He was to violate the customs of Kalgan, was he? To allow the Mule's palace to be ransacked so that a fool could write another book? The cause of science! The sacredness of knowledge! Great Galaxy! Were these catchwords to be thrown in his face in all seriousness? Besides – and his flesh pricked slightly – there was the matter of the curse. He didn't believe in it; no intelligent man could. But if he was going to defy it, it would have to be for a better reason than any the fool had advanced.

'What do *you* want?' he snapped, and Lady Callia cringed visibly in the doorway.

'Are you busy?'

'Yes. I am busy.'

'But there's nobody here, Poochie. Couldn't I even speak to you for a minute?'

'Oh, Galaxy! What do you want? Now hurry.'

Her words stumbled. 'The little girl told me they were going into the Mule's palace. I thought we could go with her. It must be gorgeous inside.'

'She told you that, did she? Well, she isn't and we aren't. Now go tend your own business. I've had about enough of you.'

'But, Poochie, why not? Aren't you going to let them? The little girl said that you were going to make an Empire!'

'I don't care what she said— What was that?' He strode to Callia and caught her firmly above the elbow, so that his fingers sank deeply into the soft flesh, 'What did she tell you?'

'You're hurting me. I can't remember what she said, if you're going to look at me like that.'

He released her, and she stood there for a moment, rubbing vainly at the red marks. She whimpered, 'The little girl made me promise not to tell.'

'That's too bad. Tell me! *Now!*'

'Well, she said the Seldon Plan was changed and that there was another Foundation somewheres that was arranging to have you make an Empire. That's all. She said Mr Munn was a very important scientist and that the Mule's palace would have proof of all that. That's every bit of what she said. Are you angry?'

But Stettin did not answer. He left the room, hurriedly, with Callia's cowlike eyes staring mournfully after him. Two orders were sent out over the official seal of the First Citizen before the hour was up. One had the effect of sending five hundred ships of the line into space on what were officially to be termed as 'war games.' The other had the effect of throwing a single man into confusion.

Homir Munn ceased his preparations to leave when that second order reached him. It was, of course, official permission to enter the palace of the Mule. He read and reread it, with anything but joy.

But Arcadia was delighted. She knew what had happened. Or, at any rate, she thought she did.

155

# 14

# ANXIETY

Poli placed the breakfast on the table, keeping one eye on the table news-recorder which quietly disgorged the bulletins of the day. It could be done easily enough without loss of efficiency, this one-eye-absent business. Since all items of food were sterilely packed in containers which served as discardable cooking units, her duties vis-à-vis breakfast consisted of nothing more than choosing the menu, placing the items on the table, and removing the residue thereafter.

She clacked her tongue at what she saw and moaned softly in restrospect.

'Oh, people are so wicked,' she said, and Darell merely hemmed in reply.

Her voice took on the high-pitched rasp which she automatically assumed when about to bewail the evil of the world. 'Now why do these terrible Kalganese' – she accented the second syllable and gave it a long 'a' – 'do like that? You'd think they'd give a body peace. But no, it's just trouble, trouble, all the time.

'Now look at that headline: "Mobs Riot Before Foundation Consulate." Oh, would I like to give them a piece of my mind, if I could. That's the trouble with people; they just don't remember. They just *don't* remember, Dr Darell – got no memory at all. Look at the last war after the Mule died – of course I was just a little girl then – and oh, the fuss and trouble. My own uncle was killed, him being just in his twenties and only two years married, with a baby girl. I remember him even yet – blond hair he had, and a dimple in his chin. I have a trimensional cube of him somewheres—

'And now his baby girl has a son of her own in the navy and most like if anything happens—

156

'And we had the bombardment patrols, and all the old men taking turns in the stratospheric defence – I could imagine what they would have been able to do if the Kalganese had come that far. My mother used to tell us children about the food rationing and the prices and taxes. A body could hardly make ends meet—

'You'd think if they had sense people would just never want to start it again; just have nothing to do with it. And I suppose it's not people that do it, either; I suppose even Kalganese would rather sit at home with their families and not go fooling around in ships and getting killed. It's that awful man, Stettin. It's a wonder people like that are let live. He kills the old man – what's his name – Thallos, and now he's just spoiling to be boss of everything.

'And why he wants to fight us, I don't know. He's bound to lose – like they always do. Maybe it's all in the Plan, but sometimes I'm sure it must be a wicked plan to have so much fighting and killing in it, though to be sure I haven't a word to say about Hari Seldon, who I'm sure knows much more about that than I do and perhaps I'm a fool to question him. And the *other* Foundation is as much to blame. *They* could stop Kalgan *now* and make everything fine. They'll do it anyway in the end, and you'd think they'd do it before there's any damage done.'

Dr Darell looked up. 'Did you say something, Poli?'

Poli's eyes opened wide, then narrowed angrily. 'Nothing, doctor, nothing at all. I haven't got a word to say. A body could as soon choke to death as say a word in this house. It's jump here, and jump there, but just try to say a word—' and she went off simmering.

Her leaving made as little impression on Darell as did her speaking.

Kalgan! Nonsense! A merely physical enemy! Those had always been beaten!

Yet he could not divorce himself from the current foolish crisis. Seven days earlier, the mayor had asked him to be

Administrator of Research and Development. He had promised an answer today.

Well—

He stirred uneasily. Why, himself! Yet could he refuse? It would seem strange, and he dared not seem strange. After all, what did he care about Kalgan. To him there was only one enemy. Always had been.

While his wife had lived, he was only too glad to shirk the task; to hide. Those long, quiet days on Trantor, with the ruins of the past about them! The silence of a wrecked world and the forgetfulness of it all!

But she had died. Less than five years, all told, it had been; and after that he knew that he could live only by fighting that vague and fearful enemy that deprived him of the dignity of manhood by controlling his destiny; that made life a miserable struggle against a foreordained end; that made all the universe a hateful and deadly chess game.

Call it sublimation; he, himself did call it that – but the fight gave meaning to his life.

First to the University of Santanni, where he had joined Dr Kleise. It had been five years well-spent.

And yet Kleise was merely a gatherer of data. He could not succeed in the real task – and when Darell had felt that as certainty, he knew it was time to leave.

Kleise may have worked in secret, yet he had to have men working for him and with him. He had subjects whose brains he probed. He had a University that backed him. All these were weaknesses.

Kleise may have worked in secret, yet he had to have men explain that. They parted enemies. It was well; they had to. He *had* to leave in surrender – in case someone watched.

Where Kleise worked with charts; Darell worked with mathematical concepts in the recesses of his mind. Kleise worked with many; Darell with none. Kleise in a University; Darell in the quiet of a suburban house.

And he was almost there.

A Second Foundationer is not human as far as his cerebrum is concerned. The cleverest physiologists, the most subtle neuro-chemist might detect nothing – yet the difference must be there. And since the difference was one of the mind, it was *there* that it must be detectable.

Given a man like the Mule – and there was no doubt that the Second Foundationers had the Mule's powers, whether inborn or acquired – with the power of detecting and controlling human emotions, deduce from that the electronic circuit required, and deduce from that the last details of the encephalograph on which it could not help but be betrayed.

And now Kleise had returned into his life, in the person of his ardent young pupil, Anthor.

Folly! Folly! With his graphs and charts of people who had been tampered with. He had learned to detect that years ago, but of what use was it. He wanted the arm; not the tool. Yet he had to agree to join Anthor, since it was the quieter course.

Just as now he would become Administrator of Research and Development. It was the quieter course! And so he remained a conspiracy within a conspiracy.

The thought of Arcadia teased him for a moment, and he shuddered away from it. Left to himself, it would never have happened. Left to himself, no one would ever have been endangered but himself. Left to himself—

He felt the anger rising – against the dead Kleise, the living Anthor, all the well-meaning fools—

Well, she could take care of herself. She was a very mature little girl.

She could take care of herself!

It was a whisper in his mind—

Yet could she?

At the moment, that Dr Darell told himself mournfully that she could, she was sitting in the coldly austere anteroom of the Executive Offices of the First Citizen of the Galaxy. For half an hour she had been sitting there, her eyes sliding slowly about

159

the walls. There had been two armed guards at the door when she had entered with Homir Munn. They hadn't been there the other times.

She was alone, now, yet she sensed the unfriendliness of the very furnishings of the room. And for the first time.

Now, why should that be?

Homir was with Lord Stettin. Well, was that wrong?

It made her furious. In similar situations in the book-films and the videos, the hero foresaw the conclusion, was prepared for it when it came, and she – she just sat there. *Anything* could happen. *Anything!* And she just sat there.

Well, back again. Think it back. Maybe something would come.

For two weeks, Homir had nearly lived inside the Mule's palace. He had taken her once, with Stettin's permission. It was large and gloomily massive, shrinking from the touch of life to lie sleeping within its ringing memories, answering the footsteps with a hollow boom or a savage clatter. She hadn't liked it.

Better the great, gay highways of the capital city; the theatres and spectacles of a world essentially poorer than the Foundation, yet spending more of its wealth on display.

Homir would return in the evening, awed?

'It's a dream-world for me,' he would whisper. 'If I could only chip the palace down stone by stone, layer by layer of the aluminium sponge. If I could carry it back to Terminus— What a museum it would make.'

He seemed to have lost that early reluctance. He was eager, instead; glowing. Arcadia knew that by the one sure sign; he practically never stuttered throughout that period.

One time, he said, 'There are abstracts of the records of General Pritcher—'

'I know him. He was the Foundation renegade who combed the Galaxy for the Second Foundation, wasn't he?'

'Not exactly a renegade, Arkady. The Mule had Converted him.'

'Oh, it's the same thing.'

'Galaxy, that combing you speak of was a hopeless task. The original records of the Seldon Convention that established both Foundations five hundred years ago, make only one reference to the Second Foundation. They say it's located "at the other end of the Galaxy at Star's End." That's all the Mule and Pritcher had to go on. They had no method of recognizing the Second Foundation even if they found it. What madness!

'They have records' – he was speaking to himself, but Arcadia listened eagerly – 'which must cover nearly a thousand worlds, yet the number of worlds available for study must have been closer to a million. And we are no better off—'

Arcadia broke in anxiously, '*Shhh-h*' in a tight hiss.

Homir froze, and slowly recovered. 'Let's not talk,' he mumbled.

And now Homir was with Lord Stettin and Arcadia waited outside alone and felt the blood squeezing out of her heart for no reason at all. That was more frightening than anything else. That there seemed no reason.

On the other side of the door, Homir, too, was living in a sea of gelatin. He was fighting, with furious intensity, to keep from stuttering and, of course, could scarcely speak two consecutive words clearly as a result.

Lord Stettin was in full uniform, six-feet-six, large-jawed, and hard-mouthed. His balled, arrogant fists kept a powerful time to his sentences.

'Well, you have had two weeks, and you come to me with tales of nothing. Come, sir, tell me the worst. Is my Navy to be cut to ribbons? Am I to fight the ghosts of the Second Foundation as well as the men of the First?'

'I ... I repeat, my lord, I am no p ... pre ... predictor. I ... I am at a complete ... loss.'

'Or do you wish to go back to warn your countrymen? To deep Space with your play-acting. I want the truth or I'll have it out of you along with half your guts.'

'I'm t ... telling only the truth, and I'll have you re ... remember, my l ... lord, that I am a citizen of the Foundation.

Y . . . you cannot touch me without harvesting m . . . m . . . more than you count on.'

The Lord of Kalgan laughed uproariously. 'A threat to frighten children. A horror with which to beat back an idiot. Come, Mr Munn, I have been patient with you. I have listened to you for twenty minutes while you detailed wearisome nonsense to me which must have cost you sleepless nights to compose. It was wasted effort. I know you are here not merely to rake through the Mule's dead ashes and to warm over the cinders you find – you come here for more than you have admitted. Is that not true?'

Homir Munn could no more have quenched the burning horror that grew in his eyes than, at that moment, he could have breathed. Lord Stettin saw that, and clapped the Foundation man upon his shoulder so that he and the chair he sat on reeled under the impact.

'Good. Now let us be frank. You are investigating the Seldon Plan. You know that it no longer holds. You know, perhaps, that *I* am the inevitable winner now; I and my heirs. Well, man, what matters it who established the Second Empire, so long as it is established. History plays no favourites, eh? Are you afraid to tell me? You see that I know your mission.'

Munn said thickly, 'What is it y . . . you w . . . want?'

'Your presence. I would not wish the Plan spoiled through overconfidence. You understand more of these things than I do; you can detect small flaws that I might miss. Come, you will be rewarded in the end; you will have your fair glut of the loot. What can you expect at the Foundation? To turn the tide of a perhaps inevitable defeat? To lengthen the war? Or is it merely a patriotic desire to die for your country?'

'I . . . I—' He finally spluttered into silence. Not a word would come.

'You will stay,' said the Lord of Kalgan, confidently. 'You have no choice. Wait' – an almost forgotten afterthought – 'I have information to the effect that your niece is of the family of Bayta Darell.'

Homir uttered a startled: 'Yes.' He could not trust himself at this point to be capable of weaving anything but cold truth.

'It is a family of note on the Foundation?'

Homir nodded, 'To whom they would certainly b ... brook no harm.'

'Harm! Don't be a fool, man; I am meditating the reverse. How old is she?'

'Fourteen.'

'So! Well, not even the Second Foundation, or Hari Seldon, himself, could stop time from passing or girls from becoming women.'

With that, he turned on his heel and strode to a draped door which he threw open violently.

He thundered, 'What in Space have you dragged your shivering carcass here for?'

The Lady Callia blinked at him, and said in a small voice, 'I didn't know anyone was with you.'

'Well, there is. I'll speak to you later of this, but now I want to see your back, and quickly.'

Her footsteps were a fading scurry in the corridor.

Stettin returned, 'She is a remnant of an interlude that has lasted too long. It will end soon. Fourteen, you say?'

Homir stared at him with a brand-new horror!

Arcadia started at the noiseless opening of a door – jumping at the jangling sliver of movement it made in the corner of her eye. The finger that crooked frantically at her met no response for long moments, and then, as if in response to the cautions enforced by the very sight of that white, trembling figure, she tiptoed her way across the floor.

Their footsteps were a taut whisper in the corridor. It was the Lady Callia, of course, who held her hand so tightly that it hurt, and for some reason, she did not mind following her. Of the Lady Callia, at least, she was not afraid.

Now, why was that?

They were in a boudoir now, all pink fluff and spun sugar. Lady Callia stood with her back against the door.

She said, 'This was our private way to me ... to my room, you

163

know, from his office. His, you know.' And she pointed with a thumb, as though even the thought of him were grinding her soul to death with fear.

'It's so lucky... it's so lucky—' Her pupils had blackened out the blue with their size.

'Can you tell me—' began Arcadia timidly.

And Callia was in frantic motion. 'No, child, no. There is no time. Take off your clothes. Please. Please. I'll get you more, and they won't recognize you.'

She was in the closet, throwing useless bits of flummery in reckless heaps upon the ground, looking madly for something a girl could wear without becoming a living invitation to dalliance.

'Here, this will do. It will have to. Do you have money? Here, take it all – and this.' She was stripping her ears and fingers. 'Just go home – go home to your Foundation.'

'But Homir – my uncle.' She protested vainly through the muffling folds of the sweet-smelling and luxurious spun-metal being forced over head.

'He won't leave. Poochie will hold him forever, but *you* mustn't stay. Oh, dear, don't you understand?'

'No.' Arcadia forced a standstill, 'I *don't* understand.'

Lady Callia squeezed her hands tightly together. 'You must go back to warn your people there will be war. Isn't that clear?' Absolute terror seemed paradoxically to have lent a lucidity to her thoughts and words that was entirely out of character. 'Now come!'

Out another way! Past officials who stared after them, but saw no reason to stop one whom only the Lord of Kalgan could stop with impunity. Guards clicked heels and presented arms when they went through doors.

Arcadia breathed only on occasion through the years the trip seemed to take – yet from the first crooking of the white finger to the time she stood at the outer gate, with people and noise and traffic in the distance was only twenty-five minutes.

She looked back, with a sudden frightened pity. 'I... I...don't know why you're doing this, my lady, but

164

thanks – What's going to happen to Uncle Homir?'

'I don't know,' wailed the other. 'Can't you leave? Go straight to the spaceport. Don't wait. He may be looking for you this very minute.'

And still Arcadia lingered. She would be leaving Homir; and belatedly, now that she felt the free air about her, she was suspicious. 'But what do you care if he does?'

Lady Callia bit her lower lip and muttered, 'I can't explain to a little girl like you. It would be improper. Well, you'll be growing up and I ... I met Poochie when I was sixteen. I can't have you about, you know.' There was a half-ashamed hostility in her eyes.

The implications froze Arcadia. She whispered: 'What will he do to you when he finds out?'

And she whimpered back: 'I don't know,' and threw her arm to her head as she left at a half-run, back along the wide way to the mansion of the Lord of Kalgan.

But for one eternal second, Arcadia *still* did not move, for in that last moment before Lady Callia left, Arcadia had seen something. Those frightened, frantic eyes had momentarily – flashingly – lit up with a cold amusement.

A vast, inhuman amusement.

It was much to see in such a quick flicker of a pair of eyes, but Arcadia had no doubt of what she saw.

She was running now – running wildly – searching madly for an unoccupied public booth at which one could press a button for public conveyance.

She was not running from Lord Stettin; not from him or from all the human hounds he could place at her heels – not from all his twenty-seven worlds rolled into a single gigantic phenomenon, hallooing at her shadow.

She was running from a single, frail woman who had helped her escape. From a creature who had loaded her with money and jewels; who had risked her own life to save her. From an entity she knew, certainly and finally, to be a woman of the Second Foundation.

\*     \*     \*

An air-taxi came to a soft clicking halt in the cradle. The wind of its coming brushed against Arcadia's face and stirred at the hair beneath the softly-furred hood Callia had given her.

'Where'll it be, lady?'

She fought desperately to low-pitch her voice to make it not that of a child. 'How many spaceports in the city?'

'Two. Which one ya want?'

'Which is closer?'

He stared at her: 'Kalgan Central, lady.'

'The other one, please. I've got the money.' She had a twenty-Kalganid note in her hand. The denomination of the note made little difference to her, but the taxi-man grinned appreciatively.

'Anything ya say, lady. Sky-line cabs take ya anywhere.'

She cooled her cheek against the slightly musty upholstery. The lights of the city moved leisurely below her.

What should she do? *What should she do?*

It was in that moment that she knew she was a stupid, *stupid* little girl, away from her father, and frightened. Her eyes were full of tears, and deep down in her throat, there was a small, soundless cry that hurt her insides.

She wasn't afraid that Lord Stettin would catch her. Lady Callia would see to that. Lady Callia! Old, fat, stupid, but she held on to her lord, somehow. Oh, it was clear enough, now. *Everything* was clear.

That tea with Callia at which she had been so smart. Clever little Arcadia! Something inside Arcadia choked and hated itself. That tea had been manoeuvred, and then Stettin had probably been manoeuvred so that Homir was allowed to inspect the Palace after all. *She*, the foolish Callia, has wanted it so, and arranged to have smart little Arcadia supply a foolproof excuse, one which would arouse no suspicions in the minds of the victims, and yet involve a minimum of interference on her part.

Then why was she free? Homir was a prisoner, of course—Unless—

Unless she went back to the Foundation as a decoy – a decoy to lead others into the hands of ... of them.

So she couldn't return to the Foundation—

'Spaceport, lady.' The air-taxi had come to a halt. Strange! She hadn't even noticed.

What a dream-world it was.

'Thanks,' she pushed the bill at him without seeing anything and was stumbling out the door, then running across the springy pavement.

Lights. Unconcerned men and women. Large gleaming bulletin boards, with the moving figures that followed every single spaceship that arrived and departed.

Where was she going? She didn't care. She only knew that she wasn't going to the Foundation! Anywhere else at all would suit.

Oh, thank Seldon, for that forgetful moment that last split-second when Callia wearied of her act because she had to do only with a child and had let her amusement spring through.

And then something else occurred to Arcadia, something that had been stirring and moving at the base of her brain ever since the flight began – something that forever killed the fourteen in her.

And she knew that she *must* escape.

That above all. Though they located every conspirator on the Foundation; though they caught her own father; she could not, dared not, risk a warning. She could not risk her own life – not in the slightest – for the entire realm of Terminus. She was the most important person in the Galaxy.

She knew that even as she stood before the ticket-machine and wondered where to go.

Because in all the Galaxy, she and she alone, except for *they*, themselves, knew the location of the Second Foundation.

# 15

# THROUGH THE GRID

TRANTOR *By the middle of the Interregnum, Trantor was a shadow. In the midst of the colossal ruins, there lived a small community of farmers ...*

ENCYCLOPEDIA GALACTICA

There is nothing, never has been anything, quite like a busy spaceport on the outskirts of a capital city of a populous planet. There are the huge machines resting mightily in their cradles. If you choose your time properly, there is the impressive sight of the sinking giant dropping to rest or, more hair-raising still, the swiftening departure of a bubble of steel. All processes involved are nearly noiseless. The motive power is the silent surge of nucleons shifting into more compact arrangements—

In terms of area, ninety-five percent of the port has just been referred to. Square miles are reserved for the machines, and for the men who serve them and for the calculators that serve both.

Only five percent of the port is given over to the floods of humanity to whom it is the way station to all the stars of the Galaxy. It is certain that very few of the anonymous many-headed stop to consider the technological mesh that knits the spaceways. Perhaps some of them might itch occasionally at the thought of the thousands of tons represented by the sinking steel that looks so small off in the distance. One of those cyclopean cylinders could, conceivably, miss the guiding beam and crash half a mile from its expected landing point – through the glassite roof of the immense waiting room perhaps – so that only a thin organic vapour and some powdered phosphates would be left behind to mark the passing of a thousand men.

It could never happen, however, with the safety devices in use; and only the badly neurotic would consider the possibility for more than a moment.

Then what *do* they think about? It is not just a crowd, you see. It is a crowd with a purpose. That purpose hovers over the field and thickens the atmosphere. Lines queue up; parents herd their children; baggage is manoeuvred in precise masses – people are *going* somewheres.

Consider then the complete psychic isolation of a single unit of this terribly intent mob that does not know where to go; yet at the same time feels more intensely than any of the others possibly can, the necessity of going somewheres; anywhere! Or almost anywhere!

Even lacking telepathy or any of the crudely definite methods of mind touching mind, there is a sufficient clash of atmosphere, in intangible mood, to suffice for despair.

To suffice? To overflow, and drench, and drown.

Arcadia Darell, dressed in borrowed clothes, standing on a borrowed planet in a borrowed situation of what seemed even to be a borrowed life, wanted earnestly the safety of the womb. She didn't know that was what she wanted. She only knew that the very openness of the open world was a great danger. She wanted a closed spot somewhere – somewhere far – somewhere in an unexplored nook of the universe – where no one would ever look.

And there she was, age fourteen plus, weary enough for eighty plus, frightened enough for five minus.

What stranger of the hundreds that brushed past her – actually brushed past her, so that she could feel their touch – was a Second Foundationer? What stranger could not help but instantly destroy her for her guilty knowledge – her unique knowledge – of knowing where the Second Foundation was?

And the voice that cut in on her was a thunderclap that iced the scream in her throat into a voiceless slash.

'Look, miss,' it said, irritably, 'are you using the ticket machine or are you just standing there?'

It was the first time she realized that she was standing in front of a ticket machine. You put a high denomination bill into the clipper which sank out of sight. You pressed the button below your destination and a ticket came out together with the correct change as determined by an electronic scanning device that never made a mistake. It was a very ordinary thing and there is no cause for anyone to stand before it for five minutes.

Arcadia plunged a two-hundred credit into the clipper, and was suddenly aware of the button labelled 'Trantor.' Trantor, dead capital of the dead Empire – the planet on which she was born. She pressed it in a dream. Nothing happened, except that the red letters flicked on and off, reading 172.18 – 172.18 – 172.18—

It was the amount she was short. Another two-hundred credit. The ticket was spit out towards her. It came loose when she touched it, and the change tumbled out afterward.

She seized it and ran. She felt the man behind her pressing close, anxious for his own chance at the machine, but she twisted out from before him and did not look behind.

Yet there was nowhere to run. They were all her enemies.

Without quite realizing it, she was watching the gigantic, glowing signs that puffed into the air: *Steffani, Anacreon, Fermus*— There was even one that ballooned, *Terminus*, and she longed for it, but did not dare—

For a trifling sum, she could have hired a notifier which could have been set for any destination she cared and which would, when placed in her purse, make itself heard only to her, fifteen minutes before take-off time. But such devices are for people who are reasonably secure, however; who can pause to think of them.

And then, attempting to look both ways simultaneously, she ran head-on into a soft abdomen. She felt the startled outbreath and grunt, and a hand come down on her arm. She writhed desperately but lacked breath to do no more than mew a bit in the back of her throat.

Her captor held her firmly and waited. Slowly, he came into focus for her and she managed to look at him. He was rather plump and rather short. His hair was white and copious, being brushed back to give a pompadour effect that looked strangely incongruous above a round and ruddy face that shrieked its peasant origin.

'What's the matter?' he said finally, with a frank and twinkling curiosity. 'You looked scared.'

'Sorry,' muttered Arcadia in a frenzy. 'I've got to go. Pardon me.'

But he disregarded that entirely, and said, 'Watch out, little girl. You'll drop your ticket.' And he lifted it from her resistless white fingers and looked at it with every evidence of satisfaction.

'I thought so,' he said, and then bawled in bull-like tones, '*Mommuh!*'

A woman was instantly at his side, somewhat more short, somewhat more round, somewhat more ruddy. She wound a finger about a stray grey lock to shove it beneath a well-outmoded hat.

'Pappa,' she said, reprovingly, 'why do you shout in a crowd like that? People look at you like you were crazy. Do you think you are on the farm?'

And she smiled sunnily at the unresponsive Arcadia, and added, 'He has manners like a bear.' Then, sharply, 'Pappa, let go the little girl. What are you doing?'

But Pappa simply waved the ticket at her. 'Look,' he said, 'she's going to Trantor.'

Mamma's face was a sudden beam, 'You're from Trantor? Let go her arm, I say, Pappa.' She turned the overstuffed valise she was carrying onto its side and forced Arcadia to sit down with a gentle but unrelenting pressure. 'Sit down,' she said, 'and rest your little feet. It will be no ship yet for an hour and the benches are crowded with sleeping loafers. You are from Trantor?'

Arcadia drew a deep breath and gave in. Huskily, she said, 'I was born there.'

And Mamma clapped her hands gleefully, 'One month we've been here and till now we met nobody from home. This is very nice. Your parents—' she looked about vaguely.

171

'I'm not with my parents,' Arcadia said, carefully.

'All alone? A little girl like you?' Mamma was at once a blend of indignation and sympathy, 'How does that come to be?'

'Mamma,' Pappa plucked at her sleeve, 'let me tell you. There's something wrong. I think she's frightened.' His voice, though obviously intended for a whisper was quite plainly audible to Arcadia. 'She was running – I was watching her – and not looking where she was going. Before I could step out of the way, she bumped into me. And you know what? I think she's in trouble.'

'So shut your mouth, Pappa. Into you, anybody could bump.' But she joined Arcadia on the valise, which creaked wearily under the added weight and put an arm about the girl's trembling shoulder. 'You're running away from somebody, sweetheart? Don't be afraid to tell me. I'll help you.'

Arcadia looked across at the kind grey eyes of the woman and felt her lips quivering. One part of her brain was telling her that here were people from Trantor, with whom she could go, who could help her remain on that planet until she could decide what next to do, where next to go. And another part of her brain, much the louder, was telling her in jumbled incoherence that she did not remember her mother, that she was weary to death of fighting the universe, that she wanted only to curl into a little ball with strong, gentle arms about her, that if her mother had lived, she might ... she might—

And for the first time that night, she was crying; crying like a little baby, and glad of it; clutching tightly at the old-fashioned dress and dampening a corner of it thoroughly, while soft arms held her closely and a gentle hand stroked her curls.

Pappa stood helplessly looking at the pair, fumbling futilely for a handkerchief which, when produced, was snatched from his hand. Mamma glared an admonition of quietness at him. The crowds surged about the little group with the true indifference of disconnected crowds everywhere. They were effectively alone.

Finally, the weeping trickled to a halt, and Arcadia smiled

172

weakly as she dabbed at red eyes with the borrowed handkerchief. 'Golly,' she whispered, 'I—'

'Shh. Shh. Don't talk,' said Mamma, fussily, 'just sit and rest for a while. Catch your breath. Then tell us what's wrong, and you'll see, we'll fix it up, and everything will be all right.'

Arcadia scrabbled what remained of her wits together. She could not tell them the truth. She could tell nobody the truth— And yet she was too worn to invent a useful lie.

She said, whisperingly, 'I'm better, now.'

'Good,' said Mamma. 'Now tell me why you're in trouble. You did nothing wrong? Of course, whatever you did, we'll help you; but tell us the truth.'

'For a friend from Trantor, anything,' added Pappa, expansively, 'eh, Mamma?'

'Shut your mouth, Pappa,' was the response, without rancour.

Arcadia was groping in her purse. That, at least, was still hers, despite the rapid clothes-changing forced upon her in Lady Callia's apartments. She found what she was looking for and handed it to Mamma.

'These are my papers,' she said, diffidently. It was shiny, synthetic parchment which had been issued her by the Foundation's ambassador on the day of her arrival and which had been countersigned by the appropriate Kalganian official. It was large, florid, and impressive. Mama looked at it helplessly, and passed it to Pappa who absorbed its contents with an impressive pursing of the lips.

He said, 'You're from the Foundation?'

'Yes. But I was born in Trantor. See it says that—'

'Ah-hah. It looks all right to me. You're named Arcadia, eh? That's a good Trantorian name. But where's your uncle? It says here you came in the company of Homir Munn, uncle.'

'He's been arrested,' said Arcadia, drearily.

'Arrested!' – from the two of them at once. 'What for?' asked Mamma. 'He did something?'

173

She shook her head. 'I don't know. We were just on a visit. Uncle Homir had business with Lord Stettin but—' She needed no effort to act a shudder. It was there.

Pappa was impressed. 'With Lord Stettin. Mm-m-m, your uncle must be a big man.'

'I don't know what it was all about, but Lord Stettin wanted *me* to stay—' She was recalling the last words of Lady Callia, which had been acted out for her benefit. Since Callia, as she now knew, was an expert, the story could do for a second time.

She paused, and Mamma said interestedly, 'And why you?'

'I'm not sure. He ... he wanted to have dinner with me all alone, but I said no, because I wanted Uncle Homir along. He looked at me funny and kept holding my shoulder.'

Pappa's mouth was a little open, but Mamma was suddenly red and angry. 'How old are you, Arcadia?'

'Fourteen and a half, almost.'

Mamma drew a sharp breath and said, 'That such people should be let live. The dogs in the streets are better. You're running from him, dear, is not?'

Arcadia nodded.

Mamma said, 'Pappa, go right to Information and find out exactly when the ship to Trantor comes to berth. Hurry!'

But Pappa took one step and stopped. Loud metallic words were booming overhead, and five thousand pairs of eyes looked startledly upwards.

'Men and women,' it said, with sharp force. 'The airport is being searched for a dangerous fugitive, and it is now surrounded. No one can enter and no one can leave. The search will, however, be conducted with great speed and no ships will reach or leave berth during the interval, so you will not miss your ship. I repeat, no one will miss his ship. The grid will descend. None of you will move outside your square until the grid is removed, as otherwise we will be forced to use our neuronic whips.'

During the minute or less in which the voice dominated the vast dome of the spaceport's waiting room, Arcadia could not

174

have moved if all the evil in the Galaxy had concentrated itself into a ball and hurled itself at her.

They could mean only her. It was not even necessary to formulate that idea as a specific thought. But why—

Callia had engineered her escape. And Callia was of the Second Foundation. Why, then, the search now? Had Callia failed? *Could* Callia fail? Or was this part of the plan, the intricacies of which escaped her?

For a vertiginous moment, she wanted to jump up and shout that she gave up, that she would go with them, that ... that—

But Mamma's hand was on her wrist. 'Quick! Quick! We'll go to the lady's room before they start.'

Arcadia did not understand. She merely followed blindly. They oozed through the crowd, frozen as it was into clumps, with the voice still booming through its last words.

The grid was descending now, and Pappa, openmouthed, watched it come down. He had heard of it and read of it, but had never actually been the object of it. It glimmered in the air, simply a series of cross-hatched and tight radiation beams that set the air aglow in a harmless network of flashing light.

It always was so arranged as to descend slowly from above in order that it might represent a falling net with all the terrific psychological implications of entrapment.

It was at waist level now, ten feet between glowing lines in each direction. In his own hundred square feet, Pappa found himself alone, yet the adjoining squares were crowded. He felt himself conspicuously isolated but knew that to move into the greater anonymity of a group would have meant crossing one of those glowing lines, stirring an alarm, and bringing down the neuronic whip.

He waited.

He could make out over the heads of the eerily quiet and waiting mob, the far-off stir that was the line of policemen covering the vast floor area, lighted square by lighted square. It was a long time before a uniform stepped into his square and carefully noted its co-ordinates into an official notebook.

'Papers!'

Pappa handed them over, and they were flipped through in expert fashion.

'You're Preem Palver, native of Trantor, on Kalgan for a month, returning to Trantor. Answer, yes or no.'

'Yes, yes.'

'What's your business on Kalgan?'

'I'm trading representative of our farm co-operative. I've been negotiating terms with the Department of Agriculture on Kalgan.'

'Um-m-m. Your wife is with you? Where is she? She is mentioned in your papers.'

'Please. My wife is in the—' He pointed.

'Hanto,' roared the policeman. Another uniform joined him.

The first one said, dryly, 'Another dame in the can, by the Galaxy. The place must be busting with them. Write down her name.' He indicated the entry in the papers which gave it.

'Anyone else with you?'

'My niece.'

'She's not mentioned in the papers.'

'She came separately.'

'Where is she? Never mind, I know. Write down the niece's name, too, Hanto. What's her name? Write down Arcadia Palver. You stay right here, Palver. We'll take care of the women before we leave.'

Pappa waited interminably. And then, long, long after, Mamma was marching toward him, Arcadia's hand firmly in hers, the two policemen trailing behind her.

They entered Pappa's square, and said, 'Is this noisy old woman your wife?'

'Yes, sir,' said Pappa, placatingly.

'Then you'd better tell her she's liable to get into trouble if she talks the way she does to the First Citizen's police.' He straightened his shoulders angrily. 'Is this your niece?'

'Yes, sir.'

'I want her papers.'

Looking straight at her husband, Mamma slightly, but no less firmly, shook her head.

A short pause, and Pappa said with a weak smile, 'I don't think I can do that.'

'What do you mean you can't do that?' The policeman thrust out a hard palm. 'Hand it over.'

'Diplomatic immunity,' said Pappa, softly.

'What do you mean?'

'I said I was trading representative of my farm co-operative. I'm accredited to the Kalganian government as an official foreign representative and my papers prove it. I showed them to you and now I don't want to be bothered any more.'

For a moment, the policeman was taken aback. 'I've got to see your papers. It's orders.'

'You go away,' broke in Mamma, suddenly. 'When we want you, we'll send for you, you ... you *bum*.'

The policeman's lips tightened. 'Keep your eye on them, Hanto. I'll get the lieutenant.'

'Break a leg!' called Mamma after him. Someone laughed, and then choked it off suddenly.

The search was approaching its end. The crowd was growing dangerously restless. Forty-five minutes had elapsed since the grid had started falling and that is too long for best effects. Lieutenant Dirige threaded his way hastily, therefore, toward the dense centre of the mob.

'Is this the girl?' he asked wearily. He looked at her and she obviously fitted the description. All this for a child.

He said, 'Her papers, if you please?'

Pappa began, 'I have already explained—'

'I know what you have explained, and I'm sorry,' said the lieutenant, 'but I have my orders, and I can't help them. If you care to make a protest later, you may. Meanwhile, if necessary, I must use force.'

There was a pause, and the lieutenant waited patiently.

Then Pappa said, huskily, 'Give me your papers, Arcadia.'

177

Arcadia shook her head in panic, but Pappa nodded his head. 'Don't be afraid. Give them to me.'

Helplessly, she reached out and let the documents change hands. Pappa fumbled them open and looked carefully through them, then handed them over. The lieutenant in his turn looked through them carefully. For a long moment, he raised his eyes to rest them on Arcadia, and then he closed the booklet with a sharp snap.

'All in order,' he said. 'All right, men.'

He left, and in two minutes, scarcely more, the grid was gone, and the voice above signified a back-to-normal. The noise of the crowd, suddenly released, rose high.

Arcadia said: 'How ... how—'

Pappa said, '*Sh-h*. Don't say a word. Let's better go to the ship. It should be in the berth soon.'

They were on the ship. They had a private stateroom and a table to themselves in the dining room. Two-light years already separated them from Kalgan, and Arcadia finally dared to broach the subject again.

She said, 'But they *were* after me, Mr Palver, and they must have had my description and all the details. Why did he let me go?'

And Pappa smiled broadly over his roast beef. 'Well, Arcadia, child, it was easy. When you've been dealing with agents and buyers and competing co-operatives, you learn some of the tricks. I've had twenty years or more to learn them in. You see, child, when the lieutenant opened your papers, he found a five hundred credit bill inside, folded up small. Simple, no?'

'I'll pay you back— Honest, I've got lots of money.'

'Well,' Pappa's broad face broke into an embarrassed smile, as he waved it away. 'For a country-woman—'

Arcadia desisted. 'But what if he'd taken the money and turned me in anyway. And accused me of bribery.'

'And give up five hundred credits? I know these people better than you do, girl.'

But Arcadia knew that he did *not* know people better. Not *these* people. In her bed that night, she considered carefully, and *knew* that no bribe would have stopped a police lieutenant in the matter of catching her unless that had been planned. They *didn't* want to catch her, yet had made every motion of doing so, nevertheless.

Why? To make sure she left? And for Trantor? Were the obtuse and soft-hearted couple she was with now only a pair of tools in the hands of the Second Foundation, as helpless as she herself?

They must be!

Or were they?

It was all so useless. How could she fight them. Whatever she did, it might only be what those terrible omnipotents wanted her to do.

Yet she had to outwit them. *Had* to! *Had* to! *Had* to!!

# 16

# BEGINNING OF WAR

For reason or reasons unknown to members of the Galaxy at the time of the era under discussion, Intergalactic Standard Time defines its fundamental unit, the second, as the time in which light travels 299,776 kilometres. 86,400 seconds are arbitrarily set equal to one Intergalactic Standard Day; and 365 of these days to one Intergalactic Standard Year.

Why 299, 776?— Or 86,400?— Or 365?

Tradition, says the historian, begging the question. Because of certain and various mysterious numerical relationships, say the mystics, cultists, numerologists, metaphysicists. Because the original home-planet of humanity had certain natural periods of rotation and revolution from which those relationships could be derived, say a very few.

No one really knew.

Nevertheless, the date on which the Foundation cruiser, the *Hober Mallow*, met the Kalganian squadron, headed by the *Fearless*, and, upon refusing to allow a search party to board, was blasted into smouldering wreckage was 185; 11692 G. E. That is, it was the 185th day of the 11,692nd year of the Galactic Era which dated from the accession of the first Emperor of the traditional Kamble dynasty. It was also 185; 419 A.S. – dating from the birth of Seldon – or 185; 348 Y.F. – dating from the establishment of the Foundation. On Kalgan it was 185; 56 F.C. – dating from the establishment of the First Citizenship by the Mule. In each case, of course, for convenience, the year was so arranged as to yield the same day number regardless of the actual day upon which the era begun.

And, in addition, to all the millions of worlds of the Galaxy, there were millions of local times, based on the motions of their own particularly heavenly neighbours.

But whichever you choose: 185; 11692–419–348–56 – or anything – it was this day which historians later pointed to when they spoke of the start of the Stettinian war.

Yet to Dr Darell, it was none of these at all. It was simply and quite precisely the thirty-second day since Arcadia had left Terminus.

What it cost Darell to maintain stolidity through these days was not obvious to everyone.

But Elvitt Semic thought he could guess. He was an old man and fond of saying that his neuronic sheaths had calcified to the point where his thinking processes were stiff and unwieldy. He invited and almost welcomed the universal underestimation of his decaying powers by being the first to laugh at them. But his eyes were none the less seeing for being faded; his mind none the less experienced and wise, for being no longer agile.

He merely twisted his pinched lips and said, 'Why don't you do something about it?'

The sound was a physical jar to Darell, under which he winced. He said, gruffly, 'Where were we?'

Semic regarded him with grave eyes. 'You'd better do something about the girl.' His sparse, yellow teeth showed in a mouth that was open in inquiry.

But Darell replied coldly, 'The question is: Can you get a Symes-Molff Resonator in the range required?'

'Well, I said I could and you weren't listening—'

'I'm sorry, Elvett. It's like this. What we're doing now can be more important to everyone in the Galaxy than the question of whether Arcadia is safe. At least, to everyone but Arcadia and myself, and I'm willing to go along with the majority. How big would the Resonator be?'

Semic looked doubtful, 'I don't know. You can find it somewheres in the catalogues.'

'About how big. A ton? A pound? A block long?'

'Oh, I thought you meant exactly. It's a little jigger.' He indicated the first joint of his thumb. 'About that.'

'All right, can you do something like this?' He sketched rapidly on the pad he held in his lap, then passed it over to the old physicist, who peered at it doubtfully, then chuckled.

'Y'know, the brain gets calcified when you get as old as I am. What are you trying to do?'

Darell hesitated. He longed desperately, at the moment, for the physical knowledge locked in the other's brain, so that he need not put his thoughts into words. But the longing was useless, and he explained.

Semic was shaking his head. 'You'd need hyper-relays. The only things that would work fast enough. A thundering lot of them.'

'But it can be built?'

'Well, sure.'

'Can you get all the parts? I mean, without causing comment? In line with your general work.'

Semic lifted his upper lip. 'Can't get fifty hyper-relays? I wouldn't use that many in my whole life.'

'We're on a defence project, now. Can't you think of something harmless that would use them? We've got the money.'

'Hm-m-m. Maybe I can think of something.'

'How small can you make the whole gadget?'

'Hyper-relays can be had micro-size ... wiring ... tubes— Space, you've got a few hundred circuits there.'

'I know. How big?'

Semic indicated with his hands.

'Too big,' said Darell. 'I've got to swing it from my belt.'

Slowly, he was crumpling his sketch into a tight ball. When it was a hard, yellow grape, he dropped it into the ash tray and it was gone with the tiny white flare of molecular decomposition.

He said, 'Who's at your door?'

Semic leaned over his desk to the little milky screen above the door signal. He said, 'The young fellow, Anthor. Someone with him, too.'

Darell scraped his chair back. 'Nothing about this, Semic, to the others yet. It's deadly knowledge, if *they* find out, and two lives are enough to risk.'

Pelleas Anthor was a pulsing vortex of activity in Semic's office, which, somehow, managed to partake of the age of its occupant. In the slow turgor of the quiet room, the loose, summery sleeves of Anthor's tunic seemed still a-quiver with the outer breezes.

He said, 'Dr Darell, Dr Semic – Orum Dirige.'

The other man was tall. A long straight nose that lent his thin face a saturnine appearance. Dr Darell held out a hand.

Anthor smiled slightly. 'Police Lieutenant Dirige,' he amplified. Then, significantly, 'Of Kalgan.'

And Darell turned to stare with force at the young man. 'Police Lieutenant Dirige of Kalgan,' he repeated, distinctly. 'And you bring him here. Why?'

'Because he was the last man on Kalgan to see your daughter. Hold, man.'

Anthor's look of triumph was suddenly one of concern, and he was between the two, struggling violently with Darell. Slowly, and not gently, he forced the older man back into the chair.

'What are you trying to do?' Anthor brushed a lock of brown hair from his forehead, tossed a hip lightly upon the desk, and swung a leg, thoughtfully. 'I thought I was bringing you good news.'

Darell addressed the policeman directly, 'What does he mean by calling you the last man to see my daughter? Is my daughter dead? Please tell me without preliminary.' His face was white with apprehension.

Lieutenant Dirige said expressionlessly, '"Last man on Kalgan" was the phrase. She's not on Kalgan now. I have no knowledge past that.'

'Here,' broke in Anthor, 'let me put it straight. Sorry if I overplayed the drama a bit, Doc. You're so inhuman about this, I forget you have feelings. In the first place, Lieutenant

Dirige is one of us. He was born on Kalgan, but his father was a Foundation man brought to that planet in the service of the Mule. I answer for the lieutenant's loyalty to the Foundation.

'Now I was in touch with him the day after we stopped getting the daily report from Munn—'

'Why?' broke in Darell, fiercely. 'I thought it was quite decided that we were not to make a move in the matter. You were risking their lives and ours.'

'Because,' was the equally fierce retort, 'I've been involved in this game for longer than you. Because I know of certain contacts on Kalgan of which you know nothing. Because I act from deeper knowledge, do you understand?'

'I think you're completely mad.'

'Will you listen?'

A pause, and Darell's eyes dropped.

Anthor's lips quirked into a half smile, 'All right, Doc. Give me a few minutes. Tell him, Dirige.'

Dirige spoke easily: 'As far as I know, Dr Darell, your daughter is at Trantor. At least, she had a ticket to Trantor at the Eastern Spaceport. She was with a Trading Representative from that planet who claimed she was his niece. Your daughter seems to have a queer collection of relatives, doctor. That was the second uncle she had in a period of two weeks, eh? The Trantorian even tried to bribe me – probably thinks that's why they got away.' He smiled grimly at the thought.

'How was she?'

'Unharmed, as far as I could see. Frightened. I don't blame her for that. The whole department was after her. I still don't know why.'

Darell drew a breath for what seemed the first time in several minutes. He was conscious of the trembling of his hands and controlled them with an effort. 'Then she's all right. This Trading Representative, who was he? Go back to him. What part does he play in it?'

'*I* don't know. Do you know anything about Trantor?'

'I lived there once.'

'It's an agricultural world, now. Exports animal fodder and grains, mostly. High quality! They sell them all over the Galaxy. There are a dozen or two farm co-operatives on the planet and each has its representatives overseas. Shrewd sons of guns, too – I knew this one's record. He'd been on Kalgan before, usually with his wife. Perfectly honest. Perfectly harmless.'

'Um-m-m,' said Anthor. 'Arcadia was born in Trantor, wasn't she, Doc?'

Darell nodded.

'It hangs together, you see. She wanted to go away – quickly and far – and Trantor would suggest itself. Don't *you* think so?'

Darell said: 'Why not back here?'

'Perhaps she was being pursued and felt that she had to double off in a new angle, eh?'

Dr Darell lacked the heart to question further. Well, then, let her be safe on Trantor, or as safe as one could be anywhere in this dark and horrible Galaxy. He groped toward the door, felt Anthor's light touch on his sleeve, and stopped, but did not turn.

'Mind if I go home with you, Doc?'

'You're welcome,' was the automatic response.

By evening, the exteriormost reaches of Dr Darell's personality, the ones that made immediate contact with other people had solidified once more. He had refused to eat his evening meal and had, instead, with feverish insistence, returned to the inch-wise advance into the intricate mathematics of encephalo-graphic analysis.

It was not till nearly midnight, that he entered the living room again.

Pelleas Anthor was still there, twiddling at the controls of the video. The footsteps behind him caused him to glance over his shoulder.

'Hi. Aren't you in bed yet? I've been spending hours on the video, trying to get something other than bulletins. It seems

185

the *F.S. Hober Mallow* is delayed in course and hasn't been heard from.'

'Really? What do they suspect?'

'What do you think? Kalganian skulduggery. There are reports that Kalganian vessels were sighted in the general space sector in which the *Hober Mallow* was last heard from?'

Darell shrugged, and Anthor rubbed his forehead doubtfully.

'Look, doc,' he said, 'why don't you go to Trantor?'

'Why should I?'

'Because you're no good to us here. You're not yourself. You can't be. And you could accomplish a purpose by going to Trantor, too. The old Imperial Library with the complete records of the Proceedings of the Seldon Commission are there—'

'No! The Library has been picked clean and it hasn't helped anyone.'

'It helped Ebling Mis once.'

'How do you know? Yes, he *said* he found the Second Foundation, and my mother killed him five seconds later as the only way to keep him from unwittingly revealing its location to the Mule. But in doing so, she also, you realize, made it impossible ever to tell whether Mis *really* did know the location. After all, no one else has ever been able to deduce the truth from those records.'

'Ebling Mis, if you'll remember, was working under the driving impetus of the Mule's mind.'

'I know that, too, but Mis' mind was, by that very token, in an abnormal state. Do you and I know anything about the properties of a mind under the emotional control of another; about its abilities and shortcomings? In any case, I will not go to Trantor.'

Anthor frowned, 'Well, why the vehemence? I merely suggested it as – well, by Space, I don't understand you. You look ten years older. You're obviously having a hellish time of it. You're not doing anything of value here. If I were you, I'd go and get the girl.'

'Exactly! It's what I want to do, too. *That's why I won't do it.*

Look, Anthor, and try to understand. You're playing – we're both playing – with something completely beyond our powers to fight. In cold blood, if you have any, you know that, whatever you may think in your moments of quixoticism.

'For fifty years, we've known that the Second Foundation is the real descendant and pupil of Seldonian mathematics. What that means, and you know that, too, is that nothing in the Galaxy happens which does not play a part in their reckoning. To us, all life is a series of accidents to be met with by improvisations. To them, all life is purposive and should be met by precalculation.

'But they have their weakness. Their work is statistical and only the mass action of humanity is truly inevitable. Now how *I* play a part, as an individual, in the foreseen course of history, I don't know. Perhaps I have no definite part, since the Plan leaves individuals to indeterminacy and free will. But I am important and they – *they*, you understand – may at least have calculated my probable reaction. So I distrust my impulses, my desires, my probable reactions.

'I would rather present them with an *im*probable reaction. I will stay here, despite the fact that I yearn very desperately to leave. No! *Because* I yearn very desperately to leave.'

The younger man smiled sourly. 'You don't know your own mind as well as *they* might. Suppose that – knowing you – they might count on what you think, merely *think*, is the improbable reaction, simply by knowing in advance what your line of reasoning would be.'

'In that case, there is no escape. For if I follow the reasoning you have just outlined and go to Trantor, they may have foreseen that, too. There is an endless cycle of double-double-double-doublecrosses. No matter how far I follow that cycle. I can only either go or stay. The intricate act of luring my daughter halfway across the Galaxy cannot be meant to make me stay where I am, since I would most certainly have stayed if they had done nothing. It can only be to make me move, and so I will stay.

'And besides, Anthor, not everything bears the breath of the
187

Second Foundation; not all events are the results of their puppeting. They may have had nothing to do with Arcadia's leave-taking, and she may be safe on Trantor when all the rest of us are dead.'

'No,' said Anthor, sharply, 'now you are off the track.'

'You have an alternative interpretation?'

'I have – if you'll listen.'

'Oh, go ahead. I don't lack patience.'

'Well, then – how well do you know your own daughter?'

'How well can any individual know any other? Obviously, my knowledge is inadequate.'

'So is mine on that basis, perhaps even more so – but at least, I viewed her with fresh eyes. Item one: She is a ferocious little romantic, the only child of an ivory-tower academician, growing up in an unreal world of video and book-film adventure. She lives in a weird self-constructed fantasy of espionage and intrigue. Item two: She's intelligent about it; intelligent enough to outwit us, at any rate. She planned carefully to overhear our first conference and succeeded. She planned carefully to go to Kalgan with Munn and succeeded. Item three: She has an unholy hero-worship of her grandmother – your mother – who defeated the Mule.

'I'm right so far, I think? All right, then. Now, unlike you, I've received a complete report from Lieutenant Dirige and, in addition, my sources of information on Kalgan are rather complete, and all sources check. We know, for instance, that Homir Munn, in conference with the Lord of Kalgan was refused admission to the Mule's Palace, and that this refusal was suddenly abrogated after Arcadia had spoken to Lady Callia, the First Citizen's very good friend.'

Darell interrupted. 'And how do you know all this?'

'For one thing, Munn was interviewed by Dirige as part of the police campaign to locate Arcadia. Naturally, we have a complete transcript of the questions and answers.

'And take Lady Callia herself. It is rumoured that she has lost Stettin's interest, but the rumour isn't borne out by facts. She not only remains unreplaced; is not only able to mediate the lord's refusal to Munn into an acceptance; but can even engineer Arcadia's escape openly. Why, a dozen of the soldiers about Stettin's executive mansion testified that they were seen together on the last evening. Yet she remains unpunished. This despite the fact that Arcadia was searched for with every appearance of diligence.'

'But what is your conclusion from all this torrent of ill-connection?'

'That Arcadia's escape was arranged.'

'As I said.'

'With this addition. That Arcadia must have known it was arranged; that Arcadia, the bright little girl who saw cabals everywhere, saw this one and followed your own type of reasoning. They wanted her to return to the Foundation, and so she went to Trantor, instead. But why Trantor?'

'Well, why?'

'Because that is where Bayta, her idolized grandmother, escaped when *she* was in flight. Consciously or unconsciously, Arcadia imitated that. I wonder, then, if Arcadia was fleeing the same enemy.'

'The Mule?' asked Darell with polite sarcasm.

'Of course not. I mean, by the enemy, a mentality that she could not fight. She was running from the Second Foundation, or such influence thereof as could be found on Kalgan.'

'What influence is this you speak of?'

'Do you expect Kalgan to be immune from that ubiquitous menace? We both have come to the conclusion, somehow, that Arcadia's escape was arranged. Right? She was searched for and found, but deliberately allowed to slip away by Dirige. By Dirige, do you understand? But how was that? Because he was our man. But how did they know that? Were they counting on him to be a traitor? Eh, doc?'

'Now you're saying that they honestly meant to recapture her. Frankly, you're tiring me a bit, Anthor. Finish your say; I want to go to bed.'

'My say is quickly finished.' Anthor reached for a small group of photo-records in his inner pocket. It was the familiar wigglings of the encephalograph. 'Dirige's brainwaves,' Anthor said, casually, 'taken since he returned.'

It was quite visible to Darell's naked eye, and his face was grey when he looked up. 'He is Controlled.'

'Exactly. He allowed Arcadia to escape not because he was our man but because he was the Second Foundation's.'

'Even after he knew she was going to Trantor, and not to Terminus.'

Anthor shrugged. 'He had been geared to let her go. There was no way *he* could modify that. He was only a tool, you see. It was just that Arcadia followed the least probable course, and is probably safe. Or at least safe until such time as the Second Foundation can modify the plans to take into account this changed state of affairs—'

He paused. The little signal light on the video set was flashing. On an independent circuit, it signified the presence of emergency news. Darell saw it, too, and with the mechanical movement of long habit turned on the video. They broke in upon the middle of a sentence but before its completion, they knew that the *Hober Mallow*, or the wreck thereof, had been found and that, for the first time in nearly half a century, the Foundation was again at war.

Anthor's jaw was set in a hard line. 'All right, doc, you heard that. Kalgan has attacked; and Kalgan is under the control of the Second Foundation. Will you follow your daughter's lead and move to Trantor?'

'No. I will risk it. Here.'

'Dr Darell. You are not as intelligent as your daughter. I wonder how far you can be trusted.' His long, level stare held Darell for a moment, and then without a word, he left.

And Darell was left in uncertainty and – almost – despair.

Unheeded, the video was a medley of excited sight-sound, as it described in nervous detail the first hour of the war between Kalgan and the Foundation.

# 17

## WAR

The mayor of the Foundation brushed futilely at the picket fence of hair that rimmed his skull. He sighed. 'The years that we have wasted; the chances we have thrown away. I make no recriminations, Dr Darell, but we deserve defeat.'

Darell said, quietly, 'I see no reason for lack of confidence in events, sir.'

'Lack of confidence! Lack of confidence! By the Galaxy, Dr Darell, on what would you base any other attitude? Come here—'

He half-led half-forced Darell toward the limpid ovoid cradled gracefully on its tiny force-field support. At a touch of the mayor's hand, it glowed within – an accurate three-dimensional model of the Galactic double-spiral.

'In yellow,' said the mayor, excitedly, 'we have that region of Space under Foundation control; in red, that under Kalgan.'

What Darell saw was a crimson sphere resting within a stretching yellow fist that surrounded it on all sides but that toward the centre of the Galaxy.

'Galactography,' said the mayor, 'is our greatest enemy. Our admirals make no secret of our almost hopeless, strategic position. Observe. The enemy has inner lines of communication. He is concentrated; can meet us on all sides with equal ease. He can defend himself with minimum force.

'We are expanded. The average distance between inhabited systems within the Foundation is nearly three times that within Kalgan. To go from Santanni to Locris, for instance, is a voyage of twenty-five hundred parsecs for us, but only eight hundred parsecs for them, if we remain within our respective territories—'

Darell said, 'I understand all that, sir.'

'And you do not understand that it may mean defeat.'

'There is more than distance to war. I say we cannot lose. It is quite impossible.'

'And why do you say that?'

'Because of my own interpretation of the Seldon Plan.'

'Oh,' the mayor's lips twisted, and the hands behind his back flapped one within the other, 'then you rely, too, on the mystical help of the Second Foundation.'

'No. Merely on the help of inevitability – and of courage and persistence.'

And yet behind his easy confidence, he wondered—

What if—

Well— What if Anthor were right, and Kalgan were a direct tool of the mental wizards. What if it was their purpose to defeat and destroy the Foundation. No! It made no sense!

And yet—

He smiled bitterly. Always the same. Always that peering and peering through the opaque granite which, to the enemy, was so transparent.

Nor were the galactographic verities of the situation lost upon Stettin.

The Lord of Kalgan stood before a twin of the Galactic model which the mayor and Darell had inspected. Except that where the mayor frowned, Stettin smiled.

His admiral's uniform glistered imposingly upon his massive figure. The crimson sash of the Order of the Mule awarded him by the former First Citizen whom six months later he had replaced somewhat forcefully, spanned his chest diagonally from right shoulder to waist. The Silver Star with Double Comets and Swords sparkled brilliantly upon his left shoulder.

He addressed the six men of his general staff whose uniforms were only less grandiloquent than his own, and his First Minister as well, thin and grey – a darkling cobweb, lost in the brightness.

Stettin said, 'I think the decisions are clear. We can afford to wait. To them, every day of delay will be another blow at their morale. If they attempt to defend all portions of their realm, they will be spread thin and we can strike through in two simultaneous thrusts here and here.' He indicated the directions on the Galactic model – two lances of pure white shooting through the yellow fist from the red ball it enclosed, cutting Terminus off on either side in a tight arc. 'In such a manner, we cut their fleet into three parts which can be defeated in detail. If they concentrate, they give up two-thirds of their dominions voluntarily and will probably risk rebellion.'

The First Minister's thin voice alone seeped through the hush that followed. 'In six months,' he said, 'the Foundation will grow six months stronger. Their resources are greater, as we all know; their navy is numerically stronger; their manpower is virtually inexhaustible. Perhaps a quick thrust would be safer.'

His was easily the least influential voice in the room. Lord Stettin smiled and made a flat gesture with his hand. 'The six months – or a year, if necessary – will cost us nothing. The men of the Foundation cannot prepare; they are ideologically incapable of it. It is in their very philosophy to believe that the Second Foundation will save them. But not this time, eh?'

The men in the room stirred uneasily.

'You lack confidence, I believe,' said Stettin, frigidly. 'Is it necessary once again to describe the reports of our agents in Foundation territory, or to repeat the findings of Mr Homir Munn, the Foundation agent now in our...uh...service? Let us adjourn, gentlemen.'

Stettin returned to his private chambers with a fixed smile still on his face. He sometimes wondered about this Homir Munn. A queer water-spined fellow who certainly did not bear out his early promise. And yet he crawled with interesting information that carried conviction with it – particularly when Callia was present.

His smile broadened. That fat fool had her uses, after all. At least, she got more with her wheedling out of Munn than he could, and with less trouble. Why not give her to Munn? He frowned. Callia. She and her stupid jealousy. Space! If he still had the Darell girl— Why hadn't he ground her skull to powder for that?

He couldn't put his finger on the reason.

Maybe because she got along with Munn. And he needed Munn. It was Munn, for instance, who had demonstrated that, at least in the belief of the Mule, there was no Second Foundation. His admirals needed that assurance.

He would have liked to make the proofs public, but it was better to let the Foundation believe in their nonexistent help. Was it actually Callia who had pointed that out? That's right. She had said.

Oh, nonsense! She couldn't have said anything.

And yet—

He shook his head to clear it and passed on.

# 18

# GHOST OF A WORLD

Trantor was a world in dregs and rebirth. Set like a faded jewel in the midst of the bewildering crowd of suns at the centre of the Galaxy – in the heaps and clusters of stars piled high with aimless prodigality – it alternately dreamed of past and future.

Time had been when the insubstantial ribbons of control had stretched out from its metal coating to the very edges of stardom. It had been a single city, housing four hundred billion administrators; the mightiest capital that had ever been.

Until the decay of the Empire eventually reached it and in the Great Sack of a century ago, its drooping powers had been bent back upon themselves and broken forever. In the blasting ruin of death, the metal shell that circled the planet wrinkled and crumpled into an aching mock of its own grandeur.

The survivors tore up the metal plating and sold it to other planets for seed and cattle. The soil was uncovered once more and the planet returned to its beginnings. In the spreading areas of primitive agriculture, it forgot its intricate and colossal past.

Or would have but for the still mighty shards that heaped their massive ruins toward the sky in bitter and dignified silence.

Arcadia watched the metal rim of the horizon with a stirring of the heart. The village in which the Palvers lived was but a huddle of houses to her – small and primitive. The fields that surrounded it were golden-yellow, wheat-clogged tracts.

But there, just past the reaching point, was the memory of the past, still glowing in unrusted splendour, and burning with fire where the sun of Trantor caught it in gleaming highlights. She had been there once during the months since she had arrived at Trantor. She had climbed onto the smooth, unjointed pavement and ventured into the silent dust-streaked structures, where the light entered through the jags of broken walls and partitions.

It had been solidified heartache. It had been blasphemy.

She had left, clangingly – running until her feet pounded softly on earth once more.

And then she could only look back longingly. She dared not disturb that mighty brooding once more.

Somewhere on this world, she knew, she had been born – near the old Imperial Library, which was the veriest Trantor of Trantor. It was the sacred of the sacred; the holy of holies! Of all the world, it alone had survived the Great Sack and for a century it had remained complete and untouched; defiant of the universe.

There Hari Seldon and his group had woven their unimaginable web. There Ebling Mis pierced the secret, and sat numbed in his vast surprise, until he was killed to prevent the secret from going further.

There at the Imperial Library, her grandparents had lived for ten years, until the Mule died, and they could return to the reborn Foundation.

There at the Imperial Library, her own father returned with his bride to find the Second Foundation once again, but failed. There, she had been born and there her mother had died.

She would have liked to visit the Library, but Preem Palver shook his round head. 'It's thousands of miles, Arkady, and there's so much to do here. Besides, it's not good to bother there. You know; it's a shrine—'

But Arcadia knew that he had no desire to visit the Library; that it was a case of the Mule's Palace over again. There was this superstitious fear on the part of the pygmies of the present for the relics of the giants of the past.

Yet it would have been horrible to feel a grudge against the funny little man for that. She had been on Trantor now for nearly three months and in all that time, he and she – Pappa and

Mamma – had been wonderful to her—

And what was her return? Why, to involve them in the common ruin. Had she warned them that she was marked for destruction, perhaps? No! She let them assume the deadly role of protectors.

Her conscience panged unbearably – yet what choice had she?

She stepped reluctantly down the stairs to breakfast. The voices reached her.

Preem Palver had tucked the napkin down his shirt collar with a twist of his plump neck and had reached for his poached eggs with an uninhibited satisfaction.

'I was down in the city yesterday, Mamma,' he said, wielding his fork and nearly drowning the words with a capacious mouthful.

'And what is down in the city, Pappa?' asked Mamma indifferently, sitting down, looking sharply about the table, and rising again for the salt.

'Ah, not so good. A ship came in from out Kalgan-way with newspapers from there. It's war there.'

'War! So! Well, let them break their heads, if they have no more sense inside. Did your pay bill come yet? Pappa, I'm telling you again. You warn old man Cosker this isn't the only co-operative in the world. It's bad enough they pay what I'm ashamed to tell my friends, but at least on time they could be!'

'Time; shmime,' said Pappa, irritably. 'Look, don't make me silly talk at breakfast, it should choke me each bite in the throat,' and he wreaked havoc among the buttered toast as he said it. He added, somewhat more moderately, 'The fighting is between Kalgan and the Foundation, and for two months they've been at it.'

His hands lunged at one another in mock-representation of a space fight.

'Um-m-m. And what's doing?'

'Bad for the Foundation. Well, you saw Kalgan; all soldiers.

197

They were ready. The Foundation was not, and so – *poof*!'

And suddenly, Mamma laid down her fork and hissed, 'Fool!'

'Huh?'

'Dumb-head! Your big mouth is always moving and wagging.'

She was pointing quickly and when Pappa looked over his shoulder, there was Arcadia, frozen in the doorway.

She said, 'The Foundation is at war?'

Pappa looked helplessly at Mamma, then nodded.

'And they're losing?'

Again the nod.

Arcadia felt the unbearable catch in her throat, and slowly approached the table. 'Is it over?' she whispered.

'Over?' repeated Pappa, with false heartiness. 'Who said it was over? In war, lots of things can happen. And . . . and—'

'Sit down, darling,' said Mamma, soothingly. 'No one should talk before breakfast. You're not in a healthy condition with no food in the stomach.'

But Arcadia ignored her. 'Are the Kalganians on Terminus?'

'No,' said Pappa, seriously. 'The news is from last week, and Terminus is still fighting. This is honest. I'm telling the truth. And the Foundation is still strong. Do you want me to get you the newspapers?'

'Yes!'

She read them over what she could eat of her breakfast and her eyes blurred as she read. Santanni and Korell were gone – without a fight. A squadron of the Foundation's navy had been trapped in the sparsely-sunned Ifni sector and wiped out to almost the last ship.

And now the Foundation was back to the Four-Kingdom core – the original Realm which had been built up under Salvor Hardin, the first mayor. But still it fought – and still there might be a chance – and whatever happened, she must inform her father. She must somehow reach his ear. She *must*!

But how? With a war in the way.

She asked Pappa after breakfast, 'Are you going out on a new mission soon, Mr Palver?'

Pappa was on the large chair on the front lawn, sunning himself. A fat cigar smouldered between his plump fingers and he looked like a beatific pug-dog.

'A mission?' he repeated, lazily. 'Who knows. It's a nice vacation and my leave isn't up. Why talk about new missions? You're restless, Arkady?'

'Me? No, I like it here. You're very good to me, you and Mrs Palver.'

He waved his hand at her, brushing away her words.

Arcadia said, 'I was thinking about the war.'

'But don't think about it. What can *you* do? If it's something you can't help, why hurt yourself over it?'

'But I was thinking that the Foundation has lost most of its farming worlds. They're probably rationing food there.'

Pappa looked uncomfortable. 'Don't worry. It'll be all right.'

She scarcely listened. 'I wish I could carry food to them, that's what. You know after the Mule died, and the Foundation rebelled, Terminus was just about isolated for a time and General Han Pritcher, who succeeded the Mule for a while, was laying siege to it. Food was running awfully low and my father says that *his* father told him that they only had dry amino-acid concentrates that tasted terrible. Why, one egg cost two hundred credits. And then they broke the siege just in time and food ships came through from Santanni. It must have been an awful time. Probably it's happening all over, now.'

There was a pause, and then Arcadia said, 'You know, I'll bet the Foundation would be willing to pay smuggler's prices for food now. Double and triple and more. Gee, if any co-operative, f'r instance, here on Trantor took over the job, they might lose some ships, but, I'll bet they'd be war millionaires before it was over. The Foundation Traders in the old days used to do that all the time. There'd be a war, so they'd sell

199

whatever was needed bad and take their chances. Golly, they used to make as much as two million dollars out of one trip – *profit*. That was just out of what they could carry on one ship, too.'

Pappa stirred. His cigar had gone out, unnoticed. 'A deal for food, huh? Hm-m-m— But the Foundation is so far away.'

'Oh, I know. I guess you couldn't do it from here. If you took a regular liner you probably couldn't get closer than Massena or Smushyk, and after that you'd have to hire a small scoutship or something to slip you through the lines.'

Pappa's hand brushed at his hair, as he calculated.

Two weeks later, arrangements for the mission were completed. Mamma railed for most of the time— First, at the incurable obstinacy with which he courted suicide. Then, at the incredible obstinacy with which which he refused to allow her to accompany him.

Pappa said, 'Mamma, why do you act like an old lady. I can't take you. It's a man's work. What do you think a war is? Fun? Child's play?'

'Then why do *you* go? Are *you* a man, you old fool – with a leg and half an arm in the grave. Let some of the young ones go – not a fat bald-head like you?'

'I'm not a bald-head,' retorted Pappa, with dignity. 'I got yet lots of hair. And why should it not be me that gets the commission? Why a young fellow? Listen, this could mean millions?'

She knew that and she subsided.

Arcadia saw him once before he left.

She said, 'Are you going to Terminus?'

'Why not? You say yourself they need bread and rice and potatoes. Well, I'll make a deal with them, and they'll get it.'

'Well, then – just one thing: If you're going to Terminus, could you ... would you see my father?'

And Pappa's face crinkled and seemed to melt into sympathy, 'Oh – and I have to wait for you to tell me. Sure, I'll see him. I'll tell him you're safe and everything's O.K., and when the war is over, I'll bring you back.'

'Thanks. I'll tell you how to find him. His name is Dr Toran Darell and he lives in Stanmark. That's just outside Terminus City, and you can get a little commuting plane that goes there. We're at 55 Channel Drive.'

'Wait, and I'll write it down.'

'No, no,' Arcadia's arm shot out. 'You mustn't write anything down. You must remember – and find him without anybody's help.'

Pappa looked puzzled. Then he shrugged his shoulders. 'All right, then. It's 55 Channel Drive in Stanmark, outside Terminus City, and you commute there by plane. All right?'

'One other thing.'

'Yes?'

'Would you tell him something from me?'

'Sure.'

'I want to whisper it to you.'

He leaned his plump cheek toward her, and the little whispered sound passed from one to the other.

Pappa's eyes were round. 'That's what you want me to say? But it doesn't make sense.'

'He'll know what you mean. Just say I sent it and that I said he would know what it means. And you say it exactly the way I told you. No different. You won't forget it?'

'How can I forget it? Five little words. Look—'

'No, no.' She hopped up and down in the intensity of her feelings. 'Don't repeat it. Don't ever repeat it to anyone. Forget all about it except to my father. Promise me.'

Pappa shrugged again. 'I promise! All right!'

'All right,' she said, mournfully, and as he passed down the drive to where the air taxi waited to take him to the spaceport, she wondered if she had signed his death warrant. She wondered if she would ever see him again.

She scarcely dared to walk into the house again to face the good, kind Mamma. Maybe when it was all over, she had better kill herself for what she had done to them.

# 19

# END OF WAR

QUORISTON, BATTLE OF *Fought on 9, 17, 377 F.E.
between the forces of the Foundation and those of Lord Stettin of
Kalgan, it was the last battle of consequence during the
Interregnum ...*

ENCYCLOPEDIA GALACTICA

Jole Turbor, in his new role of war correspondent, found his
bulk incased in a naval uniform, and rather liked it. He enjoyed
being back on the air, and some of the fierce helplessness of the
futile fight against the Second Foundation left him in the
excitement of another sort of fight with substantial ships and
ordinary men.

To be sure, the Foundation's fight had not been remarkable
for victories, but it was still possible to be philosophic about the
matter. After six months, the hard core of the Foundation was
untouched, and the hard core of the Fleet was still in being.
With the new additions since the start of the war, it was almost
as strong numerically, and stronger technically, than before
the defeat at Ifni.

And meanwhile, planetary defenses were being strengthened;
the armed forces better trained; administrative efficiency was
having some of the water squeezed out of it – and much of the
Kalganian's conquering fleet was being wallowed down
through the necessity of occupying the 'conquered' territory.

At the moment, Turbor was with the Third Fleet in the outer
reaches of the Anacreonian sector. In line with his policy of
making this a 'little man's war,' he was interviewing Fennel
Leemor, Engineer Third Class, volunteer.

'Tell us a little about yourself, sailor,' said Turbor.

'Ain't much to tell,' Leemor shuffled his feet and allowed a faint, bashful smile to cover his face, as though he could see all the millions that undoubtedly could see him at the moment. 'I'm a Locrian. Got a job in an air-car factory; section head and good pay. I'm married; got two kids, both girls. Say, I couldn't say hello to them, could I – in case they're listening.'

'Go ahead, sailor. The video is all yours.'

'Gosh, thanks.' He burbled, 'Hello, Milla, in case you're listening, I'm fine. Is Sunni all right? And Tomma? I think of you all the time and maybe I'll be back on furlough after we get back to port. I got your food parcel but I'm sending it back. We get our regular mess, but they say the civilians are a little tight. I guess that's all.'

'I'll look her up next time I'm on Locris, sailor, and make sure she's not short of food. O.K.?'

The young man smiled broadly and nodded his head. 'Thank you, Mr Turbor. I'd appreciate that.'

'All right. Suppose you tell us, then— You're a volunteer, aren't you?'

'Sure am. If anyone picks a fight with me, I don't have to wait for anyone to drag me in. I joined up the day I heard about the *Hober Mallow*.'

'That's a fine spirit. Have you seen much action? I notice you're wearing two battle stars.'

'*Ptah*.' The sailor spat. 'Those weren't battles, they were chases. The Kalganians don't fight, unless they have odds of five to one or better in their favour. Even then they just edge in and try to cut us up ship by ship. Cousin of mine was at Ifni and he was on a ship that got away, the old *Ebling Mis*. He says it was the same there. They had their Main Fleet against just a wing division of ours, and down to where we only had five ships left, they kept stalking instead of fighting. We got twice as many of their ships at *that* fight.'

'Then you think we're going to win the war?'

'Sure bet; now that we aren't retreating. Even if things got too bad, that's when I'd expect the Second Foundation to step in. We still got the Seldon Plan – and *they* know it, too.'

Turbor's lips curled a bit. 'You're counting on the Second Foundation, then?'

The answer came with honest surprise. 'Well, doesn't everyone?'

Junior Officer Tipellum stepped into Turbor's room after the visicast. He shoved a cigarette at the correspondent and knocked his cap back to a perilous balance on the occiput.

'We picked up a prisoner,' he said.

'Yes?'

'Little crazy fellow. Claims to be a neutral – diplomatic immunity, no less. I don't think they know what to do with him. His name's Palvro, Palver, something like that, and he says he's from Trantor. Don't know what in space he's doing in a war zone.'

But Turbor had swung to a sitting position on his bunk and the nap he had been about to take was forgotten. He remembered quite well his last interview with Darell, the day after war had been declared and he was shoving off.

'Preem Palver,' he said. It was a statement.

Tipellum paused and let the smoke trickle out the sides of his mouth. 'Yeah,' he said, 'how in space did you know?'

'Never mind. Can I see him?'

'Space, I can't say. The old man has him in his own room for questioning. Everyone figures he's a spy.'

'You tell the old man that I know him, if he's who he claims he is. I'll take the responsibility.'

Captain Dixyl on the flagship of the Third Fleet watched unremittingly at the Grand Detector. No ship could avoid being a source of atomic radiation – not even if it were lying an inert mass – and each focal point of such radiation was a little sparkle in the three-dimensional field.

Each one of the Foundation's ships were accounted for and no sparkle was left over, now that the little spy who claimed to be a neutral had been picked up. For a while, that outside ship had created a stir in the captain's quarters. The tactics might

204

have needed changing on short notice. As it was—

'Are you sure you have it?' he asked.

Commander Cenn nodded. 'I will take my squadron through hyperspace: radius, 10.00 parsecs; theta, 268.52 degrees; phi, 84.15 degrees. Return to origin at 1330. Total absence 11.83 hours.'

'Right. Now we are going to count on pin-point return as regards both space and time. Understand?'

'Yes, captain.' He looked at his wrist watch, 'My ships will be ready by 0140.'

'Good,' said Captain Dixyl.

The Kalganian squadron was not within detector range now, but they would be soon. There was independent information to that effect. Without Cenn's squadron the Foundation forces would be badly outnumbered, but the captain was quite confident. *Quite* confident.

Preem Palver looked sadly about him. First at the tall, skinny admiral; then at the others, everyone in uniform; and now at this last one, big and stout, with his collar open and no tie –not like the rest – who said he wanted to speak to him.

Jole Turbor was saying: 'I am perfectly aware, admiral, of the serious possibilities involved here, but I tell you that if I can be allowed to speak to him for a few minutes, I may be able to settle the current uncertainty.'

'Is there any reason why you can't question him before me?'

Turbor pursed his lips and looked stubborn. 'Admiral,' he said, 'while I have been attached to your ships, the Third Fleet has received an excellent press. You may station men outside the door, if you like, and you may return in five minutes. But, meanwhile, humour me a bit, and your public relations will not suffer. Do you understand me?'

He did.

Then Turbor, in the isolation that followed, turned to Palver, and said, 'Quickly – what is the name of the girl you abducted.'

And Palver could simply stare round-eyed, and shake his head.

'No nonsense,' said Turbor. 'If you do not answer, you will

be a spy and spies are blasted without trial in war time.'

'Arcadia Darell!' gasped Palver.

'*Well!* All right, then. Is she safe?'

Palver nodded.

'You had better be sure of that, or it won't be well for you.'

'She is in good health, perfectly safe,' said Palver, palely.

The admiral returned, 'Well?'

'The man, sir, is not a spy. You may believe what he tells you. I vouch for him.'

'That so?' The admiral frowned. 'Then he represents an agricultural co-operative on Trantor that wants to make a trade treaty with Terminus for the delivery of grains and potatoes. Well, all right, but he can't leave now.'

'Why not?' asked Palver, quickly.

'Because we're in the middle of a battle. After it is over – assuming we're still alive – we'll take you to Terminus.'

The Kalganian fleet that spanned through space detected the Foundation ships from an incredible distance and were themselves detected. Like little fireflies in each other's Grand Detectors, they closed in across the emptiness.

And the Foundation's admiral frowned and said, 'This must be their main push. Look at the numbers.' Then, 'They won't stand up before us, though, not if Cenn's detachment can be counted on.'

Commander Cenn had left hours before – at the first detection of the coming enemy. There was no way of altering the plan now. It worked or it didn't, but the admiral felt quite comfortable. As did the officers. As did the men.

Again watch the fireflies.

Like a deadly ballet dance, in precise formations, they sparked.

The Foundation fleet edged slowly backwards. Hours passed and the fleet slowly veered off, teasing the advancing enemy slightly off course, then more so.

In the minds of the dictators of the battle plan, there was a certain volume of space that must be occupied by the Kalganian ships. Out from that volume crept the Foundationers; into it slipped the Kalganians. Those that passed out again were attacked, suddenly and fiercely. Those that stayed within were not touched.

It all depended on the reluctance of the ships of Lord Stettin to take the initiative themselves – on their willingness to remain where none attacked.

Captain Dixyl stared frigidly at his wrist watch. It was 1310.

'We've got twenty minutes,' he said.

The lieutenant at his side nodded tensely, 'It looks all right so far, captain. We've got more than ninety percent of them boxed. If we can keep them that way—'

'Yes! If—'

The Foundation ships were drifting forward again – very slowly. Not quick enough to urge a Kalganian retreat and just quickly enough to discourage a Kalganian advance. They preferred to wait.

And the minutes passed.

At 1325, the admiral's buzzer sounded in seventy-five ships of the Foundation's line, and they built up to a maximum acceleration towards the front-plane of the Kalganian fleet, itself three hundred strong. Kalganian shields flared into action, and the vast energy beams flicked out. Every one of the three hundred concentrated in the same direction, towards their mad attackers who bore down relentlessly, uncaringly and—

At 1330, fifty ships under Commander Cenn appeared from nowhere, in one single bound through hyperspace to a calculated spot at a calculated time – and were spaced in tearing fury at the unprepared Kalganian rear.

The trap worked perfectly.

The Kalganians still had numbers on their side, but they were in no mood to count. Their first effort was to escape and the formation once broken was only the more vulnerable, as the

207

enemy ships bumbled into one another's path.

After a while, it took on the proportions of a rat hunt.

Of three hundred Kalganian ships, the core and pride of their fleet, some sixty or less, many in a state of near-hopeless disrepair, reached Kalgan once more. The Foundation loss was eight ships out of a total of one hundred twenty-five.

Preem Palver landed on Terminus at the height of the celebration. He found the furore distracting, but before he left the planet, he had accomplished two things, and received one request.

The two things accomplished were: 1) the conclusion of an agreement whereby Palver's co-operative was to deliver twenty shiploads of certain foodstuffs per month for the next year at a war price, without, thanks to the recent battle, a corresponding war risk, and 2) the transfer to Dr Darell of Arcadia's five short words.

For a startled moment, Darell had stared wide-eyed at him, and then he had made his request. It was to carry an answer back to Arcadia. Palver liked it; it was a simple answer and made sense. It was: 'Come back now. There won't be any danger.'

Lord Stettin was in raging frustration. To watch his every weapon break in his hands; to feel the firm fabric of his military might part like the rotten thread it suddenly turned out to be – would have turned phlegmaticism itself into flowing lava. And yet he was helpless, and knew it.

He hadn't really slept well in weeks. He hadn't shaved in three days. He had cancelled all audiences. His admirals were left to themselves and none knew better than the Lord of Kalgan that very little time and no further defeats need elapse before he would have to contend with internal rebellion.

Lev Meirus, First Minister, was no help. He stood there, calm and indecently old, with his thin, nervous finger stroking, as always, the wrinkled line from nose to chin.

'Well,' shouted Stettin at him, 'contribute something. We stand here defeated, do you understand? *Defeated!* And why? I don't know why. There you have it. I don't know why. Do *you* know why?'

'I think so,' said Meirus, calmly.

'Treason!' The word came out softly, and other words followed as softly. 'You've known of treason, and you've kept quiet. You served the fool I ejected from the First Citizenship and you think you can serve whatever foul rat replaces me. If you have acted so, I will extract your entrails for it and burn them before your living eyes.'

Meirus was unmoved. 'I have tried to fill you with my own doubts, not once, but many times. I have dinned it in your ears and you have preferred the advice of others because it stuffed your ego better. Matters have turned out not as I feared, but even worse. If you do not care to listen now, say so, sir, and I shall leave, and, in due course, deal with your successor, whose first act, no doubt, will be to sign a treaty of peace.'

Stettin stared at him red-eyed, enormous fists slowly clenching and unclenching. 'Speak, you grey slug. *Speak!*'

'I have told you often, sir, that you are not the Mule. You may control ships and guns but you cannot control the minds of your subjects. Are you aware, sir, of who it is you are fighting? You fight the Foundation, which is never defeated — the Foundation, which is protected by the Seldon Plan — the Foundation, which is destined to form a new Empire.'

'There is no Plan. No longer. Munn has said so.'

'Then Munn is wrong. And if he were right, what then? You and I, sir, are not the people. The men and women of Kalgan and its subject worlds believe utterly and deeply in the Seldon Plan as do all the inhabitants of this end of the Galaxy. Nearly four hundred years of history teach the fact that the Foundation cannot be beaten. Neither the kingdoms nor the warlords nor the old Galactic Empire itself could do it.'

'The Mule did it.'

'Exactly, and he was beyond calculation — and you are not.

What is worse, the people know that you are not. So your ships go into battle fearing defeat in some unknown way. The insubstantial fabric of the Plan hangs over them so that they are cautious and look before they attack and wonder a little too much. While on the other side, that same insubstantial fabric fills the enemy with confidence, removes fear, maintains morale in the face of early defeats. Why not? The Foundation has always been defeated at first and has always won in the end.

'And your own morale, sir? You stand everywhere on enemy territory. Your own dominions have not been invaded; are still not in danger of invasion – yet you are defeated. You don't believe in the possibility, even, of victory, because you know there is none.

'Stoop, then, or you will be beaten to your knees. Stoop voluntarily, and you may save a remnant. You have depended on metal and power and they have sustained you as far as they could. You have ignored mind and morale and they have failed you. Now, take my advice. You have the Foundation man, Homir Munn. Release him. Send him back to Terminus and he will carry your peace offers.'

Stettin's teeth ground behind his pale, set lips. But what choice had he?

On the first day of the new year, Homir Munn left Kalgan again. More than six months had passed since he had left Terminus and in the interim, a war had raged and faded.

He had come alone, but he left escorted. He had come a simple man of private life; he left the unappointed but nevertheless, actual, ambassador of peace.

And what had most changed was his early concern over the Second Foundation. He had laughed at the thought of that: and pictured in luxuriant detail the final revelation to Dr Darell, to that energetic, young competent, Anthor, to all of them—

*He* knew. He, Homir Munn, finally knew the truth.

# 20

# 'I KNOW ...'

The last two months of the Stettinian war did not lag for Homir. In his unusual office as Mediator Extraordinary, he found himself the centre of interstellar affairs, a role he could not help but find pleasing.

There were no further major battles – a few accidental skirmishes that could scarcely count – and the terms of the treaty were hammered out with little necessity for concessions on the part of the Foundation. Stettin retained his office, but scarcely anything else. His navy was dismantled; his possessions outside the home system itself made autonomous and allowed to vote for return to previous status, full independence or confederation within the Foundation, as they chose.

The war was formally ended on an asteroid on Terminus' own stellar system; site of the Foundation's oldest naval base. Lev Meirus signed for Kalgan, and Homir was an interested spectator.

Throughout all that period he did not see Dr Darell, nor any of the others. But it scarcely mattered. His news would keep – and, as always, he smiled at the thought.

Dr Darell returned to Terminus some weeks after VK day, and that same evening, his house served as the meeting place for the five men who, ten months earlier, had laid their first plans.

They lingered over dinner and then over wine as though hesitating to return again to the old subject.

It was Jole Turbor, who, peering steadily into the purple depths of the wineglass with one eye, muttered, rather than said, 'Well, Homir, you are a man of affairs now, I see. You handled matters well.'

'I?' Munn laughed loudly and joyously. For some reason, he had not stuttered in months. 'I hadn't a thing to do with it. It was Arcadia. By the by, Darell, how is she? She's coming back from Trantor, I heard?'

'You heard correctly,' said Darell, quietly. 'Her ship should dock within the week.' He looked, with veiled eyes, at the others, but there were only confused, amorphous exclamations of pleasure. Nothing else.

Turbor said, 'Then it's over, really. Who would have predicted all this ten months ago. Munn's been to Kalgan and back. Arcadia's been to Kalgan and Trantor and is coming back. We've had a war and won it, by Space. They tell you that the vast sweeps of history can be predicted, but doesn't it seem conceivable that all that has just happened, with its absolute confusion to those of us who lived through it, couldn't possibly have been predicted.'

'Nonsense,' said Anthor, acidly. 'What makes you so triumphant, anyway? You talk as though we have really won a war, when actually we have won nothing but a petty brawl which has served only to distract our minds from the real enemy.'

There was an uncomfortable silence, in which only Homir Munn's slight smile struck a discordant note.

And Anthor struck the arm of his chair with a balled and fury-filled fist, 'Yes, I refer to the Second Foundation. There is no mention of it and, if I judge correctly, every effort to have no thought of it. Is it because this fallacious atmosphere of victory that palls over this world of idiots is so attractive that you feel you must participate? Turn somersaults then, handspring your way into a wall, pound one another's back and throw confetti out the window. Do whatever you please, only get it out of your system – and when you are quite done and you are yourselves again, return and let us discuss that problem which exists now precisely as it did ten months ago when you sat here with eyes cocked over your shoulders for fear of you knew not what. Do you really think that the Mind-masters of the Second

Foundation are less to be feared because you have beaten down a foolish wielder of spaceships.'

He paused, red-faced and panting.

Munn said quietly, 'Will you hear *me* speak now, Anthor? Or do you prefer to continue your role as ranting conspirator?'

'Have your say, Homir,' said Darell, 'but let's all of us refrain from over-picturesqueness of language. It's a very good thing in its place, but at present, it bores me.'

Homir Munn leaned back in his armchair and carefully refilled his glass from the decanter at his elbow.

'I was sent to Kalgan,' he said, 'to find out what I could from the records contained in the Mule's Palace. I spent several months doing so. I seek no credit for that accomplishment. As I have indicated, it was Arcadia whose ingenious intermeddling obtained the entry for me. Nevertheless, the fact remains that to my original knowledge of the Mule's life and times, which, I submit, was not small, I have added the fruits of much labour among primary evidence which has been available to no one else.

'I am, therefore, in a unique position to estimate the true danger of the Second Foundation; much more so than is our excitable friend here.'

'And,' grated Anthor, 'what is your estimate of that danger?'

'Why, zero.'

A short pause, and Elvett Semic asked with an air of surprised disbelief, 'You mean zero danger?'

'Certainly. Friends, *there is no Second Foundation*!'

Anthor's eyelids closed slowly and he sat there, face pale and expressionless.

Munn continued, attention-centring and loving it, 'And what is more, there never was one.'

'On what,' asked Darell, 'do you base this surprising conclusion?'

'I deny,' said Munn, 'that it is surprising. You all know the story of the Mule's search for the Second Foundation. But

213

what do you know of the intensity of that search – of the single-mindedness of it. He had tremendous resources at his disposal and he spared none of it. He was single-minded – and yet he failed. No Second Foundation was found.'

'One could scarcely expect it to be found,' pointed out Turbor, restlessly. 'It had means of protecting itself against inquiring minds.'

'Even when the mind that is inquiring is the Mule's mutant mentality? I think not. But come, you do not expect me to give you the gist of fifty volumes of reports in five minutes. All of it, by the terms of the peace treaty will be part of the Seldon Historical Museum eventually, and you will all be free to be as leisurely in your analysis as I have been. You will find his conclusion plainly stated, however, and that I have already expressed. There is not, and has never been, any Second Foundation.'

Semic interposed, 'Well, what stopped the Mule, then?'

'Greaty Galaxy, what *do* you suppose stopped him? Death did; as it will stop all of us. The greatest superstition of the age is that the Mule was somehow stopped in an all-conquering career by some mysterious entities superior even to himself. It is the result of looking at everything in wrong focus.

'Certainly no one in the Galaxy can help knowing that the Mule was a freak, physical as well as mental. He died in his thirties because his ill-adjusted body could no longer struggle its creaking machinery along. For several years before his death he was an invalid. His best health was never more than an ordinary man's feebleness. All right, then. He conquered the Galaxy and, in the ordinary course of nature proceeded to die. It's a wonder he proceeded as long and as well as he did. Friends, it's down in the very clearest print. You have only to have patience. You have only to try to look at all facts in new focus.'

Darell said, thoughtfully, 'Good, let us try that, Munn. It would be an interesting attempt and, if nothing else, would help oil our thoughts. These tampered men – the records of which Anthor bought to us nearly a year ago, what of them? Help us to see them in focus.'

'Easily. How old a science is encephalographic analysis? Or, put it another way, how well developed is the study of neuronic pathways.'

'We are at the beginning in this respect. Granted,' said Darell.

'Right. How certain can we be then as to the interpretation of what I've heard Anthor and yourself call the Tamper Plateau. You have your theories, but how certain can you be. Certain enough to consider it a firm basis for the existence of a mighty force for which all other evidence is negative? It's always easy to explain the unknown by postulating a superhuman and arbitrary will.

'It's a very human phenomenon. There have been cases all through Galactic history where isolated planetary systems have reverted to savagery, and what have we learned there? In every case, such savages attribute the to-them-incomprehensible forces of Nature – storms, pestilences, droughts – to sentient beings more powerful and more arbitrary than men.

'It is called anthropomorphism, I believe, and in this respect, we are savages and indulge in it. Knowing little of mental science, we blame anything we don't know on supermen – those of the Second Foundation in this case, based on the hint thrown us by Seldon.'

'Oh,' broke in Anthor, 'then you *do* remember Seldon. I thought you had forgotten. Seldon did say there was a Second Foundation. Get *that* in focus.'

'And are *you* aware then of all Seldon's purposes. Do you know what necessities were involved in his calculations? The Second Foundation may have been a very necessary scarecrow, with a highly specific end in view. How did we defeat Kalgan, for instance? What were you saying in your last series of articles, Turbor?'

Turbor stirred his bulk. 'Yes, I see what you're driving at. I was on Kalgan towards the end, Darell, and it was quite obvious that morale on the planet was incredibly bad. I looked through their news-records and – well, they expected to be beaten. Actually, they were completely unmanned by the thought that eventually the Second Foundation would take a hand, on the side of the First, naturally.'

'Quite right,' said Munn. 'I was there all through the war. I told Stettin there was no Second Foundation and he believed me. *He* felt safe. But there was no way of making the people suddenly disbelieve what they had believed all their lives, so that the myth eventually served a very useful purpose in Seldon's cosmic chess game.'

But Anthor's eyes opened, quite suddenly, and fixed themselves sardonically on Munn's countenance. '*I say you lie.*'

Homir turned pale, 'I don't see that I have to accept, much less answer, an accusation of that nature.'

'I say it without any intention of personal offense. You cannot help lying; you don't realize that you are. But you lie just the same.'

Semic laid his withered hand on the young man's sleeve. 'Take a breath, young fella.'

Anthor shook him off, none too gently, and said, 'I'm out of patience with all of you. I haven't seen this man more than half a dozen times in my life, yet I find the change in him unbelievable. The rest of you have known him for years, yet pass it by. It is enough to drive one mad. Do you call this man you've been listening to Homir Munn? He is not the Homir Munn *I* knew.'

A medley of shock; above which Munn's voice cried, 'You claim me to be an impostor?'

'Perhaps not in the ordinary sense,' shouted Anthor above the din, 'but an impostor nonetheless. Quiet, everyone! I demand to be heard.'

He frowned them ferociously into obedience. 'Do any of you remember Homir Munn as I do – the introverted librarian who never talked without obvious embarrassment; the man of tense

216

and nervous voice, who stuttered out his uncertain sentences? Does *this* man sound like him? He's fluent, he's confident, he's full of theories, and, by Space, he doesn't stutter. *Is* he the same person?'

Even Munn looked confused, and Pelleas Anthor drove on. 'Well, shall we test him?'

'How?' asked Darell.

'*You* ask how? There is the obvious way. You have his encephalographic record of ten months ago, haven't you? Run one again, and compare.'

He pointed at the frowning librarian, and said violently, 'I dare him to refuse to subject himself to analysis.'

'I don't object,' said Munn, defiantly. 'I am the man I always was.'

'Can *you* know?' said Anthor with contempt. 'I'll go further. I trust no one here. I want everyone to undergo analysis. There has been a war. Munn has been on Kalgan; Turbor has been on board ship and all over the war areas. Darell and Semic have been absent, too – I have no idea where. Only I have remained here in seclusion and safety, and I no longer trust any of the rest of you. And to play fair, I'll submit to testing as well. Are we agreed then? Or do I leave now and go my own way?'

Turbor shrugged and said, 'I have no objection.'

'I have already said I don't,' said Munn.

Semic moved a hand in silent assent, and Anthor waited for Darell. Finally, Darell nodded his head.

'Take me first,' said Anthor.

The needles traced their delicate way across the cross-hatchings as the youngest neurologist sat frozen in the reclining seat, with lidded eyes brooding heavily. From the files, Darell removed the folder containing Anthor's old encephalographic record. He showed them to Anthor.

'That's your own signature, isn't it?'

'Yes, yes. It's my record. Make the comparison.'

The scanner threw old and new on to the screen. All six

curves in each recording were there, and in the darkness, Munn's voice sounded in harsh clarity. 'Well, now, look there. There's a change.'

'Those are the primary waves of the frontal lobe. It doesn't mean a thing, Homir. Those additional jabs you're pointing to are just anger. It's the others that count.'

He touched a control knob and the six pairs melted into one another and coincided. The deeper amplitude of primaries alone introduced doubling.

'Satisfied?' asked Anthor.

Darell nodded curtly and took the seat himself. Semic followed him and Turbor followed him. Silently the curves were collected; silently they were compared.

Munn was the last to take his seat. For a moment, he hesitated, then, with a touch of desperation in his voice, he said, 'Well now, look, I'm coming in last and I'm under tension. I expect due allowance to be made for that.'

'There will be,' Darell assured him. 'No conscious emotion of yours will affect more than the primaries and they are not important.'

It might have been hours, in the utter silence that followed—

And then in the darkness of the comparison, Anthor said huskily: 'Sure, sure, it's only the onset of a complex. Isn't that what he told us? No such thing as tampering; it's all a silly anthropomorphic notion – but look at at! A coincidence I suppose.'

'What's the matter?' shrieked Munn.

Darell's hand was tight on the librarian's shoulder. 'Quiet, Munn – you've been handled; you've been adjusted by *them*.'

Then the light went on, and Munn was looking about him with broken eyes, making a horrible attempt to smile.

'You can't be serious, surely. There is a purpose to this. You're testing me.'

But Darell only shook his head. 'No, no, Homir. It's true.'

The librarian's eyes were filled with tears, suddenly. 'I don't feel any different. I can't believe it.' With sudden conviction: 'You are all in this. It's a conspiracy.'

218

Darell attempted a soothing gesture, and his hand was struck aside. Munn snarled, 'You're planning to kill me. By Space, you're planning to kill me.'

With a lunge, Anthor was upon him. There was the sharp crack of bone against bone, and Homir was limp and flaccid with that look of fear frozen on his face.

Anthor rose shakily, and said, 'We'd better tie and gag him. Later, we can decide what to do.' He brushed his long hair back.

Turbor said, 'How did you guess there was something wrong with him?'

Anthor turned sardonically upon him. 'It wasn't difficult. You see, *I happen to know where the Second Foundation really is*.'

Successive shocks have a decreasing effect—

It was with actual mildness that Semic asked, 'Are you sure? I mean we've just got through this sort of business with Munn—'

'This isn't quite the same,' returned Anthor. 'Darell, the day the war started, I spoke to you most seriously. I tried to have you leave Terminus. I would have told you then what I will tell you now, if I had been able to trust you.'

'You mean you have known the answer for half a year?' smiled Darell.

'I have known it from the time I learned that Arcadia had left for Trantor.'

And Darell started to his feet in sudden consternation. 'What had Arcadia to do with it? What are you implying?'

'Absolutely nothing that is not plain on the face of all the events we know so well. Arcadia goes to Kalgan and flees in terror to the *very* centre of the Galaxy, rather than return home. Lieutenant Dirige, our best agent on Kalgan is tampered with. Homir Munn goes to Kalgan and *he* is tampered with. The Mule conquered the Galaxy, but, queerly enough, he made Kalgan his headquarters, and it occurs to me to wonder if he was conqueror or, perhaps, tool. At every turn, we meet with Kalgan, Kalgan – nothing but Kalgan, the world

219

that somehow survived untouched all the struggles of the warlords for over a century.'

'You're conclusion, then.'

'Is obvious,' Anthor's eyes were intense. 'The Second Foundation is on Kalgan.'

Turbor interrupted. 'I was on Kalgan, Anthor. I was there last week. If there was any Second Foundation on it, I'm mad. Personally, I think you're mad.'

The young man whirled on him savagely. 'Then you're a fat fool. What do you expect the Second Foundation to be? A grammar school? Do you think that Radiant Fields in tight beams spell out "Second Foundation" in green and purple along the incoming spaceship routes? Listen to *me*, Turbor. Wherever they are, they form a tight oligarchy. They must be as well hidden on the world on which they exist, as the world itself is in the Galaxy as a whole.'

Turbor's jaw muscles writhed. 'I don't like your attitude, Anthor.'

'That certainly disturbs me,' was the sarcastic response. 'Take a look about you here on Terminus. We're at the centre – the core – the origin of the First Foundation with all its knowledge of physical science. Well, how many of the population are physical scientists? Can *you* operate an Energy Transmitting Station? What do *you* know of the operation of a hyperatomic motor? Eh? The number of real scientists on Terminus – even on Terminus – can be numbered at less than one percent of the population.

'And what then of the Second Foundation where secrecy must be preserved. There will still be less of the cognoscenti, and these will be hidden even from their own world.'

'Say,' said Semic, carefully. 'We just licked Kalgan –'

'So we did. So we did,' said Anthor, sardonically. 'Oh, we celebrate that victory. The cities are still illuminated; they are still shooting off fireworks; they are still shouting over the televisors. But now, *now*, when the search is on once more for the Second Foundation, where is the last place we'll look;

220

where is the last place anyone will look? Right! Kalgan!

'We haven't hurt them, you know; not really. We've destroyed some ships, killed a few thousands, torn away their Empire, taken over some of their commercial and economic power – but that all means nothing. I'll wager that not one member of the real ruling class of Kalgan is in the least discomfited. On the contrary, they are now safe from curiosity. But not from *my* curiosity. What do you say, Darell?'

Darell shrugged his shoulders. 'Interesting. I'm trying to fit it in with a message I received from Arcadia a few months since.'

'Oh, a message?' asked Anthor. 'And what was it?'

'Well, I'm not certain. Five short words. But it's interesting.'

'Look,' broke in Semic, with a worried interest, 'there's something *I* don't understand.'

'What's that?'

Semic chose his words carefully, his old upper lip lifting with each word as if to let them out singly and reluctantly. 'Well, now, Homir Munn was saying just a while ago that Hari Seldon was faking when he said that he had established a Second Foundation. Now you're saying that it's not so; that Seldon wasn't faking, eh?'

'Right, he wasn't faking. Seldon said he had established a Second Foundation and so he had.'

'All right, then, but he said something else, too. He said he established the two Foundations at opposite ends of the Galaxy. Now, young man, was *that* a fake – because Kalgan isn't at the opposite end of the Galaxy.'

Anthor seemed annoyed, 'That's a minor point. That part may well have been a cover up to protect them. But after all, think— What real use would it serve to have the Mind-masters at the opposite end of the Galaxy? What is their function? To help preserve the Plan. Who are the main card players of the Plan? We, the First Foundation. Where can they best observe us, then, and serve their own ends? At the opposite end of the

Galaxy? Ridiculous! They're within fifty parsecs, actually, which is much more sensible.'

'I like that argument,' said Darell. 'It makes sense. Look here, Munn's been conscious for some time and I propose we loose him. He can't do any harm, really.'

Anthor looked rebellious, but Homir was nodding vigorously. Five seconds later he was rubbing his wrists just as vigorously.

'How do you feel?' asked Darell.

'Rotten,' said Munn, sulkily, 'but never mind. There's something I want to ask this bright young thing here. I've heard what he's had to say, and I'd just like permission to wonder what we do next.'

There was a queer and incongruous silence.

Munn smiled bitterly. 'Well, suppose Kalgan *is* the Second Foundation. *Who* on Kalgan are they? How are you going to find them? How are you going to tackle them *if* you find them, eh?'

'Ah, said Darell, 'I can answer that, strangely enough. Shall I tell you what Semic and I have been doing this past half-year? It may give you another reason, Anthor, why I was anxious to remain on Terminus all this time.'

'In the first place,' he went on, 'I've been working on encephalographic analysis with more purpose than any of you may suspect. Detecting Second Foundation minds is a little more subtle than simply finding a Tamper Plateau – and I did not actually. But I came close enough.

'Do you know, any of you, how emotional control works? It's been a popular subject with fiction writers since the time of the Mule and much nonsense has been written, spoken, and recorded about it. For the most part, it has been treated as something mysterious and occult. Of course, it isn't. That the brain is the source of a myriad, tiny electromagnetic fields, everyone knows. Every fleeting emotion varies those fields in more or less intricate fashion, and everyone should know that, too.

'Now it is possible to conceive a mind which can sense these changing fields and even resonate with them. That is, a special organ of the cerebrum can exist which can take on whatever field-pattern it may detect. Exactly how it would do this, I have no idea, but that doesn't matter. If I were blind, for instance, I could still learn the significance of photons and energy quanta and it could be reasonable to me that the absorption of a photon of such energy could create chemical changes in some organ of the body such that its presence would be detectable. But, of course, I would not be able, thereby, to understand colour.

'Do all of you follow?'

There was a firm nod from Anthor; a doubtful nod from the others.

'Such a hypothetical Mind Resonating Organ, by adjusting itself to the Fields emitted by other minds could perform what is popularly known as "reading emotion," or even "reading minds," which is actually something even more subtle. It is but an easy step from that to imagining a similar organ which could actually force an adjustment on another mind. It could orient with its stronger Field the weaker one of another mind – much as a strong magnet will orient the atomic dipoles in a bar of steel and leave it magnetized thereafter.

'I solved the mathematics of Second Foundationism in the sense that I evolved a function that would predict the necessary combination of neuronic paths that would allow for the formation of an organ such as I have just described – but, unfortunately, the function is too complicated to solve by any of the mathematical tools at present known. That is too bad, because it means that I can never detect a Mind-worker by his encephalographic pattern alone.

'But I could do something else. I could, with Semic's help, construct what I shall describe as a Mental Static device. It is not beyond the ability of modern science to create an energy source that will duplicate an encephalograph-type pattern of electromagnetic field. Moreover, it can be made to shift at complete random, creating, as far as this particular mind-sense is concerned, a sort of "noise" or "static" which masks other minds with which it may be in contact.

'Do you still follow?'

Semic chuckled. He had helped create blindly, but he had guessed, and guessed correctly. The old man had a trick or two left—

Anthor said, 'I think I do.'

'The device,' continued Darell, 'is a fairly easy one to produce, and I had all the resources of the Foundation under my control as it came under the heading of war research. And now the mayor's offices and the Legislative assemblies are surrounded with Mental Static. So are most of our key factories. So is this building. Eventually, any place we wish can be made absolutely safe from the Second Foundation or from any future Mule. And that's it.'

He ended quite simply with a flat-palmed gesture of the hand.

Turbor seemed stunned. 'Then it's all over. Great Seldon, it's all over.'

'Well,' said Darell, 'not exactly.'

'How, not exactly? Is there something more?'

'Yes, we haven't located the Second Foundation yet!'

'What,' roared Anthor, 'are you trying to say—'

'Yes, I am. Kalgan is not the Second Foundation.'

'How do *you* know?'

'It's easy,' grunted Darell. 'You see *I happen to know where the Second Foundation really is.*'

# 21

# THE ANSWER THAT SATISFIED

Turbor laughed suddenly – laughed in huge, windy gusts that bounced ringingly off the walls and died in gasps. He shook his head weakly, and said, 'Great Galaxy, this goes on all night. One after another, we put up our straw men to be knocked down. We have fun, but we don't get anywhere. Space! Maybe all planets are the Second Foundation. Maybe they have no planet, just key men spread on all the planets. And what does it matter, since Darell says we have the perfect defence?'

Darell smiled without humour. 'The perfect defence is not enough, Turbor. Even my Mental Static device is only something that keeps us in the same place. We cannot remain forever with our fists doubled, frantically staring in all directions for the unknown enemy. We must know not only *how* to win, but whom to defeat. And there *is* a specific world on which the enemy exists.'

'Get to the point,' said Anthor, wearily. 'What's your information?'

'Arcadia,' said Darell, 'sent me a message, and until I got it, I never saw the obvious. I probably would never have seen the obvious. Yet it was a simple message that went: "A circle has no end." Do you see?'

'No,' said Anthor, stubbornly, and he spoke, quite obviously, for the others.

'A circle has no end,' repeated Munn, thoughtfully, and his forehead furrowed.

'Well,' said Darell, impatiently, 'it was clear to me— What is the one absolute fact we know about the Second Foundation, eh? I'll tell you! We know that Hari Seldon located it at the opposite end of the Galaxy. Homir Munn theorized that Seldon lied about the existence of the Foundation. Pelleas

Anthor theorized that Seldon had told the truth that far, but lied about the location of the Foundation. But I tell you that Hari Seldon lied in no particular; that he told the absolute truth.

'*But*, what is the other end? The Galaxy is a flat, lens-shaped object. A cross section along the flatness of it is a circle, and a circle had no end – as Arcadia realized. We – *we*, the First Foundation – are located on Terminus at the rim of that circle. We are at an end of the Galaxy, by definition. Now follow the rim of that circle and find the other end. Follow it, follow it, follow it, and you will find no other end. You will merely come back to your starting point—

'And *there* you will find the Second Foundation.'

'There?' repeated Anthor. 'Do you mean *here*?'

'Yes, I mean here!' cried Darell, energetically. 'Why, where else could it possibly be? You said yourself that if the Second Foundationers were the guardians of the Seldon Plan, it was unlikely that they could be located at the so-called other end of the Galaxy, where they would be as isolated as they could conceivably be. You thought that fifty parsecs distance was more sensible. I tell you that that is also too far. That no distance at all is more sensible. And where would they be safest? Who would look for them here? Oh, it's the old principle of the most obvious place being the least suspicious.

'Why was poor Ebling Mis so surprised and unmanned by his discovery of the location of the Second Foundation? There he was, looking for it desperately in order to warn it of the coming of the Mule, only to find that the Mule had already captured both Foundations at a stroke. And why did the Mule himself fail in his search? Why not? If one is searching for an unconquerable menace, one would scarcely look among the enemies already conquered. So the Mind-masters, in their own leisurely time, could lay their plans to stop the Mule, and succeeded in stopping him.

'Oh, it is maddeningly simple. For here *we* are with our plots and our schemes, thinking that we are keeping our secrecy –

226

when all the time we are in the very heart and core of our enemy's stronghold. It's humorous.'

Another did not remove the scepticism from his face, 'You honestly believe this theory, Dr Darell?'

'I honestly believe it.'

'Then any of our neighbours, any man we pass in the street, might be a Second Foundation superman, with his mind watching yours and feeling the pulse of its thoughts.'

'Exactly.'

'And we have been permitted to proceed all this time, without molestation?'

'Without molestation? Who told you we were not molested? You, yourself, showed that Munn has been tampered with. What makes you think that we sent him to Kalgan in the first place entirely of our own volition – or that Arcadia overheard us and followed him on her own volition? Hah! We have been molested without pause, probably. And after all, why should they do more than they have? It is far more to their benefit to mislead us, than merely to stop us.'

Anthor buried himself in meditation and emerged therefrom with a dissatisfied expression. 'Well, then, I don't like it. Your Mental Static isn't worth a thought. We can't stay in the house forever and as soon as we leave, we're lost, with what we now think we know. Unless you can build a little machine for every inhabitant in the Galaxy.'

'Yes, but we're not quite helpless, Anthor. These men of the Second Foundation have a special sense which we lack. It is their strength and also their weakness. For instance, is there any weapon of attack that will be effective against a normal, sighted man which is useless against a blind man?'

'Sure,' said Munn, promptly. 'A light in the eyes.'

'Exactly,' said Darell. 'A good, strong blinding light.'

'Well, what of it?' asked Turbor.

'But the analogy is clear. I have a Mind Static device. It sets up an artificial electromagnetic pattern, which to the mind of a man of the Second Foundation would be like a beam of light to

227

us. But the Mind Static device is kaleidoscope. It shifts quickly and continuously, faster than the receiving mind can follow. All right, then, consider it a flickering light; the kind that would give you a headache, if continued long enough. Now intensify that light or that electromagnetic field until it is blinding – and it will become a pain, an unendurable pain. But only to those with the proper sense; *not* to the unsensed.'

'Really?' said Anthor, with the beginnings of enthusiasm. 'Have you tried this?'

'On whom? Of course, I haven't tried it. But it will work.'

'Well, where do you have the controls for the Field that surrounds the house? I'd like to see this thing.'

'Here.' Darell reached into his jacket pocket. It was a small thing, scarcely bulging his pocket. He tossed the black, knob-studded cylinder to the other.

Anthor inspected it carefully and shrugged his shoulders. 'It doesn't make me any smarter to look at it. Look Darell, what mustn't I touch? I don't want to turn off the house defense by accident, you know.'

'You won't,' said Darell, indifferently. 'That control is locked in place.' He flicked at a toggle switch that didn't move.

'And what's this knob?'

'That one varies rate of shift of pattern. Here – this one varies the intensity. It's that which I've been referring to.'

'May I—' asked Anthor, with his finger on the intensity knob. The others were crowding close.

'Why not?' shrugged Darell. 'It won't affect us.'

Slowly, almost wincingly, Anthor turned the knob, first in one direction, then in another. Turbor was gritting his teeth, while Munn blinked his eyes rapidly. It was as though they were keening their inadequate sensory equipment to locate this impulse which could not affect them.

Finally, Anthor shrugged and tossed the control box back into Darell's lap. 'Well, I suppose we can take your word for it. But it's certainly hard to imagine that anything was happening when I turned the knob.'

'But naturally, Pelleas Anthor,' said Darell, with a tight smile. 'The one I gave you was a dummy. You see I have another.' He tossed his jacket aside and seized a duplicate of the control box that Anthor had been investigating, which swung from his belt.

'You see,' said Darell, and in one gesture turned the intensity knob to maximum.

And with an unearthly shriek, Pelleas Anthor sank to the floor. He rolled in his agony; whitened, gripping fingers clutching and tearing futilely at his hair.

Munn lifted his feet hastily to prevent contact with the squirming body, and his eyes were twin depths of horror. Semic and Turbor were a pair of plaster casts; stiff and white.

Darell, sombre, turned the knob back once more. And Anthor twitched feebly once or twice and lay still. He was alive, his breath racking his body.

'Lift him on to the couch,' said Darell, grasping the young man's head. 'Help me here.'

Turbor reached for the feet. They might have been lifting a sack of flour. Then, after long minutes, the breathing grew quieter, and Anthor's eyelids fluttered and lifted. His face was a horrid yellow; his hair and body was soaked in perspiration, and his voice, when he spoke, was cracked and unrecognizable.

'Don't,' he muttered, 'don't! Don't do that again! You don't know— You don't know— Oh-h-h.' It was a long, trembling moan.

'We won't do it again,' said Darell, 'if you will tell us the truth. You are a member of the Second Foundation?'

'Let me have some water,' pleaded Anthor.

'Get some, Turbor,' said Darell, 'and bring the whiskey bottle.'

He repeated the question after pouring a jigger of whiskey and two glasses of water into Anthor. Something seemed to relax in the young man—

'Yes,' he said, wearily. 'I am a member of the Second Foundation.'

'Which,' continued Darell, 'is located on Terminus – here?'

'Yes, yes. You are right in every particular, Dr Darell.'

'Good! Now explain what's been happening this past half year. Tell us!'

'I would like to sleep,' whispered Anthor.

'Later! Speak now!'

A tremulous sigh. Then words, low and hurried. The others bent over him to catch the sound, 'The situation was growing dangerous. We knew that Terminus and its physical scientists were becoming interested in brain-wave patterns and that the times were ripe for the development of something like the Mind Static device. And there was growing enmity toward the Second Foundation. We had to stop it without ruining Seldon's Plan.

'We ... we tried to control the movement. We tried to join it. It would turn suspicion and efforts away from us. We saw to it that Kalgan declared war as a further distraction. That's why I sent Munn to Kalgan. Stettin's supposed mistress was one of us. She saw to it that Munn made the proper moves—'

'Callia is—' cried Munn, but Darell waved him silent.

Anthor continued, unaware of any interruption, 'Arcadia followed. We hadn't counted on that – can't foresee everything – so Callia manoeuvred her to Trantor to prevent interference. That's all. Except that we lost.'

'You tried to get me to go to Trantor, didn't you?' asked Darell.

Anthor nodded, 'Had to get you out of the way. The growing triumph in your mind was clear enough. You were solving the problems of the Mind Static device.'

'Why didn't you put me under control?'

'Couldn't ... couldn't. Had my orders. We were working according to a Plan. If I improvised, I would have thrown everything off. Plan only predicts probabilities ... you know that ... like Seldon's Plan.' He was talking in anguished pants, and almost incoherently. His head twisted from side to side in a restless fever. 'We worked with individuals ... not groups ...

very low probabilities involved ... lost out. Besides ... if control you ... someone else invent device ... no use ... had to control *times* ... more subtle ... First Speaker's own plan ... don't know all angles ... except ... didn't work a-a-a—' He ran down.

Darell shook him roughly, 'You can't sleep yet. How many of you are there?'

'Huh? Whatjasay ... oh ... not many ... be surprised ... fifty don't ... need more.'

'All here on Terminus?'

'Five ... six out in Space ... like Callia ... got to sleep.'

He stirred himself suddenly as though to one giant effort, and his expressions gained in clarity. It was a last attempt at self-justification, at moderating his defeat.

'Almost got you at the end. Would have turned off defenses and seized you. Would have seen who was master. But you gave me dummy controls ... suspected me all along –'

And finally he was asleep.


Turbor said, in awed tones, 'How long did you suspect him, Darell?'

'Ever since he first came here,' was the quiet response. 'He came from Kleise, he said. But I knew Kleise; and I knew on what terms we parted. He was a fanatic on the subject of the Second Foundation and I had deserted him. My own purposes were reasonable, since I thought it best and safest to pursue my own notions by myself. But I couldn't tell Kleise that; and he wouldn't have listened if I had. To him, I was a coward and a traitor, perhaps even an agent of the Second Foundation. He was an unforgiving man and from that time almost to the day of his death he had no dealings with me. Then, suddenly, in his last few weeks of life, he writes me – as an old friend – to greet his best and most promising pupil as a co-worker and begin again the old investigation.

'It was out of character. How could he possibly do such a thing without being under outside influence, and I began to

231

wonder if the only real purpose might not be to introduce into my confidence a real agent of the Second Foundation. Well it was so—'

He sighed and closed his own eyes for a moment.

Semic put in hesitantly, 'What will we do with all of them... these Second Foundation fellas?'

'I don't know,' said Darell, sadly. 'We could exile them, I suppose. There's Zoranel, for instance. They can be placed there and the planet saturated with Mind Static. The sexes can be separated, or, better still, they can be sterilized – and in fifty years, the Second Foundation will be a thing of the past. Or perhaps a quiet death for all of them would be kinder.'

'Do you suppose,' said Turbor, 'we could learn the use of this sense of theirs. Or are they born with it, like the Mule?'

'I don't know. I think it is developed through long training, since there are indications from encephalography that the potentialities of it are latent in the human mind. But what do you want that sense for? It hasn't helped *them*.'

He frowned.

Though he said nothing, his thoughts were shouting.

It had been too easy – too easy. They had fallen, these invincibles, fallen like book-villains, and he didn't like it.

Galaxy! When can a man know he is not a puppet? *How* can a man know he is not a puppet?

Arcadia was coming home, and his thoughts shuddered away from that which he must face in the end.

She was home for a week, then two, and he could not loose the tight check upon those thoughts. How could he? She had changed from child to young woman in her absence, by some strange alchemy. She was his link to life; his link to a bitter-sweet marriage that scarcely outlasted his honeymoon.

And then, late one evening, he said as casually as he could, 'Arcadia, what made you decide that Terminus contained both Foundations?'

They had been to the theatre; in the best seats with private trimensional viewers for each; her dress was new for the occasion, and she was happy.

She stared at him for a moment, then tossed it off. 'Oh, I don't know, Father. It just came to me.'

A layer of ice thickened about Dr Darell's heart.

'Think,' he said, intensely. 'This is important. What made you decide both Foundations were on Terminus?'

She frowned slightly. 'Well, there was Lady Callia. I knew *she* was a Second Foundationer. Anthor said so, too.'

'But she was on Kalgan,' insisted Darell. '*What made you decide on Terminus?*'

And now Arcadia waited for several minutes before she answered. What *had* made her decide? What had made her decide? She had the horrible sensation of something slipping just beyond her grasp.

She said, 'She knew about things – Lady Callia did – and must have had her information from Terminus. Doesn't that sound right, Father?'

But he just shook his head at her.

'Father,' she cried, 'I *knew*. The more I thought, the surer I was. It just made *sense*.'

There was that lost look in her father's eyes, 'It's no good, Arcadia. It's no good. Intuition is suspicious when concerned with the Second Foundation. You see that, don't you? It *might* have been intuition – and it might have been control!'

'Control! You mean they changed me? Oh, no. No, they couldn't.' She was backing away from him. 'But didn't Anthor say I was right? He admitted it. He admitted everything. And you've found the whole bunch right on Terminus. Didn't you? Didn't you?' She was breathing quickly.

'I know, but— Arcadia, will you let me make an encephalographic analysis of your brain?'

She shook her head violently, 'No, no! I'm too scared.'

'Of me, Arcadia? There's nothing to be afraid of. But we must know. You see that, don't you?'

\*   \*   \*

She interrupted him only once, after that. She clutched at his arm just before the last switch was thrown. 'What If I *am* different, Father? What will you have to do?'

'I won't have to do anything, Arcadia. If you're different, we'll leave. We'll go back to Trantor, you and I, and...and we won't care about anything else in the Galaxy.'

Never in Darell's life had an analysis proceeded so slowly, cost him so much, and when it was over, Arcadia huddled down and dared not look. Then she heard him laugh and that was information enough. She jumped up and threw herself into his opened arms.

He was babbling wildly as they squeezed one another, 'The house is under maximum Mind Static and your brain-waves are normal. We really have trapped them, Arcadia, and we can go back to living.'

'Father,' she gasped, 'can we let them give us medals now?'

'How did you know I'd asked to be left out of it?' He held her at arm's length for a moment, then laughed again. 'Never mind; you know everything. All right, you can have your medal on a platform, with speeches.'

'And Father?'

'Yes?'

'Can you call me Arkady from now on?'

'But— Very well, Arkady.'

Slowly the magnitude of the victory was soaking into him and saturating him. The Foundation – the First Foundation – now the only Foundation – was absolute master of the Galaxy. No further barrier stood between themselves and the Second Empire – the final fulfilment of Seldon's Plan.

They had only to reach for it—

Thanks to—

# 22

# THE ANSWER THAT WAS TRUE

An unlocated room on an unlocated world!

And a plan whose plan had worked.

The First Speaker looked up at the Student, 'Fifty men and women,' he said. 'Fifty martyrs! They knew it meant death or permanent imprisonment and they could not even be oriented to prevent weakening – since orientation might have been detected. Yet they did not weaken. They brought the Plan through, because they loved the greater Plan.'

'Might they have been fewer?' asked the Student, doubtfully.

The First Speaker slowly shook his head, 'It was the lower limit. Less could not possibly have carried conviction. In fact, pure objectivism would have demanded seventy-five to leave margin for error. Never mind. Have you studied the course of action as worked out by the Speakers' Council fifteen years ago?'

'Yes, Speaker.'

'And compared it with actual developments?'

'Yes, Speaker.' Then, after a pause.

'I was quite amazed, Speaker.'

'I know. There is always amazement. If you knew how many men laboured for how many months – years, in fact – to bring about the polish of perfection, you would be less amazed. Now tell me what happened – in words. I want your translation of the mathematics.'

'Yes, Speaker.' The young man marshalled his thoughts. 'Essentially, it was necessary for the men of the First Foundation to be thoroughly convinced that they had located *and destroyed* the Second Foundation. In that way, there would be reversion to the intended original. To all intents, Terminus would once again know nothing about us; include us in none of their calculations. We are hidden once more, and safe – at the cost of fifty men.'

'And the purpose of the Kalganian war?'

'To show the Foundation that they could beat a physical enemy – to wipe out the damage done to their self-esteem and self-assuredness by the Mule.'

'There you are insufficient in your analysis. Remember, the population of Terminus regarded us with distinct ambivalence. They hated and envied our supposed superiority; yet they relied on us implicitly for protection. If we had been "destroyed" before the Kalganian war, it would have meant panic throughout the Foundation. They would then never have had the courage to stand up against Stettin, when he *then* attacked; and he would have. Only in the full flush of victory could the "destruction" have taken place with minimum ill-effects. Even waiting a year, thereafter, might have meant a too-great cooling of spirit for success.'

The Student nodded. 'I see. Then the course of history will proceed without deviation in the direction indicated by the Plan.'

'Unless,' pointed out the First Speaker, 'further accidents, unforeseen and individual, occur.'

'And for that,' said the Student, '*we* still exist. Except?— Except— One facet of the present state of affairs worries me, Speaker. The First Foundation is left with the Mind Static device – a powerful weapon against us. That, at least, is not as it was before.'

'A good point. But they have no one to use it against. It has become a sterile device; just as without the spur of our own menace against them, encephalographic analysis will become a sterile science. Other varieties of knowledge will once again bring more important and immediate returns. So this first generation of mental scientists among the First Foundation will also be the last – and, in a century, Mind Static will be a nearly forgotten item of the past.'

'Well—' The Student was calculating mentally. 'I suppose you're right.'

'But what I want you most to realize, young man, for the sake of your future in the Council is the consideration given to the tiny intermeshings that were forced into our plan of the last decade and a half simply because we dealt with individuals. There was the manner in which Anthor had to create suspicion against himself in such a way that it would mature at the right time, but that was relatively simple.

'There was the manner in which the atmosphere was so manipulated that to no one on Terminus would it occur, prematurely, that Terminus itself might be the centre they were seeking. That knowledge had to be supplied to the young girl, Arcadia, who would be heeded by no one but her own father. She had to be sent to Trantor, thereafter, to make certain that there would be no premature contact with her father. Those two were the two poles of a hyperatomic motor; each being inactive without the other. And the switch had to be thrown – contact had to be made – at just the right moment. I saw to that!

'And the final battle had to be handled properly. The Foundation's fleet had to be soaked in self-confidence while the fleet of Kalgan made ready to run. I saw to that, also!'

Said the Student, 'It seems to me, Speaker, that you ... I mean, all of us ... were counting on Dr Darell not suspecting that Arcadia was our tool. According to *my* check on the calculations, there was something like a thirty percent probability that he *would* so suspect. What would have happened then?'

'We had taken care of that. What have you been taught about Tamper Plateaus? What are they? Certainly not evidence of the introduction of an emotional bias. That can be done without any chance of possible detection by the most refined conceivable encephalographic analysis. A consequence of Leffert's Theorem, you know. It is the removal, the cutting-out, of previous emotional bias, that shows. It *must* show.

237

'And, of course, Anthor made certain that Darell knew all about Tamper Plateaus.

'However— When can an individual be placed under Control without showing it? Where there is no previous emotional bias to remove. In other words, when the individual is a new-born infant with a blank slate of mind. Arcadia Darell was such an infant here on Trantor fifteen years ago, when the first line was drawn into the structure of the plan. She will never know that she has been Controlled, and will be all the better for it, since her control involved the development of a precocious and intelligent personality.'

The First Speaker laughed shortly, 'In a sense, it is the irony of it all that is most amazing. For four hundred years, so many men have been blinded by Seldon's words "the other end of the Galaxy." They have brought their own peculiar, physical-science thought to the problem, measuring off the other end with protractors and rulers, ending up eventually either at a point in the periphery one hundred eighty degrees around the rim of the Galaxy, or back at the original point.

'Yet our very greatest danger lay in the fact that there *was* a possible solution based on physical modes of thought. The Galaxy, you know, is not simply a flat ovoid of any sort; nor is the periphery a closed curve. Actually, it is a double spiral, with at least eighty percent of the inhabited planets on the Main Arm. Terminus is the extreme outer end of the spiral arm, and we are at the other – since, what is the opposite end of a spiral? Why, the centre.

'But that is trifling. It is an accidental and irrelevant solution. The solution could have been reached immediately, if the questioners had but remembered that Hari Seldon was a *social* scientist, not a physical scientist and adjusted their thought processes accordingly. What *could* "opposite ends" mean to a social scientist? Opposite ends on the map? Of course not. That's the mechanical interpretation only.

'The First Foundation was at the periphery, where the original Empire was weakest, where its civilizing influence was

238

least, where its wealth and culture were most nearly absent. And where is the *social opposite end of the Galaxy*? Why, at the place where the original Empire was strongest, where its civilizing influence was most, where its wealth and culture were most strongly present.

'Here! At the centre! At Trantor, capital of the Empire of Seldon's time.

'And it is so inevitable. Hari Seldon left the Second Foundation behind him to maintain, improve, and extend his work. That has been known, or guessed at, for fifty years. But where could that best be done? At Trantor, where Seldon's group had worked, and where the data of decades had been accumulated. And it was the purpose of the Second Foundation to protect the Plan against enemies. That, too, was known! And where was the source of great danger to Terminus and the Plan?

'Here! Here at Trantor, where the Empire dying though it was, could, for three centuries, still destroy the Foundation, if it could only have decided to do so.

'Then when Trantor fell and was sacked and utterly destroyed, a short century ago, *we* were naturally able to protect our headquarters, and, on all the planet, the Imperial Library and the grounds about it remained untouched. This was well-known to the Galaxy, but even that apparently overwhelming hint passed them by.

'It was here at Trantor that Ebling Mis discovered us; and here we saw to it that he did not survive the discovery. To do so, it was necessary to arrange to have a normal Foundation girl defeat the tremendous mutant powers of the Mule. Surely, such a phenomenon might have attracted suspicion to the planet on which it happened— It was here that we first studied the Mule and planned his ultimate defeat. It was here that Arcadia was born and the train of events begun that led to the great return to the Seldon Plan.

'And all those flaws in our secrecy; those gaping holes; remained unnoticed because Seldon had spoken of "the other end" in his way, and they had interpreted it in their way.'

The First Speaker had long since stopped speaking to the Student. It was an exposition to himself, really, as he stood before the window, looking up at the incredible blaze of the firmament; at the huge Galaxy that was now safe forever.

'Hari Seldon called Trantor, "Star's End,"' he whispered, 'and why not that bit of poetic imagery. All the universe was once guided from this rock; all the apron strings of the stars led here. "All roads lead to Trantor," says the old proverb, "and that is where all stars end."'

Ten months earlier, the First Speaker had viewed those same crowding stars – nowhere as crowded as at the centre of that huge cluster of matter Man calls the Galaxy – with misgivings; but now there was a sombre satisfaction on the round and ruddy face of Preem Palver – First Speaker.